Bloom
and
Doom

Beverly Allen

BERKLEY PRIME CRIME, NEW YORK

THE BERKLEY PUBLISHING GROUP
Published by the Penguin Group
Penguin Group (USA) LLC
375 Hudson Street, New York, New York 10014

USA • Canada • UK • Ireland • Australia • New Zealand • India • South Africa • China

penguin.com

A Penguin Random House Company

BLOOM AND DOOM

A Berkley Prime Crime Book / published by arrangement with the author

For information, address: The Berkley Publishing Group,
a division of Penguin Group (USA) LLC,
375 Hudson Street, New York, New York 10014.

ISBN: 978-0-425-26497-3

PUBLISHING HISTORY
Berkley Prime Crime mass-market edition / April 2014

PRINTED IN THE UNITED STATES OF AMERICA

10 9 8 7 6 5 4 3 2 1

Cover illustration by Ben Perini; *Pink rose heart* © by Titania/Shutterstock.
Cover design by Diana Kolsky.
Interior text design by Kelly Lipovich.

The wedding is off . . .

"Liv, what is it?"

"Eric had a hard time seeing because of those tinted windows. And when he got close, he saw him."

"Who?"

"Derek. Audrey, he was dead. Dead and sitting behind the steering wheel of his car."

"Maybe Derek just passed out or something."

"Audrey, there's more. When Eric got closer, he could tell something was smeared all over the windows. Audrey, it was blood, and Eric said there was a knife still . . ."

Derek was murdered. Right on the streets of Ramble. No wonder she was so shook up.

"Audrey, Eric thinks the knife was one of ours—from the shop."

"He must be mistaken." Liv ordered a dozen of those knives with the florist shop name printed on them so they wouldn't wander. And if they did wander, at least they would serve as advertisements.

She stared hard at me. And then I remembered.

"I gave Jenny a knife yesterday, but she wouldn't . . . couldn't have done anything like that."

Liv shook her head. "Audrey, Eric said the bouquet was there too, in the car. Torn to bits and covered with blood."

Acknowledgments

In the language of flowers, the Canterbury bell is a symbol of *gratitude* and *acknowledgment*. And I have a bouquet of them to hand out. I've long enjoyed reading Berkley Prime Crime mysteries, so first I'd like to thank Berkley for the opportunity to write one. And my delightful editor, Katherine Pelz, and my agent, Kim Lionetti, for making it possible.

Thanks to Janice Cline, Kathleen Hurst, Susan Johnson, Virginia Mackey, Debra Marvin, Dawn Mohr, Lisa Richardson, and Lynne Wallace-Lee for trudging through various versions of my manuscript. Your insightful comments were invaluable.

And for Christine Bress for reviewing the floral design in the book. Thanks also to the Atrium School of Floral Design, and to Brighton-Eggert Florists (Tonawanda, New York) and Jessica Carter of Sponseller's Flower Shop (Berryville, Virginia) for inviting me into their backrooms, allowing me to look around, hang out, and ask silly questions.

Also thanks to Laura Patten and T.W. Fritts of the Berryville Police Department for being so helpful. And to Lee Lofland and his fabulous Writers' Police Academy. Also Logan Van Meter of the Berryville-Clarke County Visitor

Center. While the town of Ramble is fictional, you helped me ground it more firmly in Virginia soil.

Perhaps most thanks should go to my husband, family, and friends who put up with vacant stares, furious typing, and more than one takeout meal.

Dedicated to Him who is the Author and Finisher of my faith.

Chapter 1

❧

"White roses symbolize *innocence.*"

I stripped the thorns, leaves, and guard petals from a cluster of luscious white blooms and looked up just as the photographer's flash went off, leaving a bright afterimage in the center of my field of view. I blinked hard, trying to clear my vision, then tilted my head and squinted one eye so I could see to choose a large lavender rose to form the center of the bouquet. The flash went off, blinding me again.

"Okay, Miss Bloom, I know you're not used to working with cameras around." The reporter, who'd introduced himself as Ben Hanson, shifted positions with the photographer in our tiny back room. "Just keep stepping me through the bouquet you're making."

"Call me Audrey, please." The petals in front of me were still obscured by the bright spots, but I decided I should be able to do this in my sleep by now anyway. I blinked again. "The lavender rose is the symbol of *love at first sight.*" Oh, great. I resisted the urge to wince at my own words. Love at first sight was a romantic concept I'd have to reconsider after Brad the Cad.

A deep purple iris went in next as an accent, providing just the right amount of contrast. "Iris can mean a few different things. Generally, it means *a message*. The purple iris in particular can stand for *wisdom*, an important ingredient in a marriage." One that might have helped me see through Brad.

Maybe this particular bouquet was a bad idea. But it was the only one that came to mind when Hanson casually said, "Make something original. Just throw in some of your personal favorites."

Another flash went off, followed by a disgusted sigh from the photographer. "There's just so much junk back here." He waved to the floor-to-ceiling shelves lined with vases, balloons, dried floral accents, picks, wire, floral tape, spray glitter, and ribbon of every color and size imaginable—everything it takes to keep a busy floral shop supplied.

"Just do your best," Hanson said to the photographer. "Hey"—he pointed to the Queen Anne's lace I'd incorporated while the men were talking—"isn't that the same thing that grows on the side of the road?"

"You *did* ask me to use my favorites. I used Queen Anne's lace in my first childhood bouquet, so it holds special meaning for me." A quick flash of Grandma Mae treasuring that bouquet brought a new sense of calm, despite the running voice recorder and the photographer jockeying for position. "It adds texture and softness and makes the arrangement a little more informal and fun. It symbolizes *protection*."

I added more white and lavender roses around the outside, then handed the bouquet to Hanson, so I could see how it would look held by a bride. I had to stifle a chuckle. The gaunt older man with the red beard and green suit jacket looked more like a leprechaun than a blushing bride.

The photographer couldn't resist taking his picture. I suspected blackmail as a motive.

"Are you finished?" Hanson asked, his body slumping in relief when I took the bouquet from him.

"Almost." I made one minor adjustment before heading to the walk-in cooler for ivy, which I used to rim the edges. "Another slightly old-fashioned look, but ivy is one of my favorites because it represents both *friendship* and *fidelity*."

I then tucked in some white veronica. The spiky, cone-shaped flower added dimension and interest. "Veronica represents *faithfulness*. Can never have too much of that in a relationship."

I bound the stems with floral tape, snipped them to the appropriate length, then wrapped them with satin ribbon. I fastened the ribbon with two pearl pins, then attached a premade bow of thin white ribbon and held the completed bouquet up for display. The flash went off again.

"Ooh, killer shot." The photographer held the digital camera screen out for Hanson's perusal. "Will that work?"

Hanson muttered approval. The photographer gathered his equipment and darted out the door.

"Allergies?" I asked.

"Not that I'm aware of. He's the only photographer the *Ramble On* has, and he needs to be at the mayor's press conference in five minutes."

I smiled at Hanson's reference to the small-town paper. "Tell me, how did they ever come up with that name?"

Hanson's ears turned the color of his beard. "I guess it's not the most impressive masthead. The paper was originally named the *Ramble Pilot*. But Ramblers have been calling it the *On* for over a century. The new owners just caved in." Hanson looked around the back room, littered with stems and leaves. "Say, do you have an office or someplace quiet we could sit down and finish the interview?"

"We have a table where I meet with prospective clients." When Hanson nodded, I led him past the curious glances of Liv—my cousin and business partner—and through the shop's meandering aisles.

Like many florists in an age when customers can go online and have a dozen roses overnighted directly to their homes, we'd had to diversify. We'd expanded into helium balloons—including our signature balloon bouquets—giftware, houseplants, and a small range of garden statuary. We displayed all these treasures on tired old furniture scrounged up at estate sales and refinished in white crackle paint. With the colorfully painted walls, our coolers bursting with blooms, and each of our furniture treasures laden with plants, sample arrangements, and giftware, the once run-down shop had been transformed into a garden oasis. Since it was spring, that oasis spilled over onto the sidewalk, with displays (not exceeding the local statutes) of blooming annuals and perennials ready to be transplanted into local gardens.

I ushered Hanson toward the consulting nook where "We make bridal dreams come true!" It said so right on the sign we'd mounted above the wrought-iron gazebo I'd found at an estate sale. Liv and I had flanked the structure with two homemade water features, which now displayed our collection of flowering houseplants, making the nook both charming and private. Here I would, as Liv had suggested, attempt to dazzle Hanson with my expert knowledge.

Of course, dazzling a reporter can be tough when your heel turns on the top step and he has to catch you as you stumble.

When I regained my balance, if not my composure, I took a seat opposite him at the fieldstone-topped table. "Liv told me you wanted this interview for an upcoming wedding issue. Perhaps you'd like to start with the trends we're seeing in bouquets this year?" I'd spent half the night studying bridal magazines to prepare, and I wanted to get that question out of the way before I forgot what I'd read.

"I'd like to take a different approach." Hanson stroked his beard, looking every bit like an absentminded leprechaun wondering where he'd hidden his gold. "I could pull half a dozen articles off the news service that would give me the same information. Readers will want to know the secret of your marriage success rate."

"Of my . . . what?"

"Your marriage success rate."

I fought to keep the corners of my mouth propped in a smile. I'd come close to marriage once, and I'd hardly call it a success. "I don't understand."

"Do you have any idea how many bouquets you've made for Ramble brides?"

"I guess the Rose in Bloom has supplied most of the recent weddings in Ramble—and some of the outlying areas. Well over a hundred, I'd imagine."

"A hundred and fifty-six, to be exact."

"How did you . . . ?"

"I checked with your partner. That's the reason I wanted to do this interview."

Right then, Liv caught my eye as she headed toward the gazebo with her watering can. Remarkable, considering she'd already watered the flowering plants that morning. Any more and they'd drown.

Hanson continued, "One of your clients came to me with an observation I found intriguing. She insists that none of the couples who use the Rose in Bloom for their bridal bouquets have ever split up. Olivia let me sneak a peek at the client list last week. I recognized most names as belonging to couples who are still together. Those I didn't know, I called. And none of them, including those who later moved out of Ramble, have split up."

"That's . . . wow . . . that's so nice to hear."

"It's more than nice. Do you know what the divorce rate is currently in Virginia?"

"I have no idea."

"Well . . . it's . . . I . . . never mind. I'll Google it before I write the article. But I'm pretty sure it's *not* zero. This is a statistical anomaly worth exploring, don't you think?"

"Mr. Hanson, while I'd like to think I had something to do with that, how could flowers affect divorce rates?"

My question drew Hanson's chuckle while Liv cleared her throat nearby. When I caught her eye, she gave me *the look*—the same one she'd given me when we were teenagers and I took a swing at Patti Vogt for calling me Audrey Bloomers . . . again. Liv's expression melted into a smile just as Hanson turned in her direction. She continued cheerfully dowsing the dry-loving African violets.

"Look, it's probably just a fluke," Hanson said. "But it sounded like a great angle for a story to me, and it could end up driving more business to the Rose in Bloom. People eat up that kind of thing. So let's pretend a couple comes in to order flowers. Is there something you say to them?"

"First, the groom seldom sets foot in the shop. It's the bride and her mother—often the bride and a friend. Sometimes a wedding planner."

"And you bring them back here . . ."

"They'll take a look through our books and choose something that catches their eye. Usually they come in with an idea—maybe something they've seen on the Internet or in a bridal magazine or in photos of a celebrity wedding. Right after the royal wedding, we did a few bouquets similar to Kate Middleton's."

"And then?"

"Then I tweak their ideas a bit and count up the flowers, adding in labor and materials, to give them an estimate of the cost. I start with the bride's bouquet first, then base the rest of the flowers—"

"What do you mean by tweaking?"

"I'd be lying if I didn't say most of our business involves

putting together arrangements from a picture. But I like to encourage brides to put their own personal stamp on their bouquets. As a designer, I can help them choose flowers with the right colors, sizes, and textures to complement each other or contrast in ways that make a statement."

Hanson tilted his head.

"Think about baby's breath. When's the last time you saw baby's breath not wrapped around a rose? The two flowers couldn't be more dissimilar, yet they complement each other. The baby's breath makes the rose more luscious. And the rose makes the baby's breath seem lighter and more delicate. They bring out the natural beauty in each other. And it speaks volumes."

"Sounds more like an analogy for marriage."

I laughed. "I guess it is, but don't let Liv hear you say that. She teases me when I refer to people in terms of flowers."

"And here I thought bouquets just had to be pretty."

"Most bouquets are pretty. But are they memorable? Do they speak to you? When a bouquet tells me something, then I know I've gotten it right."

"That's the second time you've talked about flowers speaking. Does anything else go into a bouquet that *speaks to you*?"

"Well, there's another thing. It may seem silly and old-fashioned, but many of the brides find it romantic . . ."

Hanson said nothing, only leaned in closer. As did Liv and her watering can. Based upon the time she'd spent hovering over the geraniums, I imagined plans for an ark were well under way.

I gulped. "I like to tweak the design based on the language of flowers."

"Language?" His creased brow made me wonder if he thought I communed with flowers. And they talked back.

"Like I said as I made my bouquet for the picture. Each

flower has at least one meaning attached. When you put them together, they can form more complex statements. The language of flowers goes back . . . well, quite a ways. The Turks were using it as early as the seventeenth century, for example. Shakespeare used it. 'There's rosemary, that's for *remembrance*; pray, love, remember: and there is pansies. That's for *thoughts*.' "

Hanson quirked an eyebrow.

"Sorry." I cleared my throat. "*Hamlet*. I got carried away. But the language of flowers reached a pinnacle during the Victorian era. During the age of chaperones, often the only way a couple could communicate what they felt was through flowers."

"How did they know what the meanings were?"

"A number of books were published on the meanings of flowers." I reached over to the small side table that held our flower books and pulled out a reprint of my favorite illustrated tome on the subject. "I still like to choose flowers that have meanings good for a marriage. Often a bride will embrace the process and choose flowers that demonstrate her personality—or characterize her relationship with her fiancé."

"Your method must make brides give some serious thought to their relationships. Perhaps that has something to do with your success rate."

I shrugged. Yes, my illustrious marriage success rate. Liv could have at least given me some warning.

Hanson combed his beard with his fingers. "I can work with that, anyway. Now, maybe a little background. What started your interest in flowers?"

"I've loved them ever since I was a little girl. Liv—Olivia Rose—and I used to run the hills outside Ramble collecting dandelions and buttercups, pussy willows and wild lilacs for our grandmother. That's her in the picture." I pointed to the display behind him.

Hanson rose to take a closer look at the photo. I took the opportunity to shoo Liv away. Except Liv didn't budge.

Hanson tapped the photo frame. "I remember your grandmother and the little cottage with the flower gardens. We did a feature on it—headlined as 'Mae's Flowers,' I think—about seven or eight years ago. Sad what's happened to the place."

I swallowed hard. "Those gardens weren't always there, you know. Grandma Mae once earned quite a reputation for growing vegetables. She switched her attention to flowers when we were young."

"Why's that?"

"Partly my fault, I'm afraid. One summer when Liv and I were visiting—I think I was six, so she must have been eight— we found some new flowers to add to a bouquet we were making. Beautiful yellow and orange blooms. We gathered all we could find and tied them with Liv's hair ribbon. We expected Grandma Mae to gush over all the pretty flowers. Instead she put her hands on her cheeks and kept repeating, 'Bless your hearts.' We'd pulled all the blooms from her vegetable garden.

"That afternoon we hopped into her old Volkswagen Bug and headed to the greenhouses for seeds and bulbs and flats of flowers. She showed us where we could plant our own flower garden. We'd add a little more every summer."

"And now you and Liv have your own florist's shop. How long has it been?"

"Five years. Well, five years since we bought the shop. It took us a while to get the business updated. The building needed more than a face-lift when we found it."

"And how's it going now?"

"Pretty well, I think. Liv manages the shop, and I coordinate the weddings. Of course we all pitch in when there's a—"

My words were interrupted by a crash, as a whole shelf of potted hibiscus tumbled to the floor beneath Liv's over-zealous watering can.

I closed my eyes and counted to ten, breathing in the calming symphony of scents that is a flower shop. Not that many of the smells came from our cut flowers, since they were all stored in the coolers. But our signature scent came from our potted flowers, floral-scented candles, potpourri, and that little bottle of magic spray we surreptitiously spritzed on the tissue paper for all our boxed roses, since roses today don't have the scent people expect them to. But when customers walk in, they invariably remark on how wonderful the flowers smell.

"Sorry about that." I sent him a pleasant smile. At least I hoped it looked like a pleasant smile. "What was the question again?"

Hanson flipped off the voice recorder. "Never mind. I have enough to make it work, and it looks like your partner may need some help cleaning up."

We shook hands, then he gingerly stepped around the floral casualties, potting soil, and shards of terra-cotta. Liv and I watched as he exited.

"Sorry." Liv picked up a plant that had miraculously remained intact and firmed the dirt with her fingers.

"You could have waited until after the interview. You know I'd tell you everything."

"Did we just meet? You know I can't wait."

That much was true. Liv always used to stalk the closets for presents. When she was a child, she'd shake and poke and pinch them. As a young teen, she'd unwrap and rewrap them. When she was in high school, I'd known her to replace the family's tape with a removable variety. Of course, she taught me all her secrets.

"When I saw the watering can," Liv said, "I figured it would look like part of the job."

"I hope you haven't drowned our entire stock." I started stacking the largest shards of terra-cotta.

"That"—Liv tapped her forehead—"is why I didn't put any water in the watering can."

"You could have given me some warning about what he wanted to talk to me about," I said. Even then, irritation was melting away. It was truly hard to be mad at bubbly, cheerful Liv.

"I figured you'd be more candid this way. And you did great. We're sure to pick up a few more wedding appointments from the article."

The bell signaled the arrival of a customer.

"You take that," I said. "I'll clean up."

A sad-looking hibiscus sat in the pile of dirt. I transferred it to a pot. With a little tender care and a bit of luck, the patient would survive. I triaged a few more before sweeping up the remaining potting soil.

While Liv cashed out the latest customer, the bell rang again.

I looked up to see a man in baker's whites standing in the door. At least I think they were baker's whites, since he wasn't Ricardo Montalban or Mr. Clean. Not all men can pull off the all-white look (case in point, Mr. Clean), but this one did. Perhaps due to the tanned muscles jutting from his short sleeves or the wavy locks of brown hair that crowned his head.

He reminded me briefly of a moonflower. Bright, strong, elusive.

He crossed the room to where I stood and towered over me. Since I'm five ten, that's quite a trick. He flashed a smile and said . . . something.

The words seemed to hang in the air, but I had no recollection of them. Perhaps because I was thinking of the meaning of the moonflower. *I only dream of love.* "I beg your pardon?" What was wrong with me?

"Is there a manager about?"

"I . . . yes . . . I'm a manager. Well, an owner . . . a co-owner. My cousin and I . . ." I cleared my throat. I needed a do-over. I swallowed and forced a smile as I stuck out my hand. "Audrey Bloom. How can I help you?"

"Nick Maxwell." He shook my hand, which we then both realized still contained remnants of potting soil.

"Oh, fiddleheads," I said, employing one of the green words that passed for cussing in our small shop. "Sorry. I'll get you a . . ." I ran to the back room, where I banged my head three times on the door of the walk-in, trying to knock sense into myself, then brought back a damp paper towel.

"Sorry," I said again. "Occupational hazard."

"No problem. For me it's usually flour."

I laughed politely and waited.

And he waited.

"Oh, the reason I came . . ." He reached into a pocket and pulled out a flyer. "I recently opened the Baby Cakes Bakery just down the street."

"The new cupcake place?"

"That's right. We started out with cupcakes. Now we're trying to branch out into weddings. Like those cupcake arrangements in the bridal magazines. And full-sized cakes, too."

"*You* read the bridal magazines?"

He raised his hands in the universal symbol of surrender. "Guilty. Another trade hazard, I'm afraid."

I chuckled. "I know. I coordinate weddings for the shop, so I have a stack of them on either side of my couch. I use them for coffee tables."

"I usually read them at the library."

"Hey, if you ever want to come over and check out the back issues, my apartment is just a couple of blocks from here." Oh, great. Without thinking, I'd just invited a stranger to my apartment. He was probably married anyway. I looked to his ring finger. Empty, but that didn't always mean anything.

"I . . . uh . . . I might just do that. By the time I get to the library, the brides have ripped out half the pictures anyway."

"And brought many of them here, I'm afraid."

Nick looked down at the flyer in his hands. "Oh, I wondered if it would be possible to place some flyers in your shop. If you want, I could put something advertising the Rose in Bloom in the bakery."

"I have some business cards."

"Great. I'll bring a stack of flyers over later today." He started backing toward the door. "Oh, I forgot. Do you have any small bouquets? Nothing fancy."

I pointed to the self-service cooler. "Something like that?"

My jaw tightened as he picked out a tasteful arrangement of tulips and daffodils. If he had a wife or girlfriend, it would be better to find out now, before I made an idiot out of myself and did something silly like . . . inviting him to my apartment to look through bridal magazines.

"He's not married," my assistant, Amber Lee, said the moment I made it to the back room. Amber Lee was a tall, African American woman with a hint of gray in her tight-cropped hair and a deep-throated laugh more infectious than pinkeye in a day care center. A lifelong resident of Ramble and former schoolteacher, she'd taught at least one child from every family and could still dish up dirt on most, but never in a mean way. She struck me as more the kindly grandmother type, looking over all her children, warts and all.

I went for innocence. "Who's not married?"

Liv laughed. "Mr. Baby Cakes, of course."

Amber Lee grinned. "Can't fool us. I saw you checking out the baker's buns." She batted her eyelashes and put a hand on her hip. " 'Why, I've got *plenty* of bridal magazines in my apartment. Stop over any time.' "

Liv swatted Amber Lee's arm. "Give the kid a break." Although only two years older, Liv had a nasty habit of referring to me as "the kid." She turned back to me. "Don't let a little teasing dissuade you. The baker is pretty—"

"Hot?" Amber Lee tried. "Sweet? Smoking? Well-done?"

I rolled my eyes. "It doesn't matter anyway. Even if I were ready for another romance, he bought flowers for someone."

"That's new," Amber Lee said. "I haven't heard anything about a girlfriend. Let me see what I can find out."

"What kind of flowers did he buy?" Liv asked.

"Pink tulips and daffodils."

"And what do those mean in that supersecret language of yours?" Liv asked.

"Pink tulips represent *care* and *compassion*. Daffodils represent *regard*. Or *vanity*."

"But if we want to sell them, we say they mean *regard*." She wagged her finger at me. "In either case, not the most romantic flowers one can choose."

I shrugged. Choosing flowers was romantic enough.

Chapter 2

I was sweeping the floral detritus, the stems, leaves, and wilted petals that collect on the floor, from the back room when the bell over the door signaled a last-minute customer.

"I'll take care of it." Liv left off counting spools of ribbon and set down her clipboard. She returned a moment later. "You're on, kid. The Whitneys are here for their bridal appointment."

I glanced at the clock, where the second hand inched toward the top of the hour. Seven p.m., our closing time. "And only four hours late. How considerate."

Liv gestured that I lower my volume, looking like a concert conductor signaling the tuba section to make a massive decrescendo. I'd know because Liv *is* the conductor of Ramble's town band. Such a petite conductor, in fact, that they had to build a special platform in the gazebo in Ramble's town square so she could be seen over the music stands.

And I do, in fact, play the tuba, which, in my defense, is a difficult instrument to play softly.

People often don't believe we're cousins. Although our mothers were identical twins, each of us got our looks from our fathers. I grew tall with dark hair and complexion. Liv was named for her olive skin, which turned out to be a mild case of jaundice that dissipated shortly after the ink on her birth certificate dried, or so the old family story goes. Instead, Liv was petite with fair hair and skin, with cute freckles that were the bane of her teen years.

"I already suggested they come back tomorrow," she said, "but you know how Ellen is. She insists it's urgent."

I thought of my aching feet. At least I could sit down during the planning appointment. "You go home to Eric. I'll lock up when we're done."

"You sure, kiddo?" Liv was already gathering her purse. "I can't understand why they even came to us, considering. Look, if you don't want to do this alone, I can stay. I'd imagine it would be a bit uncomfortable, since Jenny . . ."

"Don't dramatize it, Liv. Jenny and I were friends. We drifted apart. It happens. I got this. Now, shoo."

As Liv scooted out the back door into the alleyway, I steeled myself to meet the Whitneys, not giving in to the urge to run outside and drag Liv back. I was twenty-nine, after all, old enough to deal with difficult customers and awkward relationships. Heaven knows, I'd had my share of each.

I darted into our small restroom and changed into a lavender dress. Early in our business, Liv found an article that hypothesized that a wedding coordinator sold 28 percent more wedding flowers when dressed as for a wedding. Since I didn't have the data to argue with her, I wore a dress for bridal appointments. I ran a brush through my hair, pulled it up into a quick knot, then practiced my best friendly smile in the mirror. It would have to do.

"There you are, Audrey. I wondered if everyone had gone home." Ellen Whitney had paged halfway through our stack of bridal books. Her coral-colored sandals tapped the floor of the gazebo in nervous energy. Of course those coral sandals were topped by an extra-large coral pantsuit; a coral necklace, bracelet, and earrings; and a coral lipstick that made her Italian complexion sallow. Ellen was decidedly monochromatic, and never in a good way.

"The shop would have been dark and locked if you were just a minute later."

"Glad we made it here in time, then." Ellen continued foraging through the books, with no hint of apology for missing their earlier appointment or holding me up at this late hour. "I'd forgotten how many details there were in planning a wedding . . . and on such short notice."

I grabbed my notebook and started a clean page. "When is the big day?"

"Three weeks." Ellen didn't bat a coral-tinted eyelid. "April twenty-seventh," she added, naming a date closer to two and a half weeks away. "We wanted to avoid the hot weather."

Her daughter, Jenny, bit on a well-chewed fingernail. That might be her major source of calories these days. When Jenny and I were close, often capping a Saturday morning garage-sailing expedition (or is it sale-ing?) with a stop for chicken sandwiches and waffle fries, she equaled her mother in girth. When she lost all the extra poundage, however, she deserted me for her new anorexic friends from the fitness center. I missed my companion in cholesterol. But she'd kept off the weight, and I was happy for her.

"Mrs. Whitney," I started, "with such late notice I'm afraid—"

"Oh, but you must," Ellen insisted. "Everything else is all arranged. The church, the hall, the dresses, the cake." She counted off the items on her coral-tipped fingernails.

"All we have left is the flowers, and with you being a friend of Jenny, I assumed . . ."

Jenny slumped further into her chair. "Mother, maybe we could do imitation flowers. Some of them looked almost real."

"Imitation flowers?" Ellen bellowed. "At what is sure to be the wedding of the season? You can't marry into the Rawling family using cheap silk pansies. I'd be the laughingstock of Ramble.

"Really, Audrey." She turned to me with a smirk of challenge on her face. "You must see how an opportunity to provide the flowers for such an occasion would be a boon to your business. After all"—she gestured to the empty shop—"you're not exactly packing them in here."

I felt my cheeks turn a peony pink. *Of course the shop is empty. We're closed, you dragonwort.* Only I didn't say that. I paused for a moment, caught the calming scent of lavender still in the air, and went with that. "You didn't let me finish. Of course we'll do our best to accommodate your wishes, but with such little lead time, certain flowers, especially tropicals, might be difficult to obtain." I deliberately turned to Jenny and sent her an encouraging smile. "Now, perhaps we should start with what the bride has in mind."

Despite my attempts to direct my attention to Jenny, Ellen would have her way. When we were all done they'd ordered a lackluster bouquet composed of black and white anemones with accents of, of all things, pussy willows and scabious seed heads (even the name should give people a hint) and with more filler than my high school paper on the French Revolution. For that I'd gotten a D. But I determined to make these flowers into something wonderful. I remembered Jenny sharing stories of her embarrassment at being stuffed into too-small bridesmaid's dresses as all her thinner friends married before her. How exciting that the little wallflower would now be the blushing bride.

But Derek Rawling? The few occasions he deigned to

speak with me, he'd impressed me as being what Grandma Mae used to call wanton—the prodigal son *before* his appointment with the swine.

Ellen would consider him a good catch, though. Looks. Old money. Even if he was considerably older than Jenny. Still, no one had been able to reel in the town's resident playboy to date. I wondered what it was about the thinner, but still somewhat socially awkward, Jenny that had baited him.

The next morning as I sipped my instant coffee and added Jenny's flowers to our upcoming orders, I grew more depressed. I had stewed over it the night before with Chester. Well, I stewed while he chased his well-chewed, neon green toy mouse and played hide-and-seek with my favorite pair of earrings. I'd yet to find one of them, but I had grown more optimistic about Ellen's color scheme. I recalled a recent bouquet with similar colors—or lack thereof—and textures that made the cover of a major bridal magazine. I scavenged my apartment for the issue and saw that the writer had characterized the bouquet as "earthy, bold, and strikingly different."

For a moment I tried to convince myself that sweet Jenny could pull off earthy, bold, and strikingly different.

But worse than that, the language of the flowers was all wrong. While many guides suggest that the anemone signifies *expectation*, the old-time Victorians declared it meant *forsaken*. And the dried accents Ellen had chosen? The scabious is the symbol of *unfortunate love*. And the pussy willows represent *motherhood*. Perhaps Ellen's stamp of approval on this union? Then again, black, white, gray, brown . . . could just be another of Ellen's failed color experiments. Not a great way to start off a life together. Perhaps Jenny and I could sit down and talk about it.

The alleyway door opened and Amber Lee bustled in,

removing an old-fashioned hair bonnet and shaking the remains of our latest April shower into the utility tub. She spied my cup, glanced at the empty pot I'd spurned in favor of the quicker and easier instant, then rolled her eyes before preparing a fresh pot of real coffee.

I couldn't blame her. Both of us found the seven a.m. shift difficult. Amber Lee had kept schoolteacher's hours until two years before. She'd confided in me that she'd expected retirement to be like the summer vacations she'd long enjoyed. But by October, she was climbing the walls. She checked if the school district needed substitutes, but they talked about more budget cuts. Her love of flowers drew her to us, and we gave her an audition during one of our busy periods. She took to the job like she was born in a garden, and we'd been expanding her duties ever since.

She poured some of her high-test into my empty mug, and only then did we talk. She pointed at the paperwork. "I see Ellen and Jenny did come in yesterday after all. Did they say why they were late?" She hid a smirk behind her coffee cup.

I could sense a story coming on. "Why? What did you hear?"

"One of my former students is now a secretary down at the church. And she saw Ellen there raising a ruckus with Pastor Seymour."

I couldn't imagine anyone drawing ire from the kind-hearted, elderly minister. "What in the world about?"

"Well, it seems Ellen presented him with *her* order of service for the wedding—in fifty-two easy-to-remember steps. I guess they'd gotten to number fifteen when he fell asleep. To my way of thinking, at eighty-three, you've earned the right to nod off now and then. Let's just say Ellen was not amused. She stayed right there until he promised to study up on her list."

"Poor Pastor Seymour . . . and poor Jenny."

"I can't help thinking the kid is getting the short end of this deal." Amber Lee wagged a finger for emphasis. "And from what I heard, it *is* a deal. The word is, Ellen and old man Rawling were more involved in making this happen than Jenny and Derek."

My next sip of coffee turned bitter in my mouth. "The rumor mill doesn't always have it right, you know. Like the time everyone in town insisted Clara Kettering was dying from a large tumor and—"

"And it turned out to be triplets. I hear you. But this would explain a few things. Like why Jenny is all glum but Ellen is beaming from ear to ear. Consider who stands to benefit from this match."

I pulled on my black florist's apron and glanced at the next orders to be prepared. "But why would Jenny go along with that—and why would Derek?"

Amber Lee pulled out a step stool and retrieved a box of vases from an upper shelf. "Some are saying Jenny planned the whole thing to get her hands on Derek's money."

"That sounds like mean-spirited jealousy."

"I knew you would defend her, even after she dumped you."

I reached up to grab the box from Amber Lee. "She didn't dump me. We just . . . grew apart."

"Uh-huh. If that's the way you want it. But I agree with you," Amber Lee said. "I'll wager some old flame of Derek's started that bit. Derek has enough brokenhearted old girlfriends to string from here to Richmond. And I don't see Jenny playing the role of money-grubbing manipulator, either—at least not without a big push from mommy dearest."

"But that doesn't explain Derek's thoughts turning to orange blossoms." I sighed. I *wished* they'd ordered orange blossoms.

"That's where old man Rawling comes in, so I hear. He's been wanting good ol' Derek to settle down for quite some time now, and he has his hopes set on Jenny as the one to do it." Amber Lee set the step stool back into place.

"For Jenny's sake, I hope it works."

Amber Lee slit open the box with a utility knife. "Mark my words, Audrey. That kind only settles down when he's good and ready. Or dead."

Chapter 3

"Audrey, I loved the article about you in the paper." Pastor Seymour pumped my hand at the back of the church after the Sunday morning service. The octogenarian sported a full head of snowy white hair, greased back, as was the style decades earlier, likely when he bought the suit he was wearing. He banged his cane for emphasis. "I only wish all the couples *I* married had stayed together."

"In all fairness, Pastor, you've been at it a lot longer than I have. I'm afraid the article made it sound like I'd found some magic formula. The Botanical Dr. Dolittle, indeed."

Eric stepped forward in the queue and put his arm around Liv. "Whether it was the flowers by Audrey or the vows by Pastor Seymour, it sure worked wonders for us."

We exited the historic stone church to bright spring sunlight dappling through the opening leaves. Vibrant tulips and daffodils lined the cement walkway, the ancient lilacs at the corners of the old church were preparing to bloom, and cherry blossoms were already in the air.

"Audrey, we were thinking about a picnic today," Liv said. "Maybe grabbing some fried chicken and heading to Ramble Falls. We can celebrate the article. I have a feeling it's going to be great for business."

Eric wagged his head and wrapped his arms around Liv. "Only if you stop thinking about business for one day." He planted a kiss on the tip of her nose.

I looked at the couple and remembered their stroll down the same pathway just two years earlier—except then I was throwing rice. Well, not really rice, but the latest environmentally approved substitute. "No, you two go ahead. Enjoy your day off together."

Liv put her hand on my arm. "Are you sure?"

"Positive. I have a couple of things I wanted to do today. But if there's any fried chicken the ants don't eat, save me a drumstick."

As Liv and Eric walked hand in hand to the parking lot, I stooped to pluck a dandelion half-hidden behind a tulip.

"Audrey!"

I popped up with a smile. How genuine the smile was is up for interpretation. "Hi, Carolyn." Leave it to our mayor's daughter to catch me hunched over with my hands in the dirt.

"Do dandelions have meaning, too?"

I glanced at the cheerful yellow weed in my hand. In a way, Carolyn resembled the dandelion, with her wispy, platinum blond hair but heavier makeup, as if she were trying too hard to prove herself a flower instead of a weed. "It depends on whom you ask. The older books say *coquetry*. The newer ones suggest they represent *happiness* and *faithfulness*."

"Happiness and faithfulness . . . Maybe we should sneak a dandelion into my bouquet, too." And then she laughed. An odd, tittering laugh I hoped her groom found endearing.

If I didn't want to spoil my record, it had better be a good bouquet.

"Is everything set for the wedding?" she asked.

"All the flowers have been ordered. I think we've cornered the market on peach roses. Come Saturday, this little church is going to be a garden. It's our only big job right now, so we'll have no trouble getting it all set."

"Audrey, I'm so glad we went with you and not that cheap online florist my mother wanted to use. Although it might have been fun to assemble our own bouquets. But what would we do if they didn't turn out just right?"

I patted Carolyn's hand and reassured her that when she marched down the aisle, her flowers would be waiting for her.

I strolled past the parking lot to the street, where the Honda CR-V I shared with the business waited. Rolling down the window, I cruised past the Rockwellian landscape that is Ramble, the two-story brick and stone Main Street, complete with awnings, pots of annuals, and a park bench outside the barbershop where men gather, even when it's closed.

The conversation with Carolyn spurred the thought that maybe, business permitting, we could offer an emergency service to fix some of those untidy homemade bouquets.

And perhaps we could offer a bridesmaids' workshop, where the bridal party could come in and assemble their own bouquets under expert direction. The brides would expect to save money, but we'd probably have to charge more just to replace flowers ruined in the process. Maybe Liv could crunch the numbers.

Apparently my cousin wasn't the only one who had trouble letting go of business on her day off. It was this kind of entrepreneurial thinking that made the Rose in Bloom a success, while Liv and I subsisted just above the poverty level. After five years, the business was paying off—if only with more money to invest back into the business.

I drove by the flower shop, with its cheerful display of Easter arrangements in the two large bay windows and the flats and pots of flowering plants sitting unprotected in front of the closed shop. In five years, we'd had just one apparent instance of theft. Except, when we opened up shop, we found the twenty-dollar bill someone had slid under the door.

On an impulse, I made a U-turn and headed back toward Old Hill Road. As I wound my way up that familiar narrow road lined with alternating white and stone fences and hanging signs announcing the various names of local farms and riding stables, memories came flooding back. For the most part, they had ceased to be painful ones. Both Liv and I treasured our recollections of Grandma Mae. But I, more than Liv, also missed the little cottage where we'd spent so many happy summers. Perhaps because Liv contented herself with her own gardens now.

I pulled to the side of the road in front of Grandma Mae's tiny cottage and sighed. As I suspected, little had been done since the last time I'd passed it. The rotting porch had been removed, leaving the front door positioned a good two feet above the yard. A shattered kitchen windowpane exposed the inside to the elements, and pine needles had collected on the bowing roofline and overflowed the gutters.

I pushed open the car door and braved the jungle that used to be the lawn. Our childhood gardens were nothing more than mounds of tall grass and weeds, with an occasional hardy perennial rearing its stubborn head and demanding its share of sunshine and spring rain. I gathered a handful of lily of the valley, snipped some rhododendron blossoms, and lifted them to my nose, enjoying the heady fragrance of nostalgia more than the scent of the flowers.

Suddenly Liv and I were young again, dancing among the dandelions on the hillside, shoving buttercups under each other's chins. We'd tear across the fields then dare each other to jump the creek. Sometimes we even made it across. Then we'd run in for some of Grandma's lemonade, and she'd clean us up and gather both of us into a hug. "My Mae flowers," she'd call us in an accent all her own, as she spoiled us with cookies and homemade fudge. She'd moved from the deep South when she married, adding a faint mountain twang of Appalachia to her Southern drawl in a charming mixture everyone around her seemed to love.

I glanced down at the lily of the valley and considered its meaning. *Happiness restored.* Seven years had elapsed since Grandma Mae's passing, and five since Liv and I moved to Ramble and started the flower shop using the small inheritance and the proceeds from selling the cottage. Happiness *was* restored. Except it still saddened me to see Grandma's cottage and our gardens in such a state. That reporter was right—sad what had become of it. I couldn't rescue it, restore it to its original glory, but I might be able to prop something in that window to prevent further damage.

I trudged through the weeds and briars to the kitchen window and peered in. Recent rains had left the countertop drenched with water and the sink filled with shards of broken glass. If the window wasn't covered soon, there would be more damage to the vintage kitchen, by weather or by wild animals. I hoped a family of raccoons hadn't already taken up residence.

I looked around the yard and spotted the battered sign: "Professionally managed by Rawling Properties." Yeah, right. While Derek's property management skills failed to impress me, his sign just might be the thing to block the broken window. I returned to the CR-V, laid my gathered flowers on the passenger seat, riffled the vehicle for my little tool kit, including a small hammer and some tacks, then yanked the sign out of the yard.

The corrugated plastic rectangle fit the window as if it were designed for it. I tacked the bottom corners then looked for something to stand on to reach the top corners. I heaved myself onto the jutting threshold of the front door. I couldn't quite reach the top far corner, so I hammered a tack into the middle. I was still suspended against the house when a car rumbled up the road. Brakes slammed. I craned my neck to see who was coming, but the vehicle was obscured by a cloud of dust and cinders.

"Audrey, what do you think you're doing?" Derek Rawling banged shut the door of his fancy sports car and braved the foliage as he headed toward me. "This place doesn't belong to you anymore."

"I know that." I hopped back to the ground. "But someone has to fix the broken window. Just being a good neighbor and doing you a favor."

Derek set his jaw. "Fine, but let me." He reached up and yanked down the sign, rolling his eyes at me as he turned it right side up. Oops.

He held out a palm, and I handed him both the hammer and a tack. While he worked at affixing the sign over the broken window, I wondered what about Derek had attracted Jenny.

Sure, he was handsome, although, in his forties, considerably older than Jenny. Still, he had that tanned skin and well-groomed salt-and-pepper hair that many women find distinguished. The salt-and-pepper continued down long sideburns and into a stubbly but well-chiseled chin. His pale blue eyes would be more attractive if they weren't bloodshot. And yes, he had money and that great car. But I couldn't help but be sad.

"Take care of her," I mumbled.

"What?" Derek asked as he hammered in the last tack.

"I said that should take care of it."

Derek stood back and examined his work, then turned to me. "Audrey, I know this place must hold a lot of memories for you, but you can't hang out here. It's abandoned. It could be dangerous being out here all alone."

"But I just—"

"No buts. I'm not trying to be mean, but if I catch you here, I'll have to report you to Chief Bixby as a trespasser. Understand?"

"Understood." I snatched back my hammer and carefully made my way out of the neglected yard without looking back. Why Derek Rawling hadn't renovated or sold the cottage to some enterprising flipper instead of letting it go to seed like this, I had no idea.

"Gone to seed?" I rolled my eyes at my inadvertent joke as I steered back down the hill and into town. Maybe the bubble bursting in the real estate market when it did had something to do with the cottage's vacancy. Now if only property values and interest rates would stay low until I saved enough for a down payment.

When I entered my apartment, Chester was nowhere to be seen. Probably sleeping on my clean laundry—if I had any—or tearing my curtains to shreds.

I arranged my purloined flowers in a small bud vase, then centered them on my kitchen table. At least a few of Grandma Mae's perennials had survived.

Chester sauntered out of the bedroom, hopped onto the table, and gave the flowers a cautious sniff. I rubbed his head, then relented to his loud request for food. *I haven't eaten in weeks,* he seemed to say. Chester lies a lot.

Finally, I poured myself a bowl of cereal and settled on the sofa for a quiet afternoon of carbs and an old musical on television. *My Fair Lady* for the umpteenth time. One of my favorites. After all, in her own way, Eliza Doolittle was a florist.

When I walked into the shop on Monday at eleven, I could tell it was an unusual day. Our coolers were already decimated. Liv was stationed at the phone, a pencil stuck behind her ear—never a good sign. Amber Lee waited on customers. Yes, plural even.

"There she is." Mrs. Simmons waddled over and drew me into a hug. "Our little celebrity!" I wasn't quite sure why she called me little, since I towered over her by at least a foot. But I guessed she'd read the article.

"Thanks." I returned her hug. I refrained from addressing her by name. When I was dating her son Brad—and with an impending engagement on the horizon—she'd insisted I call her "Mom." Somehow with Brad (a.k.a. Brad the Cad) in Manhattan and us not talking, that seemed inappropriate.

"I'll have to send the article and picture to Brad." She propped a chubby hand on each of my cheeks. "He'll be so proud!" Mrs. Simmons needed a little tutoring on the meaning of "broke up."

"Audrey!" Liv called over the din in the shop.

I thanked Mrs. Simmons, excised myself, and headed to Liv just in time to spot her shoving a pencil behind her other ear.

Liv's face flushed with energy, her eyes glittering. She gestured to the bustling shop. "It's been like this all morning—not that I'm complaining. Larry is in the back room with our delivery. Could you sign off on it?" The phone rang again.

I found Larry in the back room chuckling. "Hey, pumpkin." He drew me into a hug. "Congratulations on the article. It seems to be doing your business some good."

"I guess so. I know Liv hoped we'd get a wedding booking or two out of it, but it looks like we were swamped this morning. You haven't been waiting all this time, have you?" Larry normally delivered our stock of flowers, straight from his greenhouses, early before we opened.

"Nope, in fact this is my second delivery. Liv phoned in another order when things got busy this morning."

"Then it appears to be doing *your* business some good, too."

A smile lit up Larry's round face. Since age had taken most of his blond hair, with the exception of one shock in the middle, Larry's smiling visage bore a resemblance to a field-worn Kewpie doll. His family had raised crops in the area since colonial days, once specializing in tobacco. But after an ancestor died from lung cancer, the family switched to flowers. Now with Larry in charge of the operation, his fields and greenhouses supplied all of our locally grown blooms.

I counted the new inventory against the checklist. All the items on my list were checked off, but one long cardboard box remained on the cart. I started to open it and caught just a glimpse of rose stems and leaves when Larry grabbed it back, practically shutting the box on my hand.

"Sorry about that." His fair complexion turned bright red. "Wrong order."

"Not a problem." I scrawled my signature on the checklist and pulled out my customer copy. "We've got everything on the manifest anyway."

He'd just stepped out the door when Liv returned. "I put the phone on voice mail for lunch." She plopped a sandwich on the worktable and ignored it while she started making one of the stock arrangements we try to keep in the self-service cooler.

I processed the new delivery, separating the flowers by variety into the various buckets we kept them in until we were ready to arrange them, and then lugged them into the walk-in. By the time I finished, Liv had completed her arrangement, taken one bite from her sandwich, and pulled out a small vase to start another arrangement.

"You need to eat." I pulled the vase toward me.

"I know, but we also need to take advantage of your fifteen minutes of fame while it lasts." She pulled my appointment calendar out of her apron. "We've booked six new wedding consultations just this morning."

"Six? Where are they all coming from?"

"That's just it," she said with a bite of egg salad. "Some news service picked up the story. That article appeared in half the local newspapers in the mid-Atlantic region. Which reminds me . . ." She slid a piece of scratch paper toward me. "Here's the new delivery price schedule for locations outside of our normal delivery area. And we now have a pickup option."

I glanced at the figures tallied in pencil, arranged by miles from the store. "One-hundred mile surcharge? Do you really think someone is going to drive one hundred miles for a bridal consultation?"

She tilted her head into a pixielike grin. "She'll be here at two today. I said you could squeeze her in. Oh, and Jenny called. She wants to talk to you about her order. She's going to swing by *before* seven."

"Good. I came up with an idea to tweak that awful arrangement her mother picked."

By late afternoon, my back started to ache from wrapping arrangements in plastic. Some munchkin must have designed our counter. Hunched over, I caught a glimpse of the next customer's pant leg first. White. I stood up.

Nick Maxwell held a small spring bouquet of pink roses and white daisies. Hmm. Pink roses, the symbol of *secret love*, and daisies, *cheerfulness* or *innocence*. But that assumed he knew what they meant. I fixed up the untidy arrangement as I wrapped it for him. Understandable, considering they were slinging flowers like flapjacks in the back room. But everything would be nice before it left the shop.

Every time I hazarded a glance up at him, his gaze shifted to the ground, his dark eyes barely visible under those long lashes women try to fake with mascara.

As soon as I handed him his receipt, the next customer plopped her purse onto the counter. Nick remained planted in place for a moment. "Audrey, I . . . thanks." Then he waved the flowers at me in a salute and backed out of the store.

When Jenny arrived just after six, I could spare more time. I offered her a cup of coffee. She looked like she needed it, and I felt the need of some caffeine reinforcement as well. When we were seated in the consulting nook, she stared down at the flagstone table for a few moments.

I decided to start. "I've been considering the bouquet we discussed the other day."

"Cancel it."

"Cancel?" I wondered if the mayor's wife had been talking to her about the joys of online flowers.

"The wedding is off."

"Off?" I repeated. Where was the off button on this lame echo machine? "Jenny, I'm sorry. Would you like to talk about it?"

She raised her head, met my eyes, and let out a sardonic laugh. "You know, the funny thing is we're not even technically broken up yet. I just spent all afternoon canceling the cake, the dress—everything. I figured that would make it easier to call it off with Derek." She rolled her eyes. "And tell my mother. That's going to be worse than talking to Derek, I think. She's going to flip."

Amber Lee's words about Ellen being instrumental in orchestrating the relationship sprang to mind. "Jenny, if you don't mind my asking, how did you ever get involved with Derek? I remember you once called him 'the wild one.'"

Jenny smiled, then rummaged through her purse as tears started forming. I pulled up a box of tissues I kept on hand for emotional moments. Though usually they involved mothers of the bride—either when they realized their daughters were getting married or when they realized how much it would cost them. Jenny plucked three tissues from the box.

"At first, I think I was flattered." She took a moment to wipe her tears and blow her nose. "Here's this rich, handsome guy, and he wanted to spend time with me. But, Audrey, then I got to really like him. He's witty and charming and educated and sophisticated. Except sometimes I feel a little like a country bumpkin next to him—always worried I'm going to use the wrong fork or something. And always wondering what he sees in me." Jenny pulled a strand of hair from her face. "Mother really, really likes him."

"But what happened?"

"I'm not sure anything happened. I mean, it's not like we argued, and Derek's never been anything but kind to me. I think over time I just . . . You can only put on a front for so long. And I'm not certain being witty and charming is enough." She paused for a moment, chewing on her thumbnail. "Audrey, when I get married, I want someone who loves me without making me question why. I don't want to wonder. Until I know, I think it would be a mistake."

"Jenny, you don't think this is just dormant insecurity, from . . ."

"From my fat years?" She laughed and shook her head. "I did think that for a while. But I'm pretty sure I'm not what Derek would pick for his wife, and I don't think he'd be happy for long if we went through with the wedding. I'm not sure I could keep his interest. Audrey, I want to be the face someone *wants* to come home to. I think I've known for a while it wouldn't work, but the more Mother went on and on about what a wonderful opportunity it was, the more chicken I got."

Jenny's slumped posture and downcast eyes spoke volumes. Poor little Jenny—always trying so hard to please. A move like this must have been hard for her. "For what it's worth, I think you're doing the right thing." I squeezed her hand.

"Thanks, Audrey. You've been a good friend. All my other friends will think I'm an idiot for breaking up with Derek. I'm only sorry I . . ." She swallowed hard. "Maybe when this is over you and I can get together, hit some garage sales."

"Sure thing."

She glanced at her watch. "Derek is supposed to pick me up here at seven. I'll break it off with him tonight." She sighed. "I think I'll wait until tomorrow to tell my mother. And then I'm going to need to dust off my résumé."

"I thought you had a job."

"Not one that pays all my bills, what with the cost of gas and rent—even with a roommate. I'm going to have to find a better job, a cheaper place, or pick up some part-time hours somewhere. Mother has made it clear she's tired of helping me make ends meet. Now that the wedding is off . . . well, it's not like I'm sixteen and she's obligated to support me. But *I* want to cut the strings. I don't want her support to influence my decisions again."

Ellen might not be; but I was proud of Jenny.

"Um, Audrey. There wouldn't be a job open here, would there? The shop seems awfully busy."

"Maybe. It depends on how things work out with these new wedding orders."

"I'm not sure how good I'd be with flowers, but I work hard."

I glanced at my watch. With still forty minutes before her meeting with Derek, Jenny would need something to keep her mind occupied besides biting her fingernails to the bone. "If we were able to put on a new person—and I'm not promising, mind you—you'd have to start with a lot of grunt work. But why don't we give you a brief lesson and see how you do?"

"A lesson?"

"Yeah, do you have a few minutes?"

"Sure."

"Then follow me." I led Jenny through the shop and into the back room, where Liv and Amber Lee were trying to get ahead with arrangements for the next day.

When Amber Lee looked up, I said, "Jenny is thinking about joining us, and I thought I'd give her a quick floral design lesson."

Liv raised an eyebrow but didn't say anything. When she knew the whole story, kindhearted Liv would agree.

"Now, what shall we make?" I tried to think of a suitable first lesson.

"You know, that bouquet in the paper was gorgeous," Jenny answered. "And I loved the meanings you gave all the flowers. Could we make one of those?"

"Sure." At the same time I wondered what I'd do with it. I certainly didn't need another reminder of my failed relationship with Brad on display. I showed Jenny around the cooler and had her pick out the flowers to use.

She grabbed a rose before I could warn her about the thorns, so we stopped to rinse off her bleeding fingers and bandage them. The dangers of being a rookie in the floral industry.

I demonstrated how to strip the leaves and thorns with a sharp folding knife we kept on hand for that purpose. "Here's an opportunity to get your revenge on those thorns." I handed the tool to her.

She gripped the knife awkwardly, ineffectively mirroring my movement as if she were afraid of hurting the flowers. In the battle against the thorns, the thorns won. I pulled another knife from the drawer, repeated the demonstration, and together we assembled a similar hand-tied bouquet of lavender and white roses and purple irises.

"It's so pretty," Jenny said, admiring her work. She handed it toward me.

"You keep it. Fruit of your labor. If you want, you can take the pins out and put it in a vase with water to keep it fresh. In the meantime . . ." I gathered the tools we'd used—pruning shears, floral tape, and the sharp knife—and placed them in one of the plastic shop bags. "You can borrow these tools and practice at home. Just rearrange the same flowers over again—or even use wildflowers. Come back later in the week and we'll see if we can work you into the schedule. Just expect it to be simple stuff for a while."

"Oh, thank you, Audrey!" She hugged me.

Right at seven, a distinctive horn sounded from the street. Her countenance fell. "That's Derek. I should go."

I escorted her to the front of the shop and watched as she darted between raindrops and climbed into Derek's sports car. Yes, this breakup would be painful, but Jenny would make it. And in the end, I suspected she'd not regret the decision.

Early the next morning—at least I thought it was morning; the light said yes, but my body insisted there were at least a few more hours to the night—I awoke to a loud pounding at my door. My first inclination was to ignore it. My dream haze convinced me it was just Audrey Hepburn stomping on the floor above, in a rousing rendition of "The Rain in Spain."

But a rather heavy cat landed squarely on my stomach, dug in his claws, and then tore out of the room. Paws skidded in the hallway, followed by a thump and then a crash.

I decided I'd better get up to investigate. So, using the walls for support, I staggered to the kitchen, where I found my flower arrangement from Grandma Mae's garden lying on the kitchen floor, the vase shattered. Since water that has held lily of the valley can be toxic, I grabbed some paper towels and wiped up the mess before Chester could get into it. So much for *renewed happiness.* I shivered as I also picked up the rhododendron. Why hadn't I considered its meaning before?

Beware.

And then the pounding on my door started again. Should I dial 911?

"Audrey?" The voice was Liv's. Why would she be here this early in the morning?

I opened the door and tried to open my eyes as well. "What? Liv, what's going on?"

Liv rushed past me into the kitchen, wringing her hands. When she stopped, they were shaking.

I grabbed her hands to try to warm them. "What's the matter? Has something happened to Eric?"

She started to nod. Horror filled me, but then she shook her head instead.

"Eric saw it. He's okay." Liv sat down on one of my kitchen chairs, clutching her arms to her chest, rocking back and forth. Even in the dim light of my kitchen, her skin appeared pale.

I ran to get a blanket and wrapped it around her shoulders. She clutched it to herself.

"Now, what happened?" I urged.

Liv took a deep breath. "Eric went out for a jog this morning." She shivered again. "He headed down Elm, you know, where those apartments are, and saw that sports car of Derek Rawling's."

"Jenny lives there. He must have . . ." My mind started

spinning. "Why would he spend the night if Jenny just broke up with him? Unless she chickened out."

Liv shook her head. "Eric crossed the street to get a closer look. You know guys and sports cars. When he got closer . . ."

I slid into my seat at the table just as Liv began rocking in her chair again.

"Liv, what is it?"

"Eric had a hard time seeing because of those tinted windows. And when he got close he saw him."

"Who?"

"Derek. Audrey, he was dead. Dead and sitting behind the steering wheel of his car."

"Was Eric positive? Maybe Derek just passed out or something."

"No, he was certain. Audrey, there's more. When Eric got closer, he could tell it wasn't just the tinted windows that were making it difficult to see. Something was smeared all over the windows. Audrey, it was blood, and Eric said there was a knife still . . ."

I held my breath, forcibly exhaled, then recalled what I remembered from college anatomy. No, anatomy is not required to be a florist, but few people in Ramble know I studied nursing for two years before dropping out. The reason is known by even fewer. "That must have hit an artery if it . . ."

Liv turned a decided green.

"Sorry," I said. Derek had been murdered. Right on the streets of Ramble. No wonder she was so shook up. "He wouldn't have suffered long."

"But, Audrey, Eric thinks the knife was one of ours—from the shop."

"He must be mistaken." Liv had ordered a dozen of those knives with the florist shop name printed on them so they wouldn't wander. And if they did wander, at least they would serve as advertisement.

She stared hard at me. And then I remembered.

"I gave Jenny a knife yesterday, but she wouldn't . . . couldn't have done anything like that."

Liv shook her head. "Audrey, Eric said the bouquet was there, too, in the car. Torn to bits and covered with blood."

Chapter 4

A stream of police entered and exited the Rose in Bloom like a swarm of ants attacking blossoming peonies. Okay, a rather small swarm, since the Ramble police force consisted of six officers, the chief of police, two volunteer crossing guards, and a couple of retired officers who filled in when needed. The entire force seemed to be present this morning.

The time I'd taken to calm Liv down was wasted the second she saw the uniformed officers carting items out of the shop in plastic and paper bags.

"What in the heliotrope is going on here?" Liv, both hands clenched into fists at her sides, marched into the shop and toward Kane Bixby, who leaned against the counter.

I stayed a couple of steps behind her. When Liv gets angry, she scares me, too.

Bixby, Ramble's chief of police, reached into his pocket and pulled out a folded paper. A cluster of spent tissues fell to the ground. "Search warrant."

Liv grasped the corner of the page with two fingers and scanned it—from a safe distance. "But why my shop? What could you possibly be looking for?" Another officer came from the back room carrying a paper bag with stems protruding from the top. Liv dropped the warrant and put her hands on both cheeks. "And why are you taking my flowers? You can't take our stock!"

"Trust me." Bixby retrieved a clean tissue from another pocket and wiped his red, watery eyes. "The last thing I want to do is take your flowers." He paused to stifle a sneeze.

Kane Bixby's regret appeared genuine. In the five years Liv and I had been running the shop, he'd never set foot inside or ordered anything for his wife, even though a few times we'd seen her strolling past the shop looking wistfully at our displays. We'd invited her in one day, but she'd declined, citing her husband's allergies, which she claimed were so bad, he could tell when she'd even gone near a flower shop.

In his sixties, Bixby kept himself in good physical condition. Slim, with receding gunmetal gray hair, he struck an imposing figure—except when doing an impression of a walking mucus factory. Since he seemed the type to enjoy striking an imposing figure, his allergies must have made him truly miserable.

Another officer walked by with a box containing our cutting implements, everything from our utility knives to our floral shears.

Before Liv could have a grand mal conniption, I stepped forward. "But why *all* of our tools? I can understand you taking the knives . . ."

Bixby raised one eyebrow and turned to me. "Why would you ask about the knives in particular, Audrey?"

"Oh, cut it out, Bixby," Liv said. "You know Eric told us."

"Told you that a knife marked 'The Rose in Bloom' was used as a murder weapon?"

"And so you're taking our shears, too?" I said. Liv's aggravation finally hit me.

Bixby crossed his arms in front of him. "I'd rather discuss the knife. How many are there?"

"How many . . . ?" I guessed the question hadn't sunk in.

"The red-handled knives with the name of the shop printed on the handle." Bixby spoke slowly and clearly—kind of like Mr. Rogers, but not so nice about it. "They look new. You must have special-ordered them. How many of them did you order?"

"I ordered twelve," Liv said.

"And we recovered nine in the shop," Bixby said. "Any idea where the others are?"

"I don't know," Liv said. "They wander. That's why I had the name printed on the sides." She looked at me.

I turned to stare at the floral case.

"Audrey, do you know where any of the other knives are?" Bixby asked.

I developed a sudden interest in my fingernails. I had two reasons for avoiding this question. "Well, I may have one in my other purse."

"Audrey, how could you?" Liv's voice oozed disappointment. "You know how hard it's been for me to keep those knives in-house."

"Liv, I just took it home one night when . . . let's not worry about that now, all right? I hardly think it matters since Bixby's walking off—"

"I'll have someone escort you home to pick it up after we're done here," Bixby interrupted. "But that still leaves two knives at large. Any ideas?"

At that point my uvula (for those without a medical background, it's that dangly thing that hangs in the back of your throat) spontaneously increased to twelve times its normal parameters—or at least it felt that way when I tried to swallow.

Liv and I had agreed not to mention giving the knife to Jenny unless asked directly. Was this direct enough?

"We have to tell him, kiddo." Liv patted my arm.

"Tell me what?" Bixby said.

"But it might not be the same knife," I said. "There's still two missing."

"Miss Bloom, if you know where either of the two missing knives are, I suggest you speak up."

"I lent one of them to a new employee. She needed it to practice some of the techniques I taught her."

"And that employee has a name, right?" Bixby pulled out another tissue to wipe his eyes. But despite the redness and inclination to water, they were clear and focused on me.

I swallowed. "Jenny Whitney."

"Derek's fiancée?" Bixby cocked his head to hear better, as if waiting for me to add to my statement. I declined to accommodate him. "Now, why do you suppose Jenny would need a new job if she were going to marry Derek Rawling?"

"It's not the 1950s," I said. "Today women don't stop working just because they get married."

"She planned to break it off with him," Liv volunteered.

I gave her a dirty look.

"Sorry, Audrey," Liv said.

"You heard her say that?" Bixby asked Liv.

"Not exactly," Liv told him. "Audrey did."

Bixby turned to me. "Audrey, is that what Jenny said? That she planned to break up with Derek?"

"Yes, but—" I couldn't finish my argument. Bixby had already made his way to the back room. He exited moments later with two of his officers. After a brief, hushed conference, the two men headed out the door.

Bixby turned back to me. "Thanks, Audrey. That helps a bit."

"You're thinking Jenny killed Derek," I said. "But you're

wrong. I know Jenny. She couldn't harm a fly." It was true. Anyone who'd spent enough time riding around in Jenny's car would know she was a shooer and not a swatter when it came to flies. Okay, she'd flattened that spider once, but it was big and hairy and scary looking, and I couldn't blame her a bit.

"Audrey, I'm not saying she did. It's too early in the investigation. And, while you're friends, if you step back and try to be objective, you'll see that she has motive—a failed relationship with the decedent—"

"A lot of people have failed relationships, Bixby. That doesn't mean they kill each other." Although the thought may spring to mind. I made a mental note to burn my home-made Brad-the-Cad dartboard, in case anything should happen to him one day.

"I'm not saying she plotted it. But what if Derek didn't take the breakup well? What if they struggled? Maybe she felt threatened. Audrey, it could even be self-defense."

My hand flew to my forehead, and I used my fingers to rake my hair away from my face. I stared at Bixby for a moment, then shook my head. "No, not even that. Not Jenny."

"Chief?" one of the retired officers called from the back room. Bixby left to join him.

Liv followed Bixby, and I followed Liv.

"Ladies, will you please stay out in the main part of the shop?"

Liv and I ignored Bixby's request.

I had just enough of a vantage over Liv's head to see Larry pinned against a wall by Ken Lafferty, Ramble's newest and youngest police officer.

"I caught this perp sneaking in the door from the alley." Ken's face flushed as he beamed with obvious pride.

"Let him go, boy," Bixby said. That was the first thing Bixby said that made sense since he'd arrived.

"What is going on here?" Larry asked, shaking out his arm, his eyes wide as he took in the scavenged back room.

"Never mind that," Bixby said. "You can't just walk in on police business."

"How could I know you had something going on back here?" Larry said. "I'm just here to make a delivery, as usual."

"The police cars out front should have been a hint." Lafferty rested his thumbs in his belt loops and rocked from heel to toe. If he'd aimed for an authoritative posture, he needed target practice.

"You can't see the front of the building from the back alley," Liv said. "And that's where we take all deliveries."

"How'd you even get in?" Lafferty asked. "I know I secured the door." Lafferty walked to the door and demonstrated how he had secured it—I guess a more officious way of saying he locked it.

Seconds later, the "secured" door swung open again. Amber Lee walked in, key in hand.

I couldn't help it. I laughed. Soon Liv and Larry joined in, and even Bixby stifled a chuckle while the rookie police officer's ears turned red.

"I guess you solved that mystery, Batman," Bixby told his rookie, then he turned to Liv and me. "How many keys?"

Liv started to protest, but I answered. "Just four. Liv's and mine. Larry's, for deliveries, and Amber Lee in case she's the first one here." I found the question encouraging, because it indicated that perhaps Bixby might be considering another suspect besides Jenny. Then I realized his expanded suspect list would include our staff. "Now, wait a second. You can't be implying that one of us killed Derek Rawling!"

"Rawling's dead?" Larry asked, while Amber Lee just gasped.

Bixby crossed his arms in front of him. I could see in his shrewd eyes that he was assessing their reactions. I wasn't sure if he knew Amber Lee well enough to know that she was faking surprise. Then again, with her grapevine connections, she might have known Derek was dead before Derek did.

"Yes, Derek Rawling is dead. Murdered. And I'm going to take a statement from each of you as possible witnesses."

"But I didn't see anything," Amber Lee protested.

Larry shook his head and also denied seeing anything.

Liv and I followed suit.

When the protest grew louder, Bixby whistled everyone silent. "Not that kind of witnesses. But there's a clear connection between Derek's murder and this shop, so I'll need to talk to each of the shop's employees—separately. Once that's done, you can resume business."

"Yeah, with half our flowers and none of our tools," Liv said under her breath.

"What about me?" Larry asked. "I'm not an employee. I'm just here to make a delivery."

"No deliveries until we're done with our search and have taken your statement."

"I need to turn my truck back on," Larry said, "so the flowers stay cool."

Bixby rolled his eyes. "That's fine," he relented. "In fact, maybe the back alley is a good place for y'all to wait until we're finished with our search in here."

As Liv, Amber Lee, and I reluctantly followed Larry out— and the steel door closed and locked behind us—I felt a shiver. Perhaps the chill came from stepping into the shadows behind the brick buildings or maybe because the April sun had not risen high enough in the sky to warm the area. Or maybe it was just the idea that someone in Ramble had died at the hands of someone we most likely knew. Everyone in Ramble interacted with everyone else. We shopped at each other's stores, worshipped in the same churches, and lived on the same tree-lined streets. That charming small-town feel had been the balm Liv and I found so restorative.

But it was also difficult at times. While it was true that you rejoiced together when things went well, it also happened that everyone sorrowed at the same time. Like when the owner of the local dress shop was diagnosed with ALS. The whole town rushed to her aid with benefits and offers of help, raising money for wheelchair ramps and a motorized chair. When she passed, the town mourned and then memorialized her. At that precise moment, sitting at her funeral while the whole town wept, I knew I would never leave Ramble. Other places might boast of excitement, entertainment, and drama, but Ramble was family. And you just don't leave family.

Of course, that also meant that everyone knew your business. They knew when your relationship was on the rocks, when your teenager was in trouble, or even when you put on a few pounds. But as long as they had your back, that was okay.

But now one of our own had been killed. And one of our own was a killer. That was bad enough, but until the police discovered who . . . what would suspicion do to our little town?

Larry's diesel engine rumbled to life, shaking me from my thoughts. To escape the noise and fumes, I pointed toward the end of the block where outdoor patio tables from the local coffee shop, the Brew-Ha-Ha, spilled around the corner. "Bixby will be able to see us from there when he's done tearing apart our shop."

"But he told us not to leave the alley," Larry said.

"That table is technically in the alley." Amber Lee started toward the closest one. "Works for me. I've only had one cup today, which makes me about a quart low."

The table caught the morning sun, with a full view of the alleyway, the awning-dotted Main Street, and the hills that rose on both sides of the town. The sun drove away my earlier chill. We took turns going to the empty counter. I added a cinnamon raisin bagel with cream cheese and apple jelly to my tall mocha coffee order. My empty stomach insisted.

Larry spoke first, cradling his cup of black coffee in both hands. "I can't believe this is happening."

"Did you know Derek well?" I asked.

Larry shook his head. "No, just . . . well, the additional greenhouse and fields I expanded to last year. I rented the facilities, hoping to buy. Derek manages the property . . . managed."

"Not surprising," Amber Lee added. "Old man Rawling picked up a bunch of real estate—foreclosed homes and failing businesses—at a discount when the bubble burst, and he created a job for his son in managing the properties."

"Not that Derek does much managing," I added, thinking about Grandma Mae's cottage.

"Audrey," Liv scolded.

"Sorry." I exhaled deeply into my coffee cup, feeling the steam warm my cheeks. "I guess I forgot he was dead."

Larry nodded, looking into his cup. "It's no secret that some of the properties could be better cared for. Except Rawling owns so much local real estate, it's hard to do business without him."

The counter server wandered over with two steaming coffeepots and offered refills—which we all accepted.

Liv requested decaf.

"Since when do you go unleaded?" I asked.

"I'm jittery enough as it is. I just wonder what this is going to do to Eric's work. I know people say that Derek was slow to make repairs, but when he did, he generally contracted with my husband. What if Rawling hires someone else to do the work?"

"And who would that be?" Amber Lee assured her, patting her hand. "Everyone knows Eric does the best work in town."

Liv would not be consoled. "But what if he hires someone

from outside of Ramble? Rawling owns a lot of property, from West Virginia all the way to the DC line." The pitch of her voice rose and her jaw trembled. "What if he went with a bigger construction company for all of them? We can't afford to lose income right now—"

I grabbed her other hand and held it. Perhaps too tightly. In the movies someone would have slapped her across the face to calm her. But I doubted the town of Ramble would approve of anything that dramatic. "Liv, it will be fine. Eric does great work and everyone knows it. Even if Rawling were foolish enough to hire some outsider to work in Ramble, quality always rises to the top . . . like cream."

She squeezed my hand in return—whether to show she appreciated my attempt to encourage her or in revenge, I wasn't sure. Florists develop strong fingers.

"I wonder how much of a shop we'll have left when Bixby's done." Liv craned her neck to peek down the alley. "We might need more flowers, Larry."

"They're taking your flowers?" Larry asked. "Why would they . . . ?" He blanched. "You don't think they'll search my greenhouses, do you?"

"They're only taking some of our flowers," I said. "Probably like the ones they found near the body."

"There were flowers near the body?" Amber Lee asked.

"Amber Lee, try to keep this under your hat," I said. "But Derek was found dead in his car with the bouquet that Jenny and I made yesterday."

"That's not going to be good for business if that gets out." Liv leaned forward and rubbed her temples. "Or good for Jenny."

"Well, nobody will hear it from me." Amber Lee was wide-eyed. "I may like to imbibe in a little gossip now and then, but I steer clear of anything that could ever harm someone—especially you two. So you think Jenny did this?"

I shook my head. "No, not in a million years. But you know

that's what Bixby is going to think . . . what Bixby *already* thinks." I used a napkin to wipe the sticky jelly from my fingers. "And I'm afraid I'm going to be his key witness. I saw Jenny climb into the car with Derek, with both the bouquet and the knife. That's pretty strong circumstantial evidence."

"Maybe she broke up with Derek in the car and he got violent," Amber Lee suggested. "Maybe she defended herself."

"Bixby already suggested that." I recalled how tentatively Jenny had used the knife on the flowers in the shop. I couldn't picture her using it against a human, particularly someone she had feelings for—the breakup aside.

"Or what if," Liv started, "she was upset and ran out of the car, leaving the bouquet and the knife behind?"

"That"—Amber Lee tapped the table—"is more like it. I can see her doing just that."

"Then," Liv continued, "someone saw Derek in the car. Maybe Derek offered him a ride. Maybe . . ." Liv perked up, her eyes sparkling and her tone animated. "Maybe the killer wasn't someone from Ramble after all. Maybe it was some stranger passing through. Some psycho, serial-killing tramp."

"Who just happened to be there at the right time," I said. "And whom Derek allowed in his expensive sports car. And who just happened to find a knife in the bag left behind, plunged it precisely in the right place to kill Derek almost instantly, then managed to slip away unseen, despite being saturated in blood."

Liv grasped her stomach. "Audrey . . ."

"Sorry, Liv," I said. "I'd like to think some passing stranger did this. But I just don't see how that could be." I tried to shift the subject. "But you're right. The knife and the flowers prove Jenny was in the car. They don't prove that she did it."

"So assuming Jenny didn't do it," Amber Lee said,

"someone with a motive to kill Derek must have seen him in the car . . . someone Derek knew and trusted enough to give a ride to . . ."

I nodded. "Although . . ."

All eyes at the table turned to me.

I searched for words that wouldn't turn Liv Martian green again. "Say someone wanted to kill Derek, and that someone even followed him to Jenny's. If he had come to kill Derek, why not bring a weapon more reliable and less . . . messy?"

We sat in the sun in front of the Brew-Ha-Ha for almost an hour before officers came to retrieve us, one by one, from our coffee klatch. When my turn came, I found myself facing Bixby, sitting in, of all places, my consulting nook. I found it difficult not to be distracted by the disarray and activity in the shop. I took a moment to close my eyes and focus, pretending I was running through a field of wildflowers, letting the wind billow through my hair as I twisted and belted out a song. Okay, maybe that was Julie Andrews.

"Audrey," Bixby started, and then he barely got his tissue to his nose before he let out the loudest sneeze I'd ever heard.

I studied his face. His time in our little shop had left him red eyed and tearful, and the skin under his nose was chafing away like he was an extra in some low-budget zombie movie. I dug under the table and pulled out my box of tissues.

He grabbed one and sneezed again, shattering forever my Julie Andrews moment. The hills were alive with the sound of . . . something entirely different.

"I know you're Jenny's friend," he began, his voice softer and more encouraging. "So I don't expect you to volunteer anything that would be harmful to her."

Maybe this wouldn't be so bad after all.

"But what I would like you to do is tell the truth. The whole truth. Anything you can to help us solve the case and put Derek's killer—whoever that might be—behind bars. You want that, right?"

I bobbed my head in a tentative nod. True, we both wanted the real killer caught and behind bars. Perhaps it would be best just to tell him everything I knew. I needed to give Kane Bixby more credit. The Mr. Rogers routine was working on me.

"So Jenny made an appointment to see you yesterday afternoon . . ."

"Yes." My voice came out hoarse. I wished I'd brought my coffee with me, but four cups sat heavy on my stomach. I cleared my throat. "She called earlier in the day, and Liv told me she was coming in."

"To discuss her wedding flowers?"

"That's what I assumed. I hoped to get her to change her order. Jenny's mother picked—"

"How did Jenny seem when she arrived?"

"She seemed . . ." I searched my brain for the right word. "Resolved."

"Resolved?"

"Jenny always tended to be a bit of a people pleaser . . . and indecisive. She seemed more sure of herself."

"But she didn't just want to change her order, did she?"

"No, she told me to cancel it."

"Because . . ."

I exhaled deeply. The whole truth. "Because she planned to break up with Derek."

"Did she say why?" Bixby leaned forward. "Was he cruel to her? Abusive?"

"No," I said. "At least not that I know of. She told me he was always kind to her."

Bixby seemed put off by that answer. Like it wreaked havoc with his theory. He rubbed his tissue under his nose again.

"Jenny will tell you the same thing," I added. "Just talk to her. I'm sure she can clear this whole thing up."

"Miss Bloom, this is a murder investigation, not a mis-understanding. You can be sure Miss Whitney will receive all the due process—"

"You've arrested her?"

"Let's just say we're questioning her. Formal charges will come later if—"

I stood and rapped the table. "Listen to yourself, Bixby. 'Miss Whitney.' 'Formal charges.' You've known Jenny since she was a little girl. Do you honestly think she could have done this thing?"

"Miss Bloom . . . Audrey. Please sit down."

I closed my eyes and sank back into my chair. He handed me the box of tissues and I wiped away a tear of . . . anger? Sympathy? Frustration? Even I didn't know.

"Yes, I've known Jenny her entire life," he said. "But human nature is not always so simple, and people can be capable of more than we give them credit for. Both good and evil. I have to go where the evidence leads."

"The circumstantial evidence."

Bixby waved off my comment. "That's why I'm being thorough—why I want to account for all the knives, for example, and not just assume. Can you see that?"

I exhaled. How can anyone argue with Mr. Rogers? I made a mental note to send him a cardigan for Christmas.

"Now, any idea where the last knife could be? Might a customer have gotten hold of it?"

I shook my head. "Not likely. We use them in the back of the house—maybe take them on big jobs for last-minute alterations. But we just got these a couple of weeks ago."

"So it would have to be in the possession of an employee—or someone with access to the back room."

I nodded.

"You, Liv, Amber Lee. Larry, although he's not an employee, still has access to the back room. You said Jenny was a new employee?"

"Not on the books yet. She'd only been back there once."

"Any other employees?"

"Two part-time cashiers who help us out in the evenings and make some deliveries. College students. Good kids."

"I'll need their names and addresses."

A lump formed in my throat thinking about the police arriving at their dorm rooms or frat houses.

"Anyone else been in the back room lately?"

"No, not that I . . . oh, wait . . . the reporter."

"For the article in the *On*?"

"Yes, Ben Hanson and the photographer were both back there."

Bixby nodded. "I'll check it out."

"Thanks," I whispered.

"What for?"

"For looking into other possibilities, and not just assuming Jenny did this."

"Audrey, I'm just dotting my i's and crossing my t's. Don't get your hopes up."

Mr. Rogers was gone, maybe was never there. Across from me now sat the police chief who was going to railroad my friend.

He could forget that cardigan.

Chapter 5

After retrieving my purloined shop knife for the deputy, I concluded only one thing could salvage the day. So, despite the spring shower that had rolled in, I climbed into the Rose in Bloom CR-V and headed to Five Guys for a little bacon cheeseburger and fries. Still waiting on a call from Liv to tell me that Bixby had graciously allowed us back into our own building, I decided I could enjoy my meal in the comfort of my own apartment. Maybe get at my laundry. Yeah, right.

When I opened my apartment door, Chester flew out. At least I think that was what happened. I saw only a streak of gray fur. I set my takeout bag on the porch and managed to locate him underneath my neighbor's pickup, rubbing his chin against one of the tires.

"Audrey, is that fur ball under my truck again?" My neighbor Tom appeared on cue, keys in hand. "I have to go to work."

I got down on my knees on the wet pavement. "Here,

kitty, kitty," I said, more for Tom's benefit, to impress upon him that I was making an effort. He knew as well as I did that Chester never comes when called.

Instead, Chester licked his paw, looking amused at the whole "kitty, kitty" routine. When I reached out to grab him, he darted farther under the truck.

"Chester . . ."

"Audrey, if they dock my pay, I'm going to charge you. Now get him out of there."

I slid onto my back, feeling the cool rain work its way through the fabric of my spring jacket and pants. As I inched my way under the truck, Chester came over and sniffed my hand. I made a move to grab him but ended up with a tuft of gray fur in my fingers and scratches on my arm. Meanwhile Tom's work boot tapped on the other side of the pickup.

"Tom, could you hand me that bag I brought home?"

"Your lunch?"

"I want to see if I can lure him out."

Tom unceremoniously tossed my bag under the truck. I wrestled among the fries until I found my cheeseburger. I tore a little of the meat off and waved it in Chester's direction. "Num-num?"

"Audrey!"

I ignored Tom's impatience as Chester advanced toward me and sniffed the bit of burger. When he took the bait, I grasped him firmly under both his front legs and shimmied out from underneath the truck. When I stood up, Chester safe and sound, I shivered as the spring breeze hit the cold water that had penetrated my clothing to the skin.

"Finally!" Without so much as a "thank you," or "sorry about your clothes," Tom hopped into the cab of the pickup and took off, his tires narrowly missing my lunch, I might add. I'd remember that the next time I got an inkling to practice my tuba at odd hours.

I tossed a squirmy Chester back inside while I gathered my burger and fries. I could hear him pawing at the screen door, so I stomped on the porch before entering. I don't know if Chester thought it was a game, or if the stomping transformed me into an abominable snowman or something fierce and dangerous, but he always scampered away and hid under the bed to gnaw on my shoes, allowing me to get inside without risking him escaping again. I hoped he wouldn't end up with some cat neurosis, but at least he wouldn't get run over by a car.

After changing into clean sweats, I threw my clothes on top of the overflowing laundry basket and sat down to my cold lunch and more thoughts of Jenny and Derek.

Liv rested her head on her hands and stared at the silent telephone. The only call we'd received all afternoon—after Bixby returned the shop back to us—had been from her husband, Eric, calling to see how we were.

The deluge of business generated by the newspaper article had disappeared. Even the normal trickle of afternoon customers dried to nothing.

"Look on the bright side," I said, "with no cutting tools, we'd have trouble filling orders anyway."

"Are we going to survive this?" Liv massaged her temples. "All the work we put into this place"—she gestured to the shop, where Amber Lee and I were still trying to put things back to rights—"and it could come crashing down in a moment. And there's not a blessed thing we can do about it."

"Hey." I crossed the room and put a comforting arm around her shoulder.

She burst into tears. "And I was going to add fruit baskets," she wailed. "Me and my dreams." I pulled her toward me as her tears seeped through my shirt. "Maybe I should just quit and start on those grandchildren Eric's mom keeps hinting about."

Amber Lee stole over and rubbed Liv's back with manicured nails. "Honey, one day does not a business ruin. I'm sure people are just waiting until the police car is gone, and then they'll be in here by the droves. All of Ramble will want to hear more about it, and they'll know they can come in here and talk to us. And it would only be polite to buy something in return, right?"

I bit my lower lip. "Don't forget, we'll get orders for flowers for the Rawlings once the news gets out."

Liv's eyes brightened momentarily, then she started wailing. "We prey on the dead, Audrey. What a morbid business! We should have never bought this shop. And now my stupid dream is going to cost us everything. If it weren't for my bright ideas, you could have afforded to keep Grandma's cottage. And Eric could have a wife who stayed home, cooked wholesome dinners, and gave him a quiverful of rug rats."

"Pull yourself together, woman." I was a bit taken aback. I'd never known Liv to be quite this emotional. In the privacy of the shop, unlike earlier on Ramble's main thoroughfare, I could do something to control her uncharacteristic hysterics. I grasped both her shoulders and gave her a gentle shake. "Liv, saying we profit on death is like saying a doctor profits on sickness. We provide a way for people to offer condolence and comfort through flowers. And we'll do our best to respect and support the grieving."

Liv took a deep breath and hiccupped.

"As for the rest of it, you know this shop was just as much my dream as yours. And maybe I'll own Grandma's cottage again someday, or maybe it's not meant to be. But I'm happy here, working with my cousin and best friend every day, doing what we've always loved."

Liv nodded through her tears.

"And as far as Eric is concerned, you can start on that collection of rug rats whenever you want. We can put in a little playpen by the gazebo. But since when did you cook?"

Liv sniffed and smiled. "I could always learn."

"Maybe you should go home," I suggested. "Get some rest. Amber Lee and I can put things back together here."

Liv exhaled deeply. "No, thanks, Audrey. Let me just get my head screwed on straight. You're right. We're going to get calls for funeral arrangements. And people will come in to gawk and buy." She straightened her apron. "I don't know what came over me, but I'm all right now." She gave us both a half smile and shooed us back to our work.

Moments later, the bell above the door tinkled. It wasn't a customer but Shelby, one of our part-time workers, who walked in. Although he was slight in stature, muscular arms flexed as he slipped a shop apron over his pastel-tinted sports shirt.

Shelby was only twenty-four, but a receding hairline suggested more age. The remaining dark hair was conservatively cut. He was completing his first year of studies in floral design and horticulture at Nathaniel Bacon University, located in the county seat about fifteen minutes away. He—Shelby, that is, and not Nathaniel Bacon—already displayed a gift for novel designs, 80 percent of which were executable. Unfortunately, most of our work tended to be more traditional. But when facing a customer who desired a more outside-the-box look, Shelby was already our go-to guy. As he progressed in his studies, we hoped to make him a larger part of our business— if we didn't lose him to some big-city floral design studio.

"What's going on?" he asked. "And why is my dad towing a police car away from the building?"

"Towing?" I looked through the large windows at the front of the shop to see Shelby's father, Mack, hook up a police car to his tow truck cable. My curiosity got the better of me. I headed out the door.

"Hey, Mack," I said.

"Audrey." He stole a glance at his son in the shop. I hoped one day he would reconcile to Shelby's career choice.

"What happened to the squad car? Nothing major, I hope."

He snorted and shook his head. "Just that Lafferty kid leaving the lights on again. Drained the battery. Won't even take a jump this time."

I watched as Mack maneuvered both vehicles into traffic and toward his shop on the outskirts of town. A few towns-folk, who stopped to watch the police car being towed, turned and went about their business, after a quick glance my way. Maybe Amber Lee was right. Maybe we'd see a few of them come in later to discover what had happened.

As I turned to walk inside, our other part-timer jogged up the sidewalk. Passersby parted to give him a wide berth. Darnell's muscular frame and shaved head made him an imposing figure, which I'm sure his college football team exploited. At least until he smiled. Then the fierce face melted into Ferdinand the Bull. And like Ferdinand, who desired nothing more than to sit under a tree smelling the flowers all day, Darnell had a gift—one he perpetually denied and refused to cultivate. We allowed him to think he'd just taken the job for the money.

He opened the door for me, and soon we were all gath-ered around relaying the story to our newcomers.

"So what are we supposed to tell customers when they ask about the police?" Darnell asked.

Amber Lee started. "What if we just tell them that we were supposed to provide the flowers for the upcoming wedding and that Derek was near the shop before he died? Or maybe mention that Jenny was supposed to start working here?"

My heart sank. "If we mention Jenny, it's just going to draw attention to her—and if we mention the job, the news of the breakup is sure to follow. She'll be vilified."

"Then we'll stick to the idea that we were doing the

flowers for the wedding?" Liv scanned the faces for consensus. We all nodded. "Now, we're going to have some long, difficult days ahead. There are sure to be curious customers, orders for condolence and funeral arrangements—and let's not forget the wedding on Saturday."

I took a deep breath. "Derek's funeral will be held later in the week," I said. "Hopefully not on Saturday, but even so, both events are going to be huge." I thought of Carolyn's lavish arrangements, which would require all of our efforts to execute.

"We're going to need more help," Liv said.

"There's a few kids in my design classes who might want some professional experience for their résumés," Shelby said. "With a little instruction . . ."

"And if you need some willing bodies," Darnell added, "I could recruit a few of my teammates to fetch and carry. They might jump at the chance to pick up a few bucks."

"They could be a big help delivering some of the larger arrangements," I said. "And maybe some of the prep work and cleanup."

Liv nodded. "We're going to need more flowers."

Larry poked his head in from the back room. "Did someone say more flowers? I've got your order still waiting in the truck, and if you need more than I can supply, I can recommend other growers nearby to supplement."

Liv noticeably choked up and she kissed Larry on the cheek. Maybe not the most professional of greetings, but Larry, a longtime friend of Grandma Mae's, seemed more like an uncle to us. I followed suit.

"But we're going to need more knives and stem cutters," Amber Lee said.

"Do you think we can make do with stuff from the hardware store?" Darnell asked.

"I could go with him and pick out some nice pruning shears," Shelby added.

I looked at the circle of earnest faces and felt a tickle in the back of my throat. It was our own little version of *It's a Wonderful Life*. "Now all we need is customers," I said.

Just as Shelby and Darnell headed out to the hardware store, our first post-Derek customer arrived. Nick Maxwell, still in baker's whites, stepped in and looked around the decimated shop. Seeing the empty cooler, he chose a potted red geranium. As I rang it up for him, I pondered its dual meaning—*comfort* or *stupidity*—and wondered which of the two, if either, the next few days held in store.

Chapter 6

❧

"Does the senator have anything specific in mind?" Liv asked into the phone as I raced into the shop a few minutes before eleven. Okay, maybe it was a few minutes after eleven, but Chester hid one of my comfortable working shoes again. The fur ball considered anything with laces a cat toy. At least it hadn't ended up in the toilet. This time.

Wednesday was my morning to start late, anyway. But I felt guilty doing so on a day we expected to be insanely busy, even if I was sure I'd make up for it by staying late.

Liv jotted a few notes onto her order pad. Even her posture while talking on the phone—straight backed, professional, yet somehow demure—showed the importance of the call.

She hung up the phone. "That was Senator Nash's aide."

"Senator Nash? . . . *the* Senator Nash?" Party leader with aspirations for the presidency? *That* Senator Nash? "We've never had an order from a state senator . . . I mean a national . . . a senator from our state serving in the U.S. Senate." Why did they make government so confusing?

"Actually," Liv said, pulling out another order and using it to fan her face, "we have."

"*Both* senators?"

"And a handful of representatives. Audrey, forget the idea that the business is going under. I had no idea the Rawlings were so politically connected. We've got more funeral orders than I know how to handle. I should stop taking phone orders, but I can't."

I sifted through the list of orders. "How are we going to . . . ?"

"And that's not even all of them. Amber Lee took the first stack into the back to get started. I called Shelby, and he and his classmates will be here as soon as they're done with their morning classes. Meanwhile, I sent a couple of Darnell's teammates to help Larry haul in more flowers. And a grower he knows from downstate is sending a large shipment for later today. Oh, and I expressed a few things."

"You did all this on decaf?"

"I haven't even gotten to my decaf yet," she said. "By the way, the funeral is set for Friday."

A sigh of relief escaped my lips. "At least it's not the same day as the wedding."

"About that," Liv said. "Audrey, I'm afraid we're using the wedding flowers in the funeral arrangements. I did reorder, and the new flowers should be here by Friday morning."

That was cutting it tight.

"Afternoon at the latest." She winced. "Definitely by five."

"Thanks, Liv." I shrugged. She was doing her best. "I just hope Derek's family likes peach roses."

After hand-delivering a cup of decaf to Liv as she fielded another phone call, I carried the latest stack of orders to the back room.

Amber Lee's rich brew stood waiting in the pot. I helped myself to a cup, shrugged on my apron, and then spread the orders out on the worktable to get a better look at what the day held.

The first was a standing spray arrangement. As I set the saturated foam in a plastic cage and secured it to an easel, I couldn't help but think of the meaning of the flowers I planned to use. Pale peach roses—as I had explained to Carolyn, for whom these flowers were originally ordered—were often placed in Victorian bridal bouquets to represent *modesty*. When I explained the progression of meanings as the peach darkened, Carolyn became entranced, and the order grew. Pale peach in her bouquet, with darker peach with some corals thrown in for the reception centerpieces. The corals represented *desire*. The intermediate peach, which these were, expressed *appreciation* and were often chosen to represent *the sealing of a deal*. Carolyn laughed at that—her signature irritating laugh—likening her marriage to a deal. And then she'd proceeded to order even more of them while her daddy stood by with the checkbook.

But the sealing of a deal—it seemed odd to put these flowers in a funeral arrangement. *Appreciation*, I decided, would be the better meaning. The budding white gladioli went in just after the foliage to form the lines for the display. The "flower of the gladiators" originally meant *well-armed for battle* but had come to represent *strength of character* and *sincerity*.

Orange lilies contrasted with the pure white lilies would keep the arrangement from becoming overly peachy. The white lilies signified *innocence*, but the orange . . . I struggled to push the first barely opening bloom into the form. While some modern florist had decided that the orange lily said *I burn for you*, the Victorians considered it a symbol of *hatred*. Maybe the two meanings weren't so different.

I thought of Jenny. Jenny who sat at my table and

dispassionately explained why she was canceling her wedding. She liked Derek. But she neither burned for him nor hated him. While it impressed me as a poor foundation for a marriage, it seemed equally poor as a motive for murder. Someone passionately wanted Derek dead, and that person just couldn't be Jenny.

I went back for some peach carnations and a few small white daisies to use as filler, then finished up the arrangement, tucking in some bear grass to add a little dimension. I felt Liv standing over my shoulder.

"It's lovely." Liv leaned in and squeezed my shoulders, and I shed a tear. While I'd put together any number of funeral displays since we'd purchased the shop, this was the first death since Grandma Mae's that touched me quite as personally.

I broached the subject I'd been avoiding. "Anyone hear how Jenny's doing?"

Liv's embrace grew tighter.

Amber Lee set down her tools and headed to my table. "Sorry, honey, I should have mentioned it when you came in." Amber Lee patted my hand. "Bixby took her in for questioning. Word is, that didn't go so well. She's still there."

I inhaled deeply. "She couldn't have done that awful thing."

"Bixby will learn that," Liv said. "The truth always comes out in the end."

"Does it?" I could hear the acid in my voice and immediately regretted it. Liv still thrived in that fairy-tale world where true love always wins and good triumphs. Maybe it worked that way for her. Then again, she'd never dated Brad. "Sorry."

She hugged me tighter. Our touching Hallmark moment was interrupted when the alley door opened and Darnell and two muscle-bound males, clearly his teammates, started toting in flowers.

I set down my tools. A floral delivery meant all hands were needed on deck to process the flowers. Cutting old ends off at a diagonal and soaking in preservative ensured that our stock stayed as fresh as possible for as long as possible. Liv pushed me back onto my stool.

"We're going to let Darnell and his crew take care of that, too," she said. "He knows what to do." She leaned in to whisper. "And if he doesn't get it quite right, most of these flowers are going to be out of the door before the day is over anyway."

As the last of the flowers were toted in, Liv shook her head. "We're going to need more."

Darnell nodded. "Larry is going to bring more by as soon as they're cut and loaded."

"That's what I sent you there for." Liv didn't yell or snap, but the tension and directness showed she felt her orders had not been carried out. I pitied her future kids.

Darnell spoke again. "We offered. But Larry made us wait outside the greenhouses."

While Liv went back to the shop to answer the tinkling door chime, Amber Lee turned the portable radio to a folk station. Soon stems were flying everywhere to the cadence of a dulcimer.

I went on to my next arrangement for the other esteemed senator: a similar standing spray in a different color scheme. It wouldn't do for one to outshine the other. Or clash. I chose some sunny sunflowers to form the base. Sunflowers varied in meaning based on size. The dwarf sunflower, which these were, symbolized *adoration*. The tall sunflower took on a meaning of *haughtiness*—perhaps as a result of too much adoration? I thought of Derek. Perhaps that was his problem. Too much adoration can make others jealous. Jealous of his lifestyle? His possessions?

As the young men finished up their tasks, Darnell looked around. "What next?" he asked.

I gestured to the completed arrangements. "These could be delivered to the funeral home." I didn't need to specify which one. Ramble only had one.

"Not to the funeral home," Liv said as she rounded the corner. "Apparently the Rawling family thinks funeral homes are a bit . . . tawdry."

I raised an eyebrow. I knew Rawling money had kept Derek out of public school and sent him to the most exclusive prep schools, camps, and later a string of Ivy League schools—why he needed more than one was never shared with the townsfolk. But I'd assumed death would be an equalizer. "Where on earth are they taking the body?" I asked.

"Their parlor," Liv said.

Apparently the advantages of the wealthy extended after death, not that Derek would derive any comfort from being laid out in the family parlor. Who even has a parlor anymore?

"So," Liv said to the football squad, as she retrieved fresh aprons from the basement storage room, "you'll need to put these on. No one but Darnell speaks, and you say the minimum—and always in hushed tones. And make sure you go to the back door." She lined them up for a final inspection. Good thing they were football players and used to being lined up.

No sooner had they gone when the alley door swung open. Shelby and his fellow students, two young women as different as apple pie and vodka, walked in. One was a fresh-faced young woman dressed in a denim skirt, pink floral tee, and sandy hair pulled back in a ponytail. The other wore flowers as well, but hers were tattooed all over her body and augmented with piercings much like the roses centered with Swarovski crystals some brides request.

As Liv gathered a handful of orders and assigned the newcomers to their narrow workstations, the door chimes announced a customer.

Amber Lee slipped past me. "I can watch the front of the house for a little while. I think my hands are going numb anyway." She massaged her fingers on her way to the front.

Liv gave the new crew some basic instructions. As the two new arrivals assembled their first arrangements, Liv made only minor adjustments, heaping on a spoonful of encouragement. Both young women beamed under her tutelage.

Two hours flew by like minutes, but the arrangements started collecting as fast as leaves and stems collected on the floor. I learned the peaches-and-cream girl was named Melanie, while her leather-and-lace counterpart with the pale skin and black lipstick was named Opal but answered to Opie. I wondered if that unfortunate nickname had sparked her interest in the goth look. Nevertheless, far from being withdrawn or sullen, Opie seemed respectful and friendly. Both were performing adequately and picking up speed with their experience.

Liv, on the other hand, kept looking at her watch and eyeing the back door. "I must have been out of my mind to take all those orders. Those boys will have to head right back out with the next delivery. You don't suppose anything went wrong, do you? Maybe I should give Darnell a call."

"They probably just stopped to grab a burger or something on the way back," I said, the thought spurred on by my own gurgling stomach. "Give them a few more minutes."

My statement proved to be prophetic. The boys, as we'd all begun to call them, squeezed through the back door with greasy paper bags stuffed with food. Enough for all of us, it turned out. Bless their hearts and pay them a bonus.

We set up our lunch in my consulting gazebo.

"So . . ." Liv kneaded her hands together. "How did it go at the Rawling estate?"

"We went to the back door, just as you said," Darnell started. "And then it got really confusing because they were expecting some temporary employees at the same time. And I guess the aprons are similar."

"Then some caterer arrived," Brandon, a cornerback—whatever that was—explained. "And they was luggin' food in when we was totin' in flowers. And those back halls are a might narrow."

"We spent half the time waiting in line to get in," Darnell added. "And then they made us carry the flowers to the room and set them up."

"Oh, dear." Liv wiped her lips with a napkin. "I'm so used to the funeral director placing them. Did you put the two large easel displays on either side of the casket?"

"There weren't no casket in there yet," Brandon said. "Just a pedestal. But some creepy dude in a long coat moved them around a bit. He didn't seem none too pleased. He made us move everything around half a dozen times before he just told us to go."

"And then we had to wait some more," Darnell explained, reaching for more fries, "because a big old hearse pulled in and blocked the exit."

I looked at Liv. "One of us should take the next order over."

Liv nodded. "Both of us, just this time, to get the lay of the land. We can help place the arrangements."

"I wonder if Jenny and her mother will be allowed to the viewing." And then I wondered if the real reason that the Rawling family had chosen not to use a funeral parlor was to control who could pay their respects.

"Oh, honey"—Amber Lee paused while she took a pull on her Coke—"I got some more news from one of the customers. The judge set bail pretty high. From what I hear, Ellen either can't or won't pay it."

"They must have charged her, then," Opie said as she

crunched up her burger wrapper. "But she's lucky. They don't often set bail at all in a murder investigation."

All eyes turned to stare at her.

"Hey, my dad's a lawyer. You pick up these things."

With Amber Lee in charge of our new interns, Liv and I headed to the Rawling place with a new load of completed floral arrangements.

I wended the narrow private road. We passed a riding arena, a tennis court, and what looked like a golf green all set in lush green rolling hills just outside Ramble.

"Georgian Revival, I think," Liv explained when we caught a glimpse of the house.

Pavement turned to a flagstone drive that circled a fountain before approaching the magnificent front entrance replete with grand columns. The caterer's vehicles and the hearse were parked to the side, between a freestanding three-bay garage and a side wing of the house. I pulled the CR-V into a spot next to them. Darnell and crew pulled in behind us.

We each grabbed a floral arrangement. As I considered the weight of the large arrangements the boys were carrying, I made a mental note to keep the football team on speed dial. The caterers stepped aside to allow us access, although they didn't look happy about it. We then filed through another hallway and into what turned out to be the back door of the parlor.

A long room, the parlor seemed more like a string of three living rooms in a row, each with a separate seating group in a coordinating style. It kind of reminded me of a ritzy furniture showroom. At the end, in front of a marble fireplace, the town's funeral director fussed with the casket, finished in a creamy tone that looked like it was chosen to blend in with the existing furnishings, which I noted with mixed pleasure contained a considerable amount of peach.

Elaborate white moldings and high ceilings extended the length of the room. Through the open double doors into a grand foyer, I caught just a glimpse of a crystal chandelier and curving staircase.

"Why would anyone want something so impersonal?" I whispered to Liv. Yeah . . . jealous.

"I knew the Rawlings had money," Liv said, "but I wasn't expecting Buckingham Palace."

The good news was that the room provided plenty of space for all the arrangements—and the ones still coming.

Right then the "creepy dude with the long coat," as Brandon had put it, sneaked up behind me. "Are you with the florist?" he asked. I whirled around to greet the epitome of English butlers, complete with aristocratic accent. Someone had been watching a little too much *Downton Abbey*. No wonder they needed a parlor.

"Yes." I held out my hand. "And a friend of Derek's come to pay my respects."

The butler looked apoplectic, but he did shake my hand. "Worthington," he said. I assumed that was his name. First or last, I wasn't sure. He was sixty-something, I guessed, with well-chiseled features, almost sculpted gray-brown hair, and perfectly manicured nails. Stiff and prickly as an aloe. The comparison made me shudder. Aloe was the symbol of *grief*.

"The visitation starts in half an hour," he said. "We must place the flowers and have . . . your staff . . . out of the way by then." He walked off to deal with the caterers, so I had no idea why he included himself in the "we" who had to place the flowers.

I grabbed Liv by the elbow. She was still gawking at the room like a tourist in a museum.

We huddled and came up with a plan, treating the arrangements themselves like flowers in a bouquet. The room became the vase, and we strategically placed arrangements to form a base, contrast, and filler.

Lorne Jans, Ramble's mortician, and his son, Joe, propped open the casket and fussed with the pillow arrangements the family had ordered. I'd always thought Lorne needed two other sons named Adam and Hoss. Apparently so did half the town, since Joe's nickname was Little Joe despite his gangly stature of over six feet. Little Joe reminded me of a pitcher plant or swamp lily: tall, dark, thin, and often found in dismal places. And totally lacking in romance; the Victorian guides assigned no meaning to the flower. Then again, such is the life of a mortician.

"Audrey, this rose . . ." Lorne pointed to the pillow arrangement.

"Oh, it's . . ." I fixed it in less time than it would have taken to explain about guard petals. I tucked the small heart-shaped pillow back into the casket.

Derek looked . . . I know people often say the dead look peaceful, like they're asleep. And there's a reason for those clichés, but none of that could be said without the work of a talented mortician. Otherwise the dead look gray and sunken in, or so I discovered on my one—and only—date with Little Joe.

I found my eyes drawn toward Derek's high-collar dress shirt. "You can't even see . . ."

"No," Lorne said. "You can't. When they first told me how he died, stabbed in the neck, I thought we were going to have to do a closed casket for sure. But a few stitches, a little makeup."

Liv walked over and joined us in front of the casket. "You do great work, Lorne."

"You really do." I leaned in and found the spot, right near

the collar, where the knife blade must have entered. "The wound is tiny."

"It did the trick," Lorne said. "A clean slice. Bled like crazy, though."

"Spurted," Little Joe said, over my shoulder. "From the artery. Like that hockey player who got his neck slashed with a skate."

Liv laid a hand on my arm.

"That was the jugular vein," Lorne said. "Not an artery. He wouldn't have survived the artery."

"It couldn't have been a vein," Joe insisted. "He was spurting, not gushing—all the way down the ice. The spatter pattern was all wrong—"

Liv's grip grew viselike. She started to sway.

"Are you okay?" I whispered.

"Fine," she said, but her color blanched. "I might just go wait in the van."

"Sure." I watched her walk out the door, a little unsteady. It wasn't like Liv to react like that. Florists spend a lot of time in funeral homes, after all. New babies, romance, weddings, and death: that was pretty much our business. And the normally levelheaded Liv had always been up to the challenge before.

With Liv out of earshot, I asked, "So it was definitely the carotid artery?"

"I still think it was the vein," Lorne said. "I don't think the trainer could have saved him if . . . oh, or do you mean Derek?"

"Derek."

"Definitely the artery. He lost so much blood," Lorne continued. "Very little draining to do."

I thought about the hockey player for a moment. "Lorne, you don't suppose . . . I mean, if a hockey player can be injured that way by accident . . ."

"That what happened to Derek might be accidental?" Lorne shook his head. "No, I'd say Derek's killer not only tried to kill him but picked the most vulnerable place . . . and then did it with surgical accuracy."

What came next, I knew from my earlier nursing studies. Each remaining beat of Derek's heart would have propelled the blood from his body. Liv's queasiness hit me for a minute. I hoped it wasn't caused by something in the lunch we'd eaten. Considering the week ahead, even a mild case of communal food poisoning would be disastrous.

Lorne and Little Joe finished their work, tipped their proverbial hats, and rode off into the sunset, leaving me alone in the parlor.

Dishes clinked as the caterer laid out refreshments in the dining room.

Worthington gave me the evil eye and tapped his watch. Guests for visitation would be arriving in ten minutes.

I stood back and examined the flowers one final time and noticed the dangling gladiolus in the tall spray sent by Senator Nash. I eased my way around the other arrangements and struggled with it from behind, wedged in the tiny space between the coffin, the wall, and the tall arrangement. It took me a couple of minutes. The foam we use can be unforgiving. I found the original hole made by the stem, but the flower leaned too far forward. I eventually found a better spot to place it and was about to push it in.

"Derek."

The voice made me jump. With just enough vantage between the stems in the floral arrangement, I saw a head of short gray hair leaning over the coffin.

"Derek, I . . ." The voice, which I recognized as Jonathan Rawling's, Derek's father, paused and the figure shuddered. He braced himself against the coffin, shoulders wracking with silent sobs.

I fought the impulse to rush over, put my arms around him,

and offer some words of comfort—if such things existed. Instead, I remained in place, hidden behind the foliage. I hadn't intended to eavesdrop, but now it seemed more awkward to make my presence known and interrupt.

When the voice resumed, it was hoarse and full of emotion. "You really mucked it up this time, son."

Chapter 7

Around dinnertime, I swung home to feed Chester. Granted, Chester has dry food available to him twenty-four/seven—and it shows. But without regular supplements of canned cat food, he'll do things like chew the bottom of my cabinet doors or put fang marks in my blinds. For some reason my landlord finds this annoying.

I poured out a half can of something that smelled like it washed up on the beach somewhere and grabbed a quick bowl of cereal for myself. I craved a shower before I headed back to the shop, but with Liv and company waiting for me, I settled for a quick change of clothing. I opted for more casual jeans and my neon green "Florists Rock" T-shirt. While we had plenty of work, there'd be no customers to impress. I was heading out the door, tossing a toy mouse in Chester's direction to distract him and keep him from running out again, when the telephone rang.

"Hello?"

"Audrey? This is Jenny."

I leaned down on the arm of the couch. "Jenny . . . how are you, hon?" I wasn't sure where the "hon" came from. Maybe my subconscious mind was trying to sound sympathetic.

"Audrey, this is a nightmare. I've tried to call, and no one will . . ." Jenny completed the sentence with sobs instead of words.

"Jenny, calm down. I'm here."

She began again. "I can't talk long. I'm in jail. They say someone can bring by clean underwear and socks. But Mom hung up on me. And I can't get through to Sarah at all."

Sarah was Jenny's roommate, one of the health club set.

"Would you like me to swing by your apartment and bring in some of your things?" Grandma Mae was always mortified by words such as "panty" and "bra," always substituting the more-generic "things." I guess I picked that up from her. Unmentionables should remain unmentioned.

"Yes, I mean . . ." Jenny sighed. "I guess the underwear and socks need to be new in an unopened package. But I would like someone to stop by the apartment. I'm worried about Sarah. She's not answering her phone, and after what happened to Derek, I . . . Oh, Audrey, who would do such an awful thing? There must be some kind of nut job out there. What if he got Sarah, too?"

I pinched my eyes shut momentarily, trying to blink away the brashness of the request. What do you do when you're worried about a crazed killer on the loose? Just call old Audrey, whom you haven't talked to in months, and send her into the thick of it.

Of course I agreed to check on Sarah. There's a fine line between a well-bred Southern lady and a sucker. And I'd never been very good at finding that line.

I got the size and brand information on her jail-acceptable "things," glanced at the clock, and promised they'd be there in the morning.

"Jenny," I said, tucking the paper in my pocket, "I wanted to ask you. What happened with Derek?"

"Audrey, I don't know. The police said . . . But I was so groggy. Breaking up with Derek was probably the hardest thing I ever had to do. After Derek and I talked, I took a sleeping pill and went to bed. I just wanted to get everything out of my mind."

"But the knife, Jenny. The knife that I gave you to practice with. What happened to it?"

"It was in the bag I took inside," Jenny said. "I think . . . I don't know. Everything is all blurry."

I heard some voices in the background, and Jenny said, "I have to go. Good-bye." And she hung up.

I called Liv and told her why I would be late. She understood. After all, Grandma Mae had taught her to be a Southern lady/sucker, too.

I swung by Jenny's apartment first and knocked on the door. No answer. Nothing seemed amiss. No broken-in doors. No bloodcurdling screams. I tried not to look at the place Derek's car would have been parked. But I couldn't resist. Despite the tragic circumstances, it was nothing more than a parking space—empty, potholed. Only the remains of a police flare marked the scene.

I decided to try to check on Sarah again after purchasing Jenny's things.

Ramble is known for the historic stone and brick shops that line Main Street—shops that now showcase antiques and collectibles. Some purposefully convoluted zoning laws kept chains out, for the most part, in favor of local mom-and-pop businesses. The occasional tourists, heading through for a peek at where Washington slept while doing his survey of the area—or where Civil War general Jubal Early stabled his horses—find them charming. Main Street is a great place to buy a scented candle, a knockoff butter churn, or stale fudge. And, of course, flowers. Underwear, not so much. So I headed out on the fifteen-minute drive to the Walmart in the next town over. The strip mall also boasted the nearest Chick-fil-A and Five Guys, so I made that trek often. Well, not quite a trek, more of a jaunt.

I found all of Jenny's "things" in short order.

Okay, I also picked myself up a chicken sandwich and waffle fries.

I wiped my mouth with a napkin just as I pulled into Ramble town limits. Yes, I'd timed it to a science.

The lights were dark in Jenny's apartment when I pulled up. A knock on the door, again, brought no answer.

A herd of flowerpot critters—you know, the googly-eyed animals made of painted clay flowerpots—stared up at me from the porch. Our shop carried a small selection, made by a local craftswoman. Jenny, I recalled, had once retrieved a spare key from under the frog. Or was it the pig? If she hadn't moved it.

I tried both. And found it under the bunny. Pressing the key in the lock, I turned it and heard the click as the door unlocked.

"What are you doing?"

I whipped around to see Sarah Anderson. Actually, I whipped around to see no one, but found Sarah Anderson, all five foot two of her, when I happened to glance down. Sarah was the cover model for the "petite" entry in *Webster's*. Not just short, she was thin and as cute as a proverbial button. Even now, when she was clearly returning from the gym in a tank and slim capri exercise pants. Her skin glistened and escaping tendrils of her blond hair caught every breeze.

Frankly, if I looked that cute after exercising, I might do it more often. My postexercise look was best described as a hot mess. And that was probably generous.

"I said, what are you doing?" Sarah's voice was always soft and feminine, but it bore a bit of an edge at the moment.

"Oh, I . . ." I looked down at the key. "Jenny asked me to stop by." Okay, Jenny asked me to check on her roommate, not break and enter into her apartment. "She worried when she couldn't reach you."

Sarah held out her hand and I dropped the key into it. She opened the door and I followed her in. "Jenny's worried about me?"

"She said she tried to call but couldn't reach you."

Sarah went to the fridge and pulled out an apple. "She probably tried my cell phone. But I misplaced my charger after the police searched the place. Or maybe one of them wandered off with it."

Of course the police would have searched Jenny's apartment. I followed Sarah into the kitchen. The apartment floor plan was open, so I could see and talk to her from the front door, but I craved an opportunity to get a better look around.

Not much had changed since I'd last been in the apartment, cluttered and decorated in modern garage sale—mostly by Jenny, I thought. But that wasn't what I was looking for.

"Sarah, were you home the other night when Jenny and Derek were here?"

While Sarah turned to the sink to mix some unappetizing green powder into water, I glanced around the room. The plastic shopping bag from the flower shop sat on the table next to a newspaper, a sticky cutting board, and a glass half full of water. Or was it half empty? The optimists and the pessimists could argue that later. Next to it were the pruning shears I'd lent Jenny. I could understand why the police hadn't taken them—they had nothing to do with Derek's death. Why they'd taken ours, I had no clue. Perhaps all the pollen flying in our shop just made Bixby cranky.

Sarah took a long draft of her green swill. "Not right away. When I got home from the gym, Jenny and Derek were in the living room talking. The conversation looked pretty intense, so I excused myself and took a long shower. When I came out, Derek was leaving."

"No idea what they talked about?"

"Only what Jenny told me. That she and Derek broke up. She seemed pretty upset. I mean, who wouldn't be?"

"So Derek left, and Jenny was still here? Did she go out after that?"

Sarah shook her head. "Jenny said she was tired and wanted to sleep. Said she wanted to forget this whole mess happened."

"Sarah, were there flowers in the house when you came in?"

"Bixby asked me the same question. I honestly couldn't tell you. When I walked in and saw Derek and Jenny and the expressions on their faces, I can't say I made an inventory of the room. I just wanted to get out of there. When Jenny went to bed, it sounded like a great idea to me, too. Audrey, I'd like to say Jenny never left after that point, but a long day at the gym makes me bone tired. I fell asleep as soon as my head hit the pillow."

No one with a cat ever needs an alarm clock. Six was the absolute earliest I wanted to awaken, and an extra half hour (or two) after such a long night at the shop seemed more than reasonable.

Chester never got the memo. He circled me on the bed with the motor running. When I pulled the covers tighter to my ear, he proceeded to take what cat lovers call love nibbles. Yes, he bit me.

"All right." I pushed the covers off and he raced to the kitchen. I considered closing the door and going back to sleep, but that would result in persistent paw scratching on the door until I opened it again—another cat habit my landlord was less than thrilled with.

I followed Chester to the kitchen, where he started weaving around my legs and yowling like only a true tomcat can. I refilled his dry food and water before giving him a half can of some rather surprisingly appetizing-looking beef nuggets in gravy.

After a quick shower, I rummaged up some clean working clothes, taking quick inventory in my closet to ensure I had enough to carry me through the next few hectic days. I then grabbed a dress for a bridal appointment later in the afternoon. And sighed.

My worst problems were a busy workday and a destructive cat. But Jenny was sitting in jail. And poor Derek was dead. I drew in a quick breath, exhaled it slowly, and determined I would have a good attitude. I owed it to our customers. And I owed it to Liv and our crew to set a good example. Besides, I could always collapse on Sunday.

After an invigorating two-block walk in the chilly April morning air, I beat everyone to the shop. I even put on a pot of coffee and powered up the radio before shuffling through the stack of funeral orders yet to be assembled.

When Liv arrived, a few minutes later than usual, she looked scary-pale. The only color in her face came from the dark circles under her eyes. I caught the whiff of ginger coming from her travel mug. She propped open the alleyway door to let in the cool air. We spent the next hour or so assembling the remaining orders. The blinking wall phone suggested there were more, but they would have to wait. The Rawlings had requested that their flower deliveries be made only before and after the hours they'd advertised for visitation. Any new arrangements wouldn't go out until later in the afternoon anyway.

When our delivery team arrived, they loaded the van under Liv's direction and then packed the remaining overflow into the CR-V we used for smaller deliveries. When I went to climb into the passenger seat, I found a basket arrangement neatly buckled in, instead.

"Should I strap myself to the hood?" I asked, a little more amused than irritated.

"No, the boys and I got this." Liv buckled herself in.

I looked back at the crowded van and packed CR-V. "Are you sure?"

"Yes, positive. I'd rather keep you here with Amber Lee. And maybe there's time to get Jenny's things over to her before your consulting appointment."

I glanced at my watch. "Sure I can spare the time?"

Liv rolled her eyes and then rolled up the windows before easing down the alley with her floral cargo.

Inside the shop, Amber Lee moved with amazing speed, filling the self-serve cooler and readying the shop for opening.

"So how did you like the Rawling place?" She wiped a few stray smudges from our glass counter.

"Quite a setup," I said. "Ever been there?"

"Naw, been trying to get a tour of the place from a guy in my garden club. Says he works there. His name's Worthington."

"Worthington? The butler?" Aloe guy.

"He's a butler? I thought he might be a gardener or something."

"Do you know much about him?" I asked.

"Only that he lives on the estate in his own private cottage and that he likes to garden. He talks about plants and soil but little else. Should I try to find out more?"

"I don't know," I said. "I mean, how weird would it be if the butler did it? But I wonder what he might know about Derek's death since he works with the Rawlings every day."

"I'm on it."

"Don't go to any trouble."

"No trouble at all." She winked.

I picked up a peach rose discarded because its long stem had broken, then gathered a few more flowers and arranged them into an old-fashioned nosegay bouquet. The thought of going to the police department and possibly facing Bixby intimidated me a bit. But I had an ally there, one who might be able to smooth my way and supply me with a little extra information, and one who was very fond of nosegay bouquets.

"For me, Audrey?" Mrs. June cradled the small bouquet, then lifted it to her nose and inhaled, a look of sheer ecstasy filling her wrinkled face. "Sure beats smelling sweaty cops all day." She opened her drawer, pulled out a glass bud vase, poured part of her bottled water into it, and set the flowers inside, placing them right next to the nameplate on her desk, which read "June Hoffman, receptionist."

Mrs. June had been Grandma Mae's next-door neighbor. Our grandmother had tried to coax us to address her as Miss June—as is the old Southern custom. But Mrs. June wouldn't hear of it, claiming it made her sound too much like a centerfold model.

Mrs. June had also received a number of our childhood bouquets. And she'd reward us by telling us stories about the police department—tales of vagrants and counterfeiters and bootleggers that I now wondered if she didn't get from old Jimmy Cagney movies and not real life. And stories that I doubted Grandma Mae knew about.

Now nearing the typical age of retirement, Mrs. June had outlasted several changes of administration at the Ramble Police Department. She was a rotund, jowly woman with poufy hair she kept dyed a rich "decadent mocha" (I'd seen the box), though it no longer appeared natural. A small pair of readers perched on the edge of her nose, and, like always, she'd dressed up her sweater with a chunky costume necklace and matching clip earrings that made her lobes droop low.

I leaned over and gave her a hug, sniffing in her familiar aroma consisting of a blend of the same perfume she'd worn ever since we met her, now mingled with Bengay. "How are you doing?"

"Hanging in there, kiddo, hanging in there. And thank you so much for the flowers." Her arthritic fingers stroked the rose. "But I do suspect you're here about Jenny."

I reached into her candy dish and pulled out a Hershey's Kiss. "I brought some things she asked me for and was hoping to visit with her . . . after you and I have a minute to catch up." I flashed her a smile and sank into her visitor's chair.

Mrs. June removed her readers and let them fall on the cord that hung around her neck.

"I can make sure Jenny gets her things, but I'm afraid the visit is not going to happen."

"Isn't she allowed visitors?" I asked. "Surely Bixby can't stop people from—"

Mrs. June held up a hand and looked around the room before continuing.

The Ramble Police Department had an eclectic mix of furniture and fixtures. Not being a town given to extravagance, things were replaced when completely worn-out or obsolete, meaning the building was furnished with reminders of many eras. A wall-mounted pencil sharpener that looked like it dated from the early part of the previous century. Battered mustard yellow and avocado desks that screamed the 1970s and were almost in style again. Thankfully they'd removed the seventies paneling a couple of years back in favor of the natural historic brick. Of course, new computers and copy machines looked almost anachronistic against the older furnishings.

She leaned in and continued, softly, "Nothing would give me greater pleasure than blaming Bixby. But first of all, we don't keep prisoners here. We don't even have holding cells anymore. All prisoners are taken directly to the regional detention center."

"Then I'll go there. That's, what, just ten minutes . . . ?"

Mrs. June shook her head. "It would be fruitless. My niece Brenda works there. Jenny is allowed visitors, but now she claims she doesn't want them."

"Doesn't want . . . ? That just doesn't make sense. Jenny called me."

"I know. I know." Mrs. June's eyes took on that let-me-kiss-it-and-make-it-all-better expression. "But just between you and me—and I'm only saying this because I know she's your friend—a lot of things she's been saying and doing don't make much sense. If I didn't know better . . ."

"What?"

"Well, it's just that . . . when she got here, she fell asleep in the interview room twice. Now, according to Brenda, she spends much of the time pacing her cell. And she's not eating."

"Stress? And I know she's counted calories for a few years now."

"But her meals are mostly untouched. It's almost like . . ." Mrs. June trailed off and waited. A dramatic pause. She certainly demonstrated a love for the dramatic, but I was too tired to carry out this guessing game much longer.

"Like?"

"Audrey, I've been doing this job for a long time, and I've seen suspects come and go—not all the time, mind you. But even in Ramble it happens. And back when we used to hold our own prisoners, I saw all kinds of reactions to the stress of being locked up. But this kind of reaction? I've seen it before."

Another dramatic pause. Mrs. June was a shoo-in for the Ramble Drama Guild. I waited this one out.

"And you know her pretty well. Could she have been—I hate to say it—doing drugs of some kind? Because it almost seems like she's suffering some kind of withdrawal."

I stood and did some pacing of my own. A few years ago, I would have sworn that Jenny could never be involved in drugs. But did I know the new Jenny? I knew that some women take illegal drugs to help them lose weight. Did I know for certain she hadn't been involved in drugs? Or hadn't killed Derek, for that matter? Could people change that much over such a short period of time? "You know, Jenny told me she had taken a sleeping pill. Could that have done it?"

"It'd have to be a pretty powerful sleep aid."

"You mention your drug theory to Bixby?" I asked.

"He saw everything I saw. But I certainly don't have to draw any conclusions for him."

"Good. If Bixby thought she'd been on drugs, that would give him all the more reason to suspect her guilt."

"I wish I could get her regular doctor to go see her, but there's no other sign that she's sick. I think she'd be much better off in a hospital."

"Is there anything I can do?"

"Maybe ask around. See if anyone knows what she was taking. Perhaps then we'd know how to help her. Our guys didn't find any drugs in her apartment during the search. Meanwhile, I'd pray for the little thing. Brenda said that she seemed so lost, you know what I mean."

"Will do, Mrs. June. I guess I'll run these by the regional center anyway." I lifted the Walmart bag.

"Actually, you can leave these things here with me. Lafferty has to run a drunk-and-disorderly over in a few minutes. He can take them with him."

She reached out for the bag, then looked through the items. "I'll make sure they clear these to her right away. Perhaps that would help her mood a bit. And I'll keep asking Brenda about a visit. Maybe she can work on Jenny to let you go out and see her. If she agrees, I'll call you."

"Thanks." I sat silently in the chair for a moment, wondering if I should ask the next question. I loved Mrs. June and wouldn't want to needle her for a favor that made her uncomfortable or to do anything to compromise her employment status.

"You've got something else on your mind, Audrey."

"I think Bixby's dead wrong on this one."

"Wouldn't be the first time." It wasn't that Mrs. June held Bixby in disdain because of any particular incompetence. But I knew she idolized a longtime chief of police who had served several administrations ago—her father—and no one had measured up since. At least in her eyes.

My gaze traveled to the wall, to the framed oil painting of her father in uniform. "I also don't think he's going to look for anyone else while Jenny's in custody."

"What are you getting at?"

"She needs help."

"She has a public defender, but I heard she barely said two words to her. Helping that child is not going to be easy."

I leaned forward, resting my elbows on her desk and my chin on my tented fingers. "Mrs. June, are you privy to information on the case?"

She glanced to the empty desks behind her but leaned in closer anyway. "I might be. After all, someone needs to make sure case reports are legible, filed correctly, and photocopied. I guess it would depend on what you were after."

"I'm trying to understand what happened after Jenny left

the flower shop. I know she had the knife and the bouquet when she left. And that looks bad—she and Derek in the car with the bouquet and the knife. If they had a violent argument there, it's everything in one tidy package—means, motive, opportunity. But they didn't break up in Derek's car. Jenny's roommate said Jenny and Derek were talking in the apartment—that Derek left and Jenny went to bed. I guess I'd like to know more about the crime scene and what Bixby found in the car."

Mrs. June wheeled on her chair to a credenza behind her desk and sifted through a number of folders before wheeling back toward me.

"I won't show you the crime scene photographs," she said. "They're pretty gruesome. But there's an inventory sheet here of everything found in the car. And a report describing the scene. I shouldn't show you that, either, though."

"Okay, don't show it to me. But they found a bouquet in the car, right?"

"Yes, or rather, the remnants of one. It looked like it was tore up pretty good. Petals everywhere."

"That doesn't make sense to me. Who would vent their rage against flowers? Except maybe a displeased bridezilla or two I may have encountered over the years."

"Or maybe a bride who just called off her engagement."

"Oh, that doesn't look good for Jenny, does it?"

"The weird thing was that someone tore it up *after* Derek was murdered. But not long after."

"How could they tell that?"

"There was blood underneath the petals, like they were tossed on top of Derek's body—and on the stems where the killer grasped them."

"The killer's hands must have been covered in blood, then. How could he get away without being seen?"

"That's why Jenny is a prime suspect. The theory is that

after her roommate went to bed, Jenny sneaked out and killed Derek—who was still in the car in front of her place, for some reason. Then she went straight back into the apartment, changed, cleaned up, disposed of the incriminating clothing, bleached everything, then went to sleep and waited for the police to show up, thinking that her roommate could alibi her."

"But that's idiotic."

Mrs. June gave a halfhearted nod. "Nevertheless, that's the working theory."

"Did they find anything in the apartment to corroborate that?"

"No bloody path leading to Jenny's bedroom door, if that's what you mean. And no bloody clothes. Only recent evidence of bleach in the tub and on the floor. And a suspicious spot they cut out of the rug and sent off to the state lab for testing. But there's no law against cleaning with bleach, or all of our grandmothers would have ended up in the clink years ago."

"The thing that I don't understand, though, is . . . the knife being in the car."

"Oh, Audrey, dear. I can understand that would be disconcerting, since you gave it to Jenny. But you can't blame yourself."

"I don't." At least I hadn't until Mrs. June suggested it. "But I gave Jenny a bag full of tools and a bouquet. The bag is in her apartment; the shears are in the apartment. How did the bouquet and knife end up in the car if Jenny is not the killer?"

Mrs. June's brows furrowed before she leafed through her file again, licking her fingers to help her turn pages. "Audrey, did you give her a roll of green florist's tape?"

"Yes, but I don't recall seeing it in the apartment."

"It's on the inventory list of items found in the car."

Shortly after, I exited the brick government building back

onto Ramble's sunny Main Street. I was still shaking my head. Even if I had read Jenny all wrong, and she *had* gone back out to kill Derek after Sarah went to bed, why would she take the bouquet? And why in the world would she take the florist's tape?

Chapter 8

"I'm sure everything will be stunning." I referred to the tropical bouquets and centerpieces as my latest bridal client signed her check for the deposit. I was less sure how a beach-themed wedding with leis and tiki torches and a whole pig roast would go over in Ramble, almost one hundred miles from the nearest beach. Or how trucking in and dumping all that sand would be looked upon by the staff of the couple's chosen venue, the exclusive Ashbury Inn, where, according to Kathleen Randolph, local historian and owner of the restored historic inn, George Washington once slept. And where his ghost was reported to walk the halls, rattling doors and stealing the pricey hand soap out of the guest rooms.

For a moment, I even pondered how our esteemed first president would view the wedding frenzy created by today's brides, each demanding her perfect day, regardless of the cost. But I drove that thought from my head. Part of that frenzy would pay my gas bill this winter so I wouldn't freeze like the revolutionary troops at Valley Forge.

I rose to escort the beach-bunny bride out of the consulting nook when clanking on the iron steps announced another visitor.

"Audrey, I demand to speak with you." Ellen Whitney, eyes bloodshot and gaze unsteady, stood at the top of the steps. Her color of the day was lime green. Or maybe it was yesterday's color because Ellen was quite in disarray, clothing wrinkled, makeup nonexistent, and hair, well, her beautician would be mortified. And while I can't say I'd been in many distilleries to make an accurate comparison, she smelled as if she'd taken the grand tour of one and knocked back a vat or two when the guides weren't looking.

"Of course. We've just finished here." I turned to the startled bride, smiled, and shook her hand. "Congratulations again."

"Thanks." She giggled and tucked her receipt into her purse before squeezing past Ellen.

"Yeah, congratulations." Ellen's slurred voice echoed through the store. "Enjoy your little wedding. Maybe I'll come. You'll know me. I'll be sitting in the back wearing black. You know why?"

Ellen waited for an answer, but the bride wisely exited the store. I caught a glimpse of Liv mouthing "Sorry" to me.

"*You* know why?" Ellen asked me instead. "Because they're doomed. Doomed, I say, right from the very beginning. And do you know why?" Ellen took a step toward me, but as she did, her foot twisted beneath her and she barely caught herself on the gazebo railing. She turned back and shook her finger at the floor where she'd lost her balance. "You should get that fixed, Audrey. Someone could break a leg or something."

I glanced at the perfectly flat area of floor and practiced customer service with a smile. "I'll take care of it. Now, what can I do for you today, Mrs. Whitney?"

She staggered over to the table and collapsed into a chair. "I came to get my money back."

"Oh, I'm sorry, Mrs. Whitney. If you had called, I could have saved you a trip. You see, I already gave Jenny her money back when she canceled the order."

It took Ellen at least twenty seconds to process what I'd told her. "All of it?"

"All but the nonrefundable portion."

"Well, give me that, then." She pounded her fist on the table for emphasis, then winced. Not a good thing to do on a fieldstone table.

I considered defining "nonrefundable" for her, but since twenty-five dollars wouldn't send us into bankruptcy, and the family had been through so much . . . Besides, twenty-five bucks was a small price to pay to get a drunken, belligerent Ellen out of the shop. As she staggered behind me to the counter, I insisted she sign a receipt for the money. I doubted she'd remember I gave it to her. Not in this state of mind.

"There you go, Mrs. Whitney." I counted the bills out for her and watched as she tucked them into her purse, along with her copy of the receipt. "Have a nice day."

"Serves you right, you know that."

I smiled and hoped she'd turn and leave. Fat chance.

"And do you know why?"

Here we go again, I thought.

"All that hoopla about those magic bouquets of yours. Well, it didn't work this time, did it? It didn't work for my Jenny." Her voice cracked with pain. "Why, Audrey? Why didn't it work for Jenny?"

And with that, she crumpled to the floor.

* * *

All I can say is that sometimes it's nice having a good portion of a college football team on staff—albeit temporarily. I'd been a little concerned about them missing so much class time, but they'd all assured me they could watch their lectures online. It took Darnell and his cohorts, and a cup of Amber Lee's high-test, to get Ellen on her feet again. And even then she wobbled, supported with a little help on either side by two young football players.

"Can we get her home, do you think?" I couldn't think of any place to let her sleep it off in our shop—unless we draped her over the fieldstone table in the consulting nook. "What about if we lay her in the back of the delivery van?"

Liv glanced at her watch. "The delivery van is already loaded to take to the Rawlings'. The CR-V, too. And I need the boys to carry for me if we're going to get those arrangements set up before the afternoon visitation hours." Liv's hand flew to her forehead. "I don't know what to do. Ellen's timing stinks."

"Don't treat me like a baby. I can get home." Ellen shook off her supporters, then fumbled in her purse and pulled out a set of car keys. "Without any help from you." She held up the keys and lurched forward. "And do you know why?"

Darnell snatched the keys from her hand and held them high out of her reach.

Ellen made a jump for them, but the sudden motion made her wobble. "Oh, dear. I'm a little dizzy." Then she passed out, cold. At least the football players used their quick reflexes to catch her before she reached the ground.

At that moment, the bell over the door sounded. What a time for a customer!

I whirled around to see Nick Maxwell. His eyes scanned the situation, Darnell's two friends struggling to support the dead weight that was Ellen Whitney. I guess it's safe to say, in the brief time since we'd met, I hadn't made the best impression on the handsome baker. But then again, what did I care? I wasn't ready for another relationship anyway. Was I?

"I see Ellen came for her refund," Nick said.

"How did you know that?" I asked.

"She hit the bakery three hours ago and talked me out of the fifty-dollar deposit on the cake. Looks like she drank it."

"Audrey," Liv interrupted, "I need to get those flowers delivered now. I should have left ten minutes ago."

Maybe Ellen would end up draped across the fieldstone table after all.

"Do you need help with her?" Nick asked.

Liv pounced on that simple offer. And I'm not sure how it happened, but soon it was decided that Nick and I would see Ellen home in the back of the bakery truck. If Liv had taken up matchmaking again, I could think of an infinite number of better ways than escorting a belligerent drunk home.

He pulled his truck into the back alley. I recalled seeing the white box truck with the cupcake logo before but wondered how I'd missed the large sliding glass windows on the side.

"I just had those installed last week." He pointed them out as he rounded to the back and opened the doors. "I'd like to take the cupcakes mobile. Maybe hit some local events this year. Ball games. The summer concerts."

"Good idea." I could imagine all the belts in Ramble being loosened a notch just at the prospect.

That also explained the stainless steel counter inside the truck, just below the window. Racks were affixed to the area just behind the driver.

"It looks new back here," I said. "Are you sure you want to do this?"

He shrugged as the football players deposited Ellen onto the carpeted floor. "I was going to replace the factory carpet with a surface that's nonskid, yet easier to clean, so if . . ." He left the rest unsaid. Better that way.

He drove, gently negotiating the streets and hills of Ramble while I rode in the back with Ellen. I felt a bit like an ambulance attendant. I wondered if maybe I should check her vitals, hook up an IV, or randomly yell "stat" like they did on the TV shows. Yet her steady snore assured me she was alive and breathing. Only when the snore stopped did I lean over.

She mumbled something incoherent, belched, then started snoring again.

Minutes later, the truck stopped, the motor grew silent, and Nick Maxwell opened the back door. He rubbed his hands together. "So, how do you want to do this?"

I jiggled the keys that Darnell had confiscated. "I guess we should open up the house first."

He offered his hand to help me down from the back of the truck. I surreptitiously wiped my palm on my clothing. I was not going to repeat that potting soil fiasco. I grasped his hand—strong and warm. I guess bakers must develop strong hands, too. Then I *tried* to climb gracefully from the back of the truck and down the two feet to Ellen's unkempt stone driveway.

Yeah, that bad.

I guess I should explain that I still wore my dress and heels because of my scheduled bridal appointment. And high heels and stone driveways just don't mix. My left foot landed squarely enough, but my right heel sliced against a large stone, leaving me toppling, just as badly as Ellen had. If it weren't for Nick, who caught me.

Okay, maybe escorting a drunk woman home *is* good matchmaking. Score one for Liv. Because—cue the violins—we had a moment. One of those corny movie moments where I look up at him, and the entire world melts away except the warmth of his body next to mine as I stare into his limpid eyes. Whatever "limpid" means. But all the world was suspended and empty and faded into the background. Nothing mattered that moment but Nick and me.

Until Ellen belched loudly, then vomited all over Nick's truck.

Cut the violins.

Quite a bit of time had passed since I'd been in the Whitney home. After Jenny's dad died, Ellen and her daughter had moved into the nondescript ranch home just outside Ramble, one of a dozen identical affordable homes built on postage-stamp lots, manufactured with the lowest-end material possible. Bottom-of-the-line carpets, discounted linoleum, particleboard. And tiny.

The nice thing about Ellen's vomiting episode was that it meant she was conscious—or, rather, semiconscious—when we got her into the house. We each took an arm and were able to direct her up the steps.

While I got Ellen undressed and settled in bed, Nick took a roll of paper towels we found in her kitchen and headed out to his truck.

By this time, Ellen had transitioned from angry to weepy.

"You're a good girl, Audrey," she told me, squeezing my chin. "Your mama must be proud."

I inhaled sharply. "Let's not go there right now. You should be proud, too. Jenny is a sweet girl. The chief will figure out she didn't do this thing."

"She is. She's a good girl." Ellen curled into a ball. "I know she's a good girl."

I sat at the edge of her bed. "Then why won't you go see her?" I asked. Now might be the time to ask the questions—when Ellen was less likely to keep her guard up and might not even recollect what I asked.

"She won't want to see me. I messed it all up."

"Messed what up?"

"Messed it *all* up," she insisted.

This was not working. "What did you do to mess it all up?" Surely she couldn't mean she'd killed Derek.

"I encouraged her. Encouraged her, that's what I did."

"Encouraged her to do what?"

"To set her cap for Derek. She never would have . . ." Ellen trailed off into a round of bawling.

I waited, making soothing sounds and rubbing her arm.

"She liked him. She didn't know that *like* sometimes just needs a little push to become *love*. So I pushed her—just a little bit. It's like that sometimes, isn't it, Audrey?"

"I guess it is."

"And Derek wasn't so bad. He'd settle down like his father, with the help of the right woman—at least that's what Jonathan Rawling told me. Told me that's what happened to him. And he could provide a good life for Jenny, too. That's why I did it. Do you believe me, Audrey?"

"Of course."

"And gambling's not so terrible. Most people gamble a little, don't they? The lottery. Bingo. Why, even a lot of churches sponsor raffles. There are worse habits for a man to have, aren't there?"

"I suppose." It wasn't much of a segue, but I thought I'd give it a try. "Speaking of habits, Ellen"—I winced—"was Jenny taking any kind of drugs that you know of? Prescription, I mean, or . . ."

She seemed not to hear me as she snuggled under her covers and spoke to her pillow. "She'd settle him down, and he'd give her a good life. That's all I wanted. All those plans, all that work to get them together. And now he blames me."

"Who?"

"Jonathan. That man was sweet as pie just a week ago. He and his wife even invited me to tea. Tea. We had scones. Have you ever eaten a scone, Audrey? I mean a real scone."

I shushed her and pulled her shades to cut out the afternoon sunlight.

"With clotted cream," she mumbled as I closed her door, leaving her to sleep it off.

When I stepped out of the bedroom, I found Nick was in the kitchen, stripping off a pair of loose-fitting food service gloves. He tossed them in the kitchen trash can, then washed his hands in the sink. "How'd it go?"

"She'll sleep it off now," I said. "I hope."

"Do we dare leave her keys?" Nick asked.

"I don't see why not. Her car must still be parked somewhere in town, and that's a long walk from here. She can pick it up later when she's sober."

"I couldn't help but overhear what she said." Nick held the door open for me. "Sad."

"You know, Ellen hasn't been to see Jenny. I thought she was mad at her. But it sounds more like she's blaming herself for trying to get Derek and Jenny together."

"I heard that part—something about gambling." He held the passenger-side door open for me. No riding in the back this time. The smell had crept into the cab of the truck, so I rolled down my window.

When Nick climbed in, he did the same. "It's not true, though."

"Derek didn't gamble? Or was he involved in more than gambling?"

Nick laughed as he backed out of the driveway and turned onto the road. "I'm afraid I didn't know Derek well enough to answer that. I just meant that sometimes a little gambling isn't a little thing—and it takes more than the right woman to make it all work."

I'd been thinking the same thing, so I just nodded.

"My uncle, he started out with just lottery tickets. He'd blow twenty a week on them. And then something awful happened. He won. Won a million-dollar instant prize."

"Awful because . . ."

"At first it didn't seem so bad. He paid off his house, bought new cars for himself and his wife. Sent his kids to college. Did all those things people say they'll do if they win it big. Except he kept buying lottery tickets. Then a trip to Atlantic City. Then Vegas, with enough little wins to keep him coming back. In just a few years, the money had all trickled through his fingers. He took out a mortgage on his house, trying to win the money back, then got involved in a number of get-rich schemes—some of them on the shady side. Soon my aunt left him. Now he has nothing. So it kind of fits."

"Fits?"

"If Derek had a gambling problem, then he likely had a money-acquisition problem. Who knows what he was involved in, what kinds of shady deals he might have been part of?"

"So you're thinking one of his shady gambling connections might have killed him." I stared out the window, watching the green hills and white-fenced farms of Virginia streak by the passenger window. It made sense—at least more sense than Jenny killing Derek.

But with the chief investigating Jenny, someone needed to investigate Derek. I contemplated how to do this. Derek's parents. Derek's business associates. Derek's well-heeled friends.

Before long, Nick pulled into the alley behind the Rose in Bloom.

"Thanks so much for helping me." I reached for the door handle.

"No problem," he said.

"Except for the carpet."

"I'll just rip it out a little earlier than I planned. Nothing to worry about—and certainly not your fault."

I smiled at him.

"Audrey?"

"Yes?"

"I've been meaning . . . well, there's something I'd like to ask you."

I turned toward him and pulled a strand of hair behind my ear. This might be it. Did he feel that moment, too, the electrical charge between us? And more important, was I ready to date again? And was he even free to date? After all, he must have given all those flowers to somebody.

"I was thinking that . . . well, when you mentioned the bridal magazines, I thought that maybe . . ."

He turned forward, staring straight ahead, and tapped the steering wheel. He bit his lower lip before continuing. "Well, since you do flowers and I do cake, I thought that maybe we could collaborate . . ."

"Collaborate?"

"Yeah. Like decorating cakes and cupcakes with fresh flowers. So they match the bouquets and centerpieces. It could be a great service for both of us to add."

He turned back to me, his eyes pleading. It was my turn to stare out the front window. I'd have to call an electrician about my faulty romantic electricity meter. I'd been certain that he felt a spark, too.

"Sure. We could do that." I reached out to open my door, and he switched off the engine. When he climbed out of the cab, I turned back.

"You don't need to walk me in. I'm fine from here."

"I just remembered what I came here for in the first place. I was hoping you might have some small bouquets ready."

Oh, yes, the mysterious recipient of Nick's flowers. What a nice guy, coming in to buy flowers but still taking time out to help me carry Ellen Whitney home.

Whoever this mystery lady was, I hoped she appreciated him.

Chapter 9

After Nick purchased a cute little bouquet of delphinium (*fun, levity*) and daisies (*cheerfulness, innocence*) and left, I felt like such a slacker. Of course, my feet screamed in my shoes and I would have loved a nap, but I feared I hadn't done my share around the shop. While I'd been running errands for Jenny and escorting her drunken mother back home, Liv, Amber Lee, and Shelby had constructed even more funeral arrangements. They also must have taken in another order of flowers from somewhere, since our cooler still bulged with new blooms to work with. The fact that not a peach rose was among them I found a tad disconcerting. Of course, Liv was now assembling arrangements with the phone tucked against her shoulder, taking orders and fielding questions while her fingers worked automatically.

Still, I had a nagging feeling that although we'd done so much for the funeral already, we hadn't officially paid our respects to the Rawling family.

"Liv, what do you say we take this next batch over a little early? Then the second the last guest leaves, we can cart the flowers in."

Liv sagged onto her worktable. This work was taking a lot out of her, and I hated to add more to her plate. I saw her glance at the stack of work orders still remaining, if not growing.

"You should do it," Shelby said. "We'll have more help. The girls are coming back tonight, and I told them to expect it to be an all-nighter. They were pretty excited about the prospect." He gave us a look down his nose. "Little do they know."

"And I'd be happy to hold down the shop," Amber Lee said. "I hate to wish ill of somebody, but if more important people in town died, I'd be able to replace my roof. Leastwise, now I can afford a repair."

From anyone else, the statement might seem mercenary. But I suspected Amber Lee was helping us not to feel guilty about all the long hours we were putting them through, letting us know that they were willing and being compensated for their work.

"You're right," Liv said. "We'll go a little early."

After a quick freshening up, Liv and I were presentable to visit the Rawling estate. Well, without time for a full spa makeover and a NYC shopping excursion with a personal style consultant, we did the best we could.

We left Darnell in charge of the running van parked in the back while we walked around to the front porch, probably best called a veranda, unless some architect had coined some even more highfalutin name. We joined other arriving guests who'd left their high-end car with a servant who parked it. Valet parking. Who knew? I wondered if you were supposed to tip them. Good thing we parked out back.

As we walked in the double doors to the foyer (pronounced "fo-yay," I learned last time), Worthington's eyebrows rose almost imperceptibly, but he did nothing more than direct us into the parlor.

Friends and family milled around, surrounded by flowers, reminding me how many trips Liv had taken since the last time I'd been there. She'd done a fantastic job. Across the foyer, other guests served themselves from trays of pastries and sandwiches. Miranda Rawling held court in a Queen Anne chair—which probably traced its origins back to Queen Anne herself—near the casket.

I looked again at Derek.

"How natural he looks. Doesn't he look natural?"

I winced at the remark of the older gentleman behind me. Nothing was natural about this whole situation. Derek didn't belong dressed in his best suit, lying in a casket in the parlor. He belonged racing down the streets of Ramble in that silly car of his.

But if the answer to Derek's death lay in his life—in his gambling or other associates, as Nick suggested—I'd need to know more about Derek, certainly more than his lifeless form could tell me. I started to make my way over to Miranda Rawling.

Miranda's dark hair was cut into a chic bob. Since every hair was always in place, I once wondered if she wore a wig made of some space-age technology that appeared natural but always bounced into shape. But no, she was just the kind of person who is naturally all put together. Her hair, her jewelry, her clothing, her makeup, were all flawless. All the time.

This day, she wore a tailored navy suit with a demure gold and blue sapphire necklace and earrings, which caught every ray of light and brought out the color in her cool blue eyes, so similar to Derek's. Matching blue pumps looked like they never stepped outside, much less managed Ellen Whitney's stone driveway. As we approached her, she glanced at her watch, probably thinking we were early for a delivery.

Liv offered her hand. "We're so sorry about Derek."

Miranda grasped it. "Thank you, my dear. That's so nice of you to say."

Of course, Liv stole my line, and I refused to remark on how good or natural Derek looked. So I just stood there and nodded. So much for being the intrepid investigator. But how did one, in polite company, ask someone's mother about who might have killed her son? Or about what kinds of secrets he was keeping that could have led to his death? Grandma Mae hadn't covered that in any of our etiquette lessons.

Or maybe she had. One might ask like any Southern lady did. The indirect way, of course.

"It's hard to imagine anyone doing something so vicious to someone so young and with so much promise as Derek." That was a start.

Instead of meeting my statement with a squeeze of the hand and a "thank you for coming," as she had all expressions of sympathy since we'd arrived, Miranda Rawling swallowed hard and blinked back tears. Her response was barely audible. "I tried to warn him."

"Excuse me?"

"I did. I tried to talk Derek out of the wedding, warned him not to trust that girl. But he and his father were so taken by that sweet little act of hers."

"Act?" Repeat what they say as a question. Somehow I mixed my Southern lady methods with Psychology 101. A potent combination. If anyone ever truly rules the whole world, a soft-spoken Southern woman with a degree in psychology would be the most likely candidate. And nobody will even know they're being ruled. In fact, maybe it's already happening.

"When you get older you'll realize people aren't always what they seem." She lowered her voice again, drawing us closer. "Looked all wholesome and innocent, that one. Jonathan assured me that she would be a good influence on Derek." Miranda's features turned hard and her eyes flashed.

"He talked like my boy was some hoodie-wearing, tattoo-covered delinquent and that girl was some kind of angel, rather than the conniving, manipulating gold digger she turned into."

"Jenny?"

"Who else?" Miranda looked up, but she spoke to the air just to my right. "I know she's a friend of yours, Audrey." She turned her gaze back to me and pressed my hand. "But I won't hold that against you. She fooled so many."

That was big of her. But then I kicked myself for my snarky thought. If she believed Jenny guilty, it *was* big of her. "Thank you," I stammered. "I must admit, though, I'm still not convinced. I mean, I know what it looks like, but all the evidence seems so circumstantial. I don't understand how. Or why."

"I do. And it's far from just circumstantial. When the chief saw what I'd found . . ."

When she trailed off and looked around, I waited. While I didn't think Miranda would respond to nosy questions from her florist, she struck me as a woman who'd get her points across in her own time.

She remained silent as Worthington picked up some discarded dishware set on a nearby table. When he passed out of earshot, she continued. "I was looking for Derek's tie—the one his father picked for him had a snag, so I made the funeral director change it. I found her so-called love letters hidden in his closet. In a bag hanging under one of his suit jackets. It's where he used to hide all those mag . . . well, let's just say boys will be boys."

"Why would he hide letters from his fiancée? Are you sure they were from Jenny?"

"Well, they weren't signed with her name—just some nickname. Bunny. What grown woman in her right mind calls herself Bunny? Maybe she fancied herself some kind of sex kitten. The letters were rather . . . explicit."

"But how does that tie Jenny in to Derek's murder?" Liv asked, while I wondered when I last heard someone use the term "sex kitten."

Miranda wiped an imaginary crumb from her lapel. "I couldn't bring myself to read all the letters, you understand. But I did skim them. And what started out all lovey-dovey quickly turned demanding. Demanding that he come see her. Demanding that he spend all his time with her. Threatening him if he didn't . . . Threatening herself."

"But Jenny planned to break up with him," I said.

"Oh, Audrey." Miranda shook her head. "Oldest ploys in the book. Make yourself unavailable, and the men come running. Make yourself pathetic, and they run to protect you."

I guess Miranda and I learned from different books. Maybe that was my problem. I came off as too available and men stayed away. And maybe not pathetic enough, but I wasn't sure I wanted to go there.

"If only Derek had come to me, trusted me with the letters earlier. Maybe I could have helped him. Women can see through other women much more clearly, don't you agree?"

Possibly. But if Jenny was a domineering killer, my feminine intuition needed a tune-up. Still, I reasoned that if I could take a peek at those letters, I could get a better idea where Jenny's head was at the time. Or maybe understand more about their relationship—or even what else Derek was involved in. "Where are these letters now?"

"Why, with Chief Bixby, of course."

Of course.

Before our visit ended, I managed to score a scone. It was as good as Ellen Whitney claimed. Still warm. Dense, but not hard. Slightly crumbly, slightly chewy, with a to-die-for citrus glaze giving it just the right amount of sweetness.

Soon visitors cleared out. The caterers cleaned up the refreshments for the afternoon and began to lay out the refreshments for the evening. Liv, Darnell, and I toted in even more flowers. Liv brought along a pail of assorted blooms so we could fix anything damaged in transport or wilted from sitting in the room for a while. But little of that was needed.

When we'd arranged everything to our satisfaction, which even got a nod from the reticent Worthington, we packed up and headed out. Darnell drove the van back to the store, and Liv and I followed. As we approached the turnoff to Old Hill Road, I flipped my turn signal on.

"Where are we going?" Liv asked. "Listen, kiddo. Don't tell me you want to moon over that cottage again. And when there's so much to do."

"No, you were there when Miranda told us about the letters she found."

"Yes, and why all the questions?"

"I hardly asked any questions, if you recall."

Liv crossed her arms in front of her. "You and I both know that you didn't have to. But I could see you were digging for something. But what has that got to do with Grandma Mae's cottage?"

"We're not going to Grandma Mae's cottage. We're going to Mrs. June's house."

"Mrs. June? Oh, Audrey. Tell me you're not planning to pump that old woman for information."

"Better not let her hear you call her an old woman. And I doubt pumping will be necessary. I talked to her this morning, and she's as concerned about Jenny as I am—and just as convinced that Bixby's barking up the wrong tree."

"But should we get involved? Surely the police . . ."

I sent her a withering glance—possibly the worst look you can give a florist.

"Okay, maybe not the police. But there's got to be someone

else. Maybe Jenny's lawyer could hire a private investigator or something."

"Jenny's lawyer is a public defender who hasn't even been able to manage bail. Even if they did hire a PI, it would be someone who didn't know Jenny, didn't know Derek, and didn't know Ramble." And Ramble wouldn't know him— which would slow down the process even more. Small towns work that way.

"Still . . ." Liv hesitated as I negotiated Mrs. June's gravel driveway. "What makes you think you can clear Jenny? Or are you trying to play detective and figure out who killed Derek?"

I turned off the engine and looked at her. "Liv, I don't know that I can. And I assure you that I'm not playing. I only know I need to try."

Liv and I stared at each other. In another time or place, our staring contest would have melted into childish giggles. But not this time. She reached into the backseat and gathered flowers from the bucket.

"What are you doing?" I asked.

"Well, we might not have to pump information from Mrs. June, but it never hurts to prime a little."

I hadn't the heart to tell Liv that I'd already given Mrs. June flowers earlier. But those were for her office. I doubted she'd complain about flowers for her home.

Seconds later, we were knocking on Mrs. June's back door.

When she swung it open, Mrs. June looked just like I always remembered her at home. Relaxed, wearing a cozy flowered housecoat and fuzzy pink slippers.

"Why, Audrey, what a pleasure to see you again so soon." She stepped back so we could enter. "And Liv, it's great to see you."

Liv leaned in to kiss Mrs. June on the cheek, then handed her the impromptu bouquet. It looked casual and lovely and set off the colors of Mrs. June's kitchen, and she oohed and aahed over them for a good minute before she invited us to sit at her kitchen table. Her signature orange chocolate cake beckoned from under a glass cover, and soon we had large slices sitting in front of us while Mrs. June ran fresh tap water into a vase.

"Now, to what do I owe this visit?" She placed the bouquet in the center of the table. "Or do I even need to ask?"

Liv spoke first. "We were just over at the Rawling place to pay our respects to Derek and thought we'd stop by and say hello."

Liv also had the Southern lady trick down to a charm, but it proved unnecessary with Mrs. June.

"Cut the malarkey. I know that act. You learned it from your grandmother." She laughed. "I was fairly good at it myself, in my day. But I'm an old woman now." As if to prove it, she sank into the chair. "So if you don't mind, can we skip the verbal gymnastics and just cut to the chase?"

"Miranda Rawling mentioned something about letters she found in Derek's closet," I said. "Letters she insists are from Jenny."

"And I suppose you're curious about what they said?" Her face was serious, but the twinkle in her eye gave her away.

"Miranda indicated that they implicated Jenny, gave her a motive for Derek's death."

Mrs. June sighed. "To answer the question you're too shy—or cunning—to ask, yes, I've seen them. Bixby asked me to photocopy them so he could log the originals into evidence. I can't say I read every word. I was only supposed to make sure all the words were legible so he could use the copies in the investigation. But it helps to be a speed reader."

It was true. I'd seen her flipping pages faster than anyone I'd ever known. Mrs. June always had a book in her hand,

and always a different one. I was surprised the Ramble Public Library could keep up with her.

"The only thing the prosecution will have a hard time doing," she said, "is proving those letters were from Jenny."

"Miranda said they were signed with a nickname."

"Bunny." Mrs. June snorted. "And the letters were all computer printed, in some curly, girlie font designed to look like handwriting. Which is kind of weird to begin with."

"The font?"

"The letters. You young people are always e-mailing today, and texting. And sending instant messages or . . . what do they call it . . . tweeting. I still don't get that. But if it was twenty years ago—maybe even thirty—I would have understood letters."

"Jenny is a little old-fashioned," I started. But I never knew her to send a letter. Except the letter where she basically dumped me. But that had at least been handwritten.

"But the letters were incriminating?" Liv asked.

Mrs. June bit her upper lip. At this point, I knew I simply had to wait. While all those TV investigators seem all bluster and questions, Grandma Mae had taught us that sometimes silence proved more effective—that other people would want to fill in the space with words—and you could learn all kinds of things just by sitting back and listening. So I took another bite of my cake.

Mrs. June didn't disappoint. "Mind you, if this gets back to Bixby, I could lose my job."

Liv rushed in to swear that she wouldn't tell a soul. With my mouth full of cake, I raised my hand in an oath.

"The letters were . . . disturbing. They started out normal enough, maybe a tad brazen. But then . . ." She turned to me. "Audrey, are you sure Jenny wasn't on drugs? Because there's a major personality shift in those letters. Drugs could explain everything. Including how she's acting now."

I sat back. "Mrs. June, when I knew Jenny, I'd say no

way. But I haven't spent much time with her over the last year or so. I just can't put my mind around her doing that, though." Then again, we were supposed to be best friends forever, and I couldn't have imagined her dumping me like she did. But this wasn't junior high anymore. Not that BFFs worked out that well in junior high. "Maybe if you could tell me how the letters changed."

Liv kicked me under the table. Too direct?

Mrs. June didn't seem to notice. She leaned in. "They got juicier and juicier. Like those soap operas on steroids." She leaned back and fanned herself with a napkin. "I'd hate to be the one to read those out loud in court.

"And then, she starts talking about getting married. Things like, when they're married . . . and here she turns into some June Cleaver. Talking about making chicken, collard greens, and biscuits, and having ten kids."

Which sounded more like Jenny. "So that can give Bixby enough to suspect Jenny," I said.

"It would help if someone found the answers to these letters." She paused while cutting herself another tiny sliver of cake. "But they don't end there."

Miranda had already suggested the letters contained threats, but I wanted to hear Mrs. June's interpretation, so I tilted my head and raised my eyebrows and let her go on.

"The last few months are the ones that are damning—pardon my French. Threatening sometimes, peachy keen other times. Like she somehow lost contact with reality and rode any wave she could climb onto. Like one of those split-personality types. I almost expected to see a different name down at the bottom. And they went on that way—sometimes more than one letter a day. Sometimes June Cleaver and sometimes, I don't know, one of those hockey-mask-wearing, chain-saw-carrying psychos from those blood-and-guts movies."

"So the letters contain threats."

"I'll say." Her eyes sparkled, but then she stopped, cast

me a sympathetic look, and patted my hand. "I'm sorry. I don't mean to get all excited, but I've been working for the Ramble police for a lot of years, and this is the most excitement we ever got. I almost forgot she was your friend."

Mrs. June took a deep breath and then exhaled. "Maybe, based on those letters, the lawyer might consider a psychological defense."

"I'd like to see Jenny," I said. "None of this makes sense with the girl I know. But perhaps if I could visit with her and listen to her, maybe I could get a handle on . . ."

Mrs. June shook her head. "She's just curled up in a little ball—at least that's how Brenda found her when she took in her food. They put her on a suicide watch, but I wish someone would call her doctor in. If she asked to see one, they'd allow it. But she still insists she doesn't want or need to see one—or anyone else, for that matter."

I could see why Mrs. June was convinced drugs were involved. And that could explain the rapid personality shift.

My heart sank. I had hoped to find more information that would clear Jenny. Instead, everything just seemed to be piling up against her.

Chapter 10

"But I bought two of them." Mrs. Burke pointed to the rose-patterned pens in the stand next to the cash register.

"And I put them in your bag," Amber Lee answered. "I recall clearly."

"But they weren't in the bag when I got home." Mrs. Burke straightened to her full height—an intimidating four feet, nine inches.

Amber Lee held her ground. "We're not responsible for items you may have lost on the way home."

"Just a minute," Liv interrupted.

Amber Lee stepped back. She looked a little miffed but held her tongue.

"May I see the bag?" Liv said.

Mrs. Burke produced the Rose in Bloom bag.

Liv took it, running her hand along the bottom before her fingers found a hole in the seam.

Amber Lee sighed and looked down.

"My associate is right, of course," Liv said, sparing Amber Lee some embarrassment. "We're not responsible for any item lost after it leaves the shop. But since, in this case, your pens appear to have slipped through a defective bag, perhaps this time you could choose another?"

Mrs. Burke's eager hands played across the selection of pens and chose two with white roses hand-painted on a wood barrel. I heard Amber Lee's quick intake of breath. I suspected the lost pens had been a cheaper variety.

Mrs. Burke appeared appeased and chatted with Liv on the way to the door.

After escorting the woman out, Liv rolled her eyes, breaking the tension and coaxing a wave of laughter from Amber Lee and the rest of the staff who were now spying from the back room.

"Now that I have you all gathered here," Liv said, with a bit of a smirk on her face, "if you're bagging merchandise for a customer, check the bags. This last order contained some defective ones. I tried to weed through them, but apparently I missed a few."

Liv glanced at her watch, then flipped the sign to "Closed," causing a round of applause. She took a low dramatic bow. "We may be closed, but we've got a full night of work ahead of us. So I hope you all brought your energy drinks and most comfortable shoes.

"So let's crank up the radio and get started. Everybody gets to choose their favorite station for an hour. Then we'll try to wrap it up and get at least a few hours of sleep."

I did a quick head count. Although there were nine of us (Liv and me, Amber Lee, Shelby, Melanie, and Opie, all set up in various workstations around the store, and Darnell and his two teammates, assigned to fetch and carry and clean and run out for more food as needed) those "few hours of sleep" would be limited to a catnap. The thought of nine solid hours of floral design was exhausting—especially since we'd repeat it again the following day.

"Oh, and Audrey? The peach roses are here."

I hightailed it to the walk-in. Although not from our usual supplier, the peach roses were just as vivid and fresh. I heaved a huge sigh of relief.

"With the rest of us working on funeral arrangements," Liv said, "I think I can spare you and Amber Lee if you want to get a jump on the wedding flowers."

Avoiding the crammed back room, Amber Lee and I set up an impromptu station in the consulting nook. The music of the hour was bluegrass. I had a hard time hearing anything but the mandolin, but that was okay. It gave me time to think. About the day—long. About the work ahead—impossible. About my own life—did I even want to venture down that alley? The alternative was thinking about Jenny, but that was even more discouraging than my own life at this instant.

I'd decided to start with the reception centerpieces. Carolyn had picked tall, elaborate arrangements. Years ago, table flowers used to be wide arrangements, maybe with a candle popped into the middle, low enough that the guests could see over and converse. Until some florist discovered you could put a full tall arrangement in an even taller pillar vase and allow the flowers to tower over the guests' heads. Of course, that tall vase required a large base, and the flowers needed to be fairly symmetrical. I had yet to see one come crashing down, but I'd imagine the results would be disastrous.

Since the flowers for these arrangements are not placed in the vase but, rather, in a smaller container that rests on top, Amber Lee and I were able to construct them while seated. I kicked off my shoes and stretched my toes. Heavenly.

I demonstrated the first centerpiece, so Amber Lee could

pick up and mimic the design. Bells of Ireland added the visual interest and seemed well suited to a wedding as they foretold *good luck*. White lilies, of course, meant *purity* or *sweetness* and made an interesting contrast with the darker peach roses that symbolized *desire*. I guessed purity and desire were a good combination for a wedding, even if no one noticed the significance but me.

The white snapdragon gave me pause, since it could mean *presumption* or even *deception*. But it also carried the meaning of *gracious lady*. What could be more typically Southern? So I tucked it in with little reservation.

As we filled in the remaining space with green Fuji mums, I had to chuckle. If a Victorian maid were to receive one of these mums, sometimes called spider mums, she might have started packing her bags. The message was *elope with me*.

I could imagine what a sudden elopement would do to the mayor's blood pressure after all the planning and expense. But in a wedding arrangement, the flower could also symbolize *liveliness*. Carolyn had jumped on the idea of including this flower, with a flush on her face. At that point, I was glad she didn't clue me in on her reasoning. Too much information.

As the reception arrangements grew in number, I sent the boys out to see if they could scavenge some cardboard boxes from the back alley or perhaps the grocery store. We'd be filling our coolers with complete funeral and wedding arrangements, and flowers don't stack well. Liv slipped them some money and asked them to come back with pizza as well.

Before too long, in a familiar environment with plenty for my hands to do, my mood lightened. As Grandma Mae always said, "Idle hands are the devil's workshop." I reasoned there might be something to all those old Southern Mama–isms she passed down.

At least I didn't have a scowl on my face at ten-something, when a tap on the front door drew my attention. The radio had shifted to an old standards station, and Frank Sinatra belted out some corny song about the coffee in Brazil. Since most of our staff were still in the back room, I stood up, stretched, and went to the front door. The darkness of the night compared to the brightness of the shop made it difficult to see who was there.

But the closer I got to the door, the more I began to recognize the figure. Nick Maxwell, minus his baker's whites. Well, before anyone gets the wrong mental image, he was wearing khaki pants and a sports shirt. And he looked just as good, if not better, in colors besides white.

"Hi," he said shyly when I cracked open the door. "I saw the lights on."

"We're closed." Lame. But after a long day it was the best I could do.

"I know that," he said. "What I mean is, I just finished stripping out the carpet in the truck. When I saw the light, I figured you'd have a lot going on over here . . ." He seemed to look past me into the shop.

My tired brain refused to complete his sentences. I supposed that was a bad sign, wasn't it? Aren't compatible people always saying how they can complete each other's sentences? But then again, since he had a girlfriend, it didn't matter how compatible we were. Why did my brain keep going there?

"I thought," he continued, "maybe you'd like more help. I don't know flowers, but I'm a quick learner and good with my hands."

"I'm sure you are." Did I say that out loud?

"And . . ." He offered up two bakery boxes. "I brought some new cupcake flavors I've been working on. I thought I might find some beta testers here."

"We're not going to turn down those," I said. "Come on in."

I introduced him to our staff, both permanent and temporary. Moments later, the boys returned with the pizzas, and we cleared off a display table to accommodate them, some two-liter bottles of soda, and Nick's cupcakes. I found a stack of paper plates left over from another all-night session and some extra plastic cups. No napkins, so we'd have to make do with paper towels.

Since all our table and counter space was taken up with floral arrangements in various stages of construction, most of us found spaces on the shop floor to sit. I joined Liv, leaning my tired back up against the main counter.

Nick fixed a small plate and sank down across from me. I looked up at him just when Frankie slid into a rendition of "The Way You Look Tonight," which made it difficult to look at him at all.

Melanie broke the silence and asked about the upcoming football season. And soon the boys were up and trying to impress the girls—at least I think that was why they were demonstrating football plays in a florist shop.

The goth, Opie, covered her eyes. "How do you do that without getting hurt? All that tackling, ramming each other. I'm surprised you don't break your necks."

"Not if you do it right." Darnell picked up a plastic pot and tucked it under his arm. "The key is to lead with your shoulder, not with your head. That way you have a broader surface to transfer force, and stress isn't placed on the neck or spinal column."

The football players demonstrated this in several variations, each one rowdier than the previous. If they were skilled florists, I'd love to be able to harness that energy. On the last play, Nick reached in and rescued a bucket of gerbera daisies somewhere around the five-yard line.

While Liv flagged them all for unnecessary roughness, I snagged myself a chocolate cupcake. Beta testing, indeed. What was so unusual about a chocolate cupcake? And then

I took a bite. The filling was something like a cherry cheese-cake, and it was topped with a thick and luscious ganache. It was so wonderful, I didn't want to swallow. I threw my head back and moaned in ecstasy.

"There'd better be more like that," Amber Lee said. "I want a bite of paradise, too."

When I opened my eyes, everyone was staring at me.

Nick laughed. "That's a good name. Maybe I'll call them a 'bite of paradise,' rather than 'Black Forest cheesecake.' Although . . . that's the reaction I was going for."

My cheeks flamed again, but my embarrassment proved short-lived. Soon everyone clamored around for their "bite of paradise," and there was more moaning going on than Ramble had seen in a long time, at least since that food poisoning incident at the Moose lodge dinner.

Nick joined Amber Lee and me in the consulting nook, chatting amiably while he stripped leaves and thorns from our roses. I can't say his hands survived unscathed, but he picked it up quickly enough.

"How was business at the shop today, Amber Lee?" I asked. She'd waited on customers and acquainted herself with a good portion of the business in the past, but we hadn't left her in charge for any longer than a break time—until this week.

"I think I did okay," Amber Lee said. "Except maybe that last customer."

"Who was that?" Nick asked.

"Mrs. Burke," Amber Lee answered. "Gave me flash-backs. I remember teaching her kids. She'd always end up in my classroom arguing with me and asking me to raise their grades. They were smart kids, mind you, but a grade is a grade."

Nick nodded. "I think she just likes to get all she's entitled to, and then some. She'll come in the bakery and spend half an hour trying to pick out the biggest cupcakes. I mean, they're barely different at all, but she's got to have the ones she picks."

"And she did rip us off," Amber Lee said. "The replacement pens she picked cost two dollars more than the original ones. We should've charged her the difference."

"Maybe," I said. "But in retail, it's not about fairness. It's a small town. We want the customers to keep coming back, not hop on the highway and buy their flowers from some grocery store. We'll make it up in the end."

"It's good business in a small town," Nick added. "Going the extra mile sometimes. Like seeing Mrs. Whitney home today."

"I'm so sorry about your carpeting." I patted his wrist. I shouldn't have done it. The old thrill of the touch came back. Anticipation, like climbing to the top of a roller coaster . . . but getting stuck at the top, waiting for two hours, and then riding in a lift with a sweaty construction worker with a receding hairline and a beer gut. Which is why I don't ride roller coasters anymore.

"Ellen was in a sorry state when she left here, that's for sure," Amber Lee said. "Her husband would be rolling in his grave to see her back to drinking."

"Back to drinking?" I asked. I'd known her to take a nip or two, but I'd never seen her that flat-out drunk. Grandma Mae would have said she was "drunk as Cooter Brown." Who Cooter Brown was, we never did figure out.

"Back when they were running the restaurant, she'd dip into the wine," Amber Lee said. "Her husband sent her to one of those high-priced rehab places near DC, where all the politicians and their wives go on the quiet and say they're at some spa. They could afford it when he was healthy and the restaurant was booming."

"Restaurant?" Nick asked.

"Yeah," Amber Lee said, "a little Italian place just out-side town. The spaghetti and meatballs would keep you filled for a week."

"Ramble has an Italian restaurant?" Nick asked. "How did I miss that?"

"It's not there anymore," I said. "But it was quite the place to go when I moved here. Jenny told me that the Whitney family had all been restaurateurs—only more home-style Southern foods. When he married an Italian woman, his family were all up in arms. Could she cook?"

Amber Lee laughed. "But the joke was on them. She could cook like a dream. So they set up this restaurant and expanded and expanded. Despite the family warnings that any place serving polenta instead of corn bread didn't stand a chance around here, it seems like people were tired of the same old, same old. They'd eat anything Ellen dished out. That place was hopping all the time."

"Then what happened?" Nick asked.

"George Whitney got sick." Amber Lee assumed a more somber tone. "Cancer. He passed away quick. Ellen kept the place going for a few months, but it just went downhill. You could see her heart wasn't in it. And then she just let the staff go and barred the doors."

And Ellen hadn't been the only one to cut ties. Jenny gave me the old heave-ho about that time.

"It was tough on Jenny, too," I said. "All that upheaval. She grew up working in that restaurant. I think she bused tables as soon as she could walk."

"How's Jenny doing?" Nick asked.

"From what I hear, not well," I said.

"What's the deal with the letters?" Amber Lee asked.

"You heard about the letters?" I asked. Of course she had. Amber Lee heard everything and saw everything. And often shared everything.

"It's making the rounds," she admitted.

"What letters?" Nick asked.

"Some spicy letters from Jenny to Derek, turning a little pathological at the end," Amber Lee summed it up.

"That's pretty much it, but there's no proof that Jenny wrote those letters," I said. "At least, she never signed them with her name. Besides, from what I hear, they were quite . . . explicit. And—I'm sorry—if anything, the Jenny I knew always seemed a bit of a prude."

Nick frowned. "So it's possible someone else wrote them. Maybe someone from Derek's secret life."

"Secret life?" Amber leaned forward.

I waved it off. "Ellen intimated that Derek had a gambling problem. So maybe the letters could be from someone associated with that lifestyle. Or who said the letters were new? Maybe they were from some old flame. Derek had a reputation for getting around."

"A player," Nick said, with just the right note of disapproval. It was getting pretty hard not to like this guy.

Amber Lee shook her head. "If you're looking at old flames as suspects, the list is going to include almost half the population of Ramble—including the mayor's daughter."

I looked down at my half-completed table centerpiece and swallowed hard. "I'd forgotten that Carolyn dated Derek."

"From what I gather," Amber Lee said, "Carolyn did it to please her father, but she and Derek didn't hit it off. At least that's what her cousin told me."

"If the mayor's daughter ran with Derek," Nick said, "maybe she could shed more light . . ."

The sentence trailed off, and we all worked silently for a while. Maybe quizzing Carolyn would prove fruitful. Perhaps she'd have some idea who could have written such letters to Derek . . . if she hadn't written them herself. She certainly wasn't as prudish as Jenny, but I wouldn't call her crude, either. But then again, it's hard to know what someone might write or do when they thought no one else would see.

But how do you interrogate the mayor's daughter the week of her wedding?

Nick must have been thinking, too. "Why would Derek keep the letters if they were from an old flame?"

For almost a minute, the question hung in the air.

"Because they meant something to him?" I proposed.

"Or . . . he could profit from them," Nick added.

"Blackmail?" Amber Lee's gaze shot to the ceiling.

"If they're as steamy as everybody says, yeah, why not?" Nick said. "We know Derek had a gambling problem. And that means he'd always be looking for a source of income."

"So," I added, "he saves these old letters, written by someone concerned about her reputation, and then Derek uses them to raise capital to feed his gambling addiction? That's repugnant." And a motive. A good one. And one that pointed at someone other than Jenny, since the Whitneys no longer had that kind of money.

I leaned back to consider. If I took this half-formed idea to Bixby, he'd ignore it. The chief wouldn't want to ruffle the mayor's feathers for such a far-fetched idea. Not that I intended to ruffle any feathers, either. But I could keep my eyes open and poke around a little. And since I would be involved in the wedding, as both florist and guest, it couldn't hurt to be extra vigilant.

"Do you need more flowers?" Nick asked.

"Maybe some more snapdragons and a few more bells of Ireland." I held up a few so he could see them. He grabbed them to take with him. Good idea. Otherwise, I could imagine him coming back with gladioli.

Instead, he emerged with the proper blooms and one bird of paradise.

"I just had a great idea. What would you think if we put a bird of paradise on a bite of paradise? As a decoration?"

It sounded like one of those two-in-the-morning ideas. One that would not seem so great in the light of day. It didn't even seem that great to me at the moment. "It would be remarkable, but I wouldn't do it."

I'm not sure where a crest is on a male human, but his was fallen.

"Not only is it one of our more expensive blooms, since it's tropical, but it's also toxic."

"Surely people wouldn't eat it."

I neglected to tell him of one wedding where a couple of the groom's fraternity buddies consumed half their table centerpiece between dinner courses. "They might not have to. A little sap of some flowers is all you need. I keep a list of edible flowers. If you still want to collaborate, I can make you a copy."

At the mention of collaboration, Amber Lee pushed herself up using the table. "I'm sorry, Audrey, but I think these old bones need to get some rest."

Nick also stood up. "Need a ride home?"

I liked those old-fashioned manners.

"No, it's just a few blocks and my car's out back," she said. "I'll see you in the morning." She winked at me, then waved and headed to the back room.

The wink did it; I caved under the added pressure that Amber Lee put on me by contriving to leave us alone. Nick and I had been working companionably for hours, but now my palms broke into a sweat and my mouth went dry. I raced to find something to say, something witty and charming and maybe a tad flirtatious. But my mind drew a complete blank.

"Are you okay?" he asked.

"Perhaps a bit tired," I said. An understatement, I assure you. I rotated my shoulder blade and heard a crack.

He stood up and came behind my chair, placed his hands on my shoulders, and started a massage that—

"Just a little to the left." As my muscles relaxed under his touch, I let out an unconscious moan.

"Hey, keep it G-rated in there," Darnell called out.

Opie then proceeded to elbow him in the ribs.

Chapter 11

❧

My brain refused to process the sound. It was either a knock on the door or my neighbor Tom was getting back at me by constructing a new deck in the middle of the night. But the source of the sound was closer than that. Considering I'd slept only a few hours and the alarm had not yet gone off, it took a good while before curiosity won out over the gravity holding down my eyelids.

I opened my eyes to the streetlight peeking through the slats of my bedroom blinds. Chester swatted at some insect that encroached on his territory. The sound that had awakened me turned out to be the blinds slapping against the window. At least through the gap I could see that the heavy rain that had fallen most of the night had diminished into a misty drizzle.

I glanced at the clock. Ten measly minutes left to sleep. "Stop," I called out in my most feeble voice. Surely Chester would show some sympathy. After all, cats are all about sleep. When that didn't work, I pulled my pillow over my face. It dulled the slapping but not the huge crash that followed.

I sat up to see Chester rolling on the floor, head, feet, and tail entwined in the cording and slats of what once were my blinds. The intruding fly zoomed around his head in an almost taunting flight pattern, then took off into the hallway. Served Chester right.

Chester took off after the fly, dragging the blinds several feet before he extricated himself.

I let my head crash back down on the pillow. This was a perfect day for calling in sick, going back to bed, and waking up to pancakes at around three in the afternoon. Unfortunately sick time is not a luxury the self-employed can enjoy. And since the missing shades left a beam of lamplight that honed in on my pillow like a laser-guided . . . laser, I heaved myself out of bed.

After a shower—at least I think I remembered taking a shower . . . my first coherent recollection was standing in my bathroom soaking wet and stark naked, so the odds were pretty good there—I toweled off and dressed in a conservative black dress.

Shoes were more difficult. This was sure to be a high-class event. I opted for my nicest black shoes, a pair of nondescript pumps that were so high that I could barely walk in them. I grabbed a pair of cheap black flats to wear while setting up.

Liv had informed me the previous night that the Rawlings wanted all the flowers that had been delivered to the house—and any new additions—taken to the graveside area, where a tent had been set up. For this massive relocation project, we'd enlisted a couple of borrowed trucks—Larry's and Eric's.

And while the football players would do most of the heavy lifting, Liv and I would be directing the effort.

When I arrived at the shop, Eric stood outside in the alley

barking orders to the boys as they loaded arrangements into Larry's truck. *All* the arrangements. I made them put the wedding centerpieces back in the cooler.

"Where's your wife this morning?" I was grateful for Eric's enthusiastic help, but without Liv's direction, not to mention her kid-glove treatment of our already tired and underpaid staff, it was a case of force misapplied. Like hammering in a tack with a jackhammer or opening an envelope with a machete.

"Sleeping," he said.

"Sleeping?"

Whether it was at the incredulity in my voice or the slap of my jaw hitting the floor or the look of panic in my eyes, Eric hustled to explain.

"She sneaked into bed late and set her alarm. I turned it off."

"You . . . turned it off?" I wasn't sure who would be more upset over this: me, Liv, or Eric's mom—after Liv killed him.

"Yes." Eric squared his shoulders. "She's been dragging all week. She needed more sleep, and I aimed to make sure she got it." His tone was challenging, daring me to cross a line.

"Eric," I said softly instead, "I understand, and I wish I had someone to turn off my alarm for me, too." Or kill my cat. "But how do you think Liv is going to feel when she wakes up and figures out what you did?"

"Pretty angry." It was Liv's voice, and we turned to see her walking out the back door, arms crossed on her chest. But as she got closer to Eric, her expression softened. "But also touched that you care." She tipped herself up on her toes to kiss Eric on his scruffy cheek.

"I tried so hard to let you sleep," Eric said.

"I know, which is why I set a backup alarm. I appreciate the thought, but this is my business, too. And we're going to have our insanely busy times. In a few days, this will all be a memory, and I'll take some extra hours off. Promise."

I'd believe that when I saw it. But it seemed to appease Eric, who then went off in search of bagels when his next question, "Did you eat anything?" was answered evasively.

"Sorry about that, Audrey." Liv leaned in for a hug. "He can get overprotective sometimes."

"No problem," I said. "Everyone needs an Eric in their life. I just hope mine shows up before I'm on social security."

Soon we and our crew were on our way, happily with bagels and coffee, to the small cemetery just outside town.

Or, rather, I was happy. Liv sipped her decaf and toyed with her bagel.

"Maybe Eric had the right idea." I noted the dark circles under her eyes and the gray pallor of her normally rosy skin. "Are you all right?"

Liv let out a slow breath. "Probably just all the junk food and late hours last night. I'll be fine."

"Maybe you should get a nap after we set up. There's no need for all of us to stay for the ceremony. And I'm sure with all the extra help, I could handle the wedding arrangements."

Liv shook her head. "I was the one who put us behind in the wedding plans because I couldn't stop taking funeral orders. I'm not going to make you do all the work to catch up while I take a break. You know it's true. You'd have all the wedding flowers done by now."

Hard to argue with that. Waiting until the last minute used to be a habit for me, but I'd grown out of that a little. Still, that procrastination had taught me something. I knew I could rally at the end if I needed to. And with the funeral and the wedding back-to-back like this, we'd need to.

The sun began to streak through pink clouds as we found the funeral tent, more like a cross between a gazebo and a pavilion but the size of a circus tent—with room for three hundred close friends and family.

Thin, translucent ribbons of a misty fog lingered,

hovering over the wet grass. Workers were busy aligning perfect rows of white wooden chairs, so we parked our truck behind the rental truck and hopped out. Liv and I took one quick circuit around the site, discussing tactics for arranging. We decided on a semicircular wall of flowers behind the grave and arching down on either side. A semicircle of smaller arrangements would flank the casket. They would be free-form here, mixing and mingling colors as though we'd just plopped them in the first place we found. Of course, we wouldn't do that. Arranging flowers casually, to look like you didn't care, took more work than most people realized.

Just the brief walk through the grass was enough to soak my suede flats. A breeze kicked up, swirling the remnants of the morning fog. A chill ran up my spine, and I wished I'd thought to bring a sweater and waterproof shoes. But as soon as we got to work in earnest and the sun continued to ascend at a rapid pace, the air grew rather warm and I appreciated the breeze. The wet shoes, not so much.

We sent the boys back in one of the empty trucks just as people started to arrive. It seemed too early for mourners. I worried we'd gotten the hours wrong, but then I saw one of the new arrivals lugging a cello toward the pavilion. Soon a string quartet was tuning and warming up.

I recognized one violinist, probably in his fifties, with short-cropped hair, a splotchy pockmarked face, and a long neck with a pronounced Adam's apple. I'd run into him at several events and tried to give him a wide berth. When he saw my gaze travel in his direction, he winked at me. If that was all he tried to do, I'd be lucky. He gave roving violinists a bad name by "accidentally" getting his bow caught in ladies' hemlines on more than one occasion.

I'd first met him at tryouts for the town band, where he plays the bassoon. As a relative newcomer to town, I'd been flattered when he asked all kinds of questions about my tuba and music education. I first pegged him as a harmless music aficionado. When he leaned over, hand on my knee, and rapturously declared how sensual an instrument the tuba was when played with such passion and joie de vivre, I saw his true colors—letch blue. I mean, I can oompah a Souza march with the best of them, but it's never inspired anything in men but an incredulous "You play the tuba?" or "Doesn't that thing get heavy for you?" Or, more often, "That must take a lot of hot air."

Five minutes later, a harpist also arrived, and a large, full harp was carried carefully from the gravel road, down a brief hill, and set into place in the pavilion.

The next car to arrive, a compact Honda Civic, pulled off the roadway and onto the grass, stopping just a few yards from the tent. A young red-headed woman hopped out of the driver's seat, jogged to the passenger side, and opened the door. Pastor Seymour neglected her offered assistance and instead planted his quad cane firmly into the grass and heaved himself up. Again the young woman offered her arm, but he refused. I wondered if she was the pastor's new secretary and Amber Lee's former student and current source of information. She parked the car on the gravel road, and he hobbled toward the pavilion.

"Pastor Seymour," I called out, then ran to greet him. Liv did the same, and we positioned ourselves on either side. He wouldn't accept assistance walking, I knew, but in the event that he lost his footing or hit a rut, between the two of us, we could keep him upright.

"How are you this morning, sir?" I said.

He paused for a moment, drew himself up to full height, and sucked in a deep breath of morning air. "Grateful," he said with a decisive nod. Whether he was grateful for the morning or grateful to be able to still enjoy it, he never said. But this was his stock answer whenever anyone asked how he was, and he lived his life graciously, as if he meant it.

"Well, it looks like I have two lovely escorts this morning." He winked, but, unlike the violinist's, I knew his wink carried nothing but kindhearted friendship.

When we arrived at the back row of chairs, he levered himself into one, struggling to catch his breath in the gusty breeze, which seemed determined to become a full-blown windstorm. "Sad occasion for it, though. I just met with the young man the other day. He was going to be married, you know. Would rather have a wedding, I think."

I slid into the chair next to him. "He was going to marry Jenny. And now the poor thing is in jail."

Pastor Seymour turned a set of clear brown eyes in my direction. His body may have grown feeble, and he napped more than he used to, but his mind proved sharp and lively. I suspected if he rambled a bit, he used it to his advantage, to say some of the things that he'd been too timid or tactful to say in years gone by. "I tried to visit Jenny," he said. "It's a good thing, visiting people in prison. The Lord said what we do to one of the least of these, we do to him. She wouldn't see me, though. Wouldn't see anybody, I hear."

"I know," I said. "I tried, too."

He patted my hand. "That's a good thing."

"Pastor Seymour, I don't think she killed Derek."

Pastor Seymour nodded and closed his eyes. For a moment, I worried that he'd already started one of his unplanned naps. But his words came anyway, soft and melancholy.

"Audrey, I've been preaching for over sixty years now, and been honored to officiate at more weddings than you can shake a stick at. I've seen all kinds of couples leave down that aisle, cheered on by their family and friends. Some went on to enjoy kids and grandkids and great-grandkids. Others, you just knew they had little chance of making it. A few of those turned around, you see, when one or the other grew up and took some responsibility. So when two young folk come to me to get married, I don't turn too many of them down. If I do, they'll just run off and get someone else to hitch them up. But I still try to teach them something . . ." He closed his eyes and trailed off, and I thought he was finished. Or sleeping again.

"But Jenny and Derek, that was an odd pair. So I laid it on thick. I talked all about the duties of marriage, cautioned them not to enter unadvisedly, painted a vivid picture of what an unhappy marriage can be."

"You tried to dissuade them," I said.

"I don't know that I'd use quite those words. Let's just say I put more emphasis on the negatives of marriage—how confining and conflicting it can be when married to the wrong person."

He could use whatever words he wanted. I figured he did right by Jenny. "You know, I think your words had an impact. Jenny called off the wedding."

"Huh . . . and here I thought I wasn't getting through." He shook his head. "She could have been stuck with that man for life."

My quick intake of breath drew a chuckle from him. "Yeah," he said, "I learned a thing or two about character over the years. Derek was what we used to call a wolf. Not that I like to speak ill of the dead, mind you. Still . . ." He gestured to the coffin, suspended over its future resting place. "I think I'd rather have a wedding." He sat there for several moments longer, staring at the casket, then he turned to me. "I wouldn't worry about Jenny, though, dear. These things have a way of working themselves out."

The young woman who had driven him appeared over my shoulder.

"Audrey, have you met my new assistant, Shirley? I've gone all modern, so don't call her a secretary."

Shirley reached out and shook my hand with a firm grip. "That's because no secretary would put up with what I do."

The words were teasing and brought a smile to the old man's lips.

"She keeps me in line," he said with a twinkle.

"That's quite a job," I said.

"Chauffeur, dispensary, masseuse," she said.

"Masseuse?" I said.

"I studied physiotherapy. It's good for arthritis and all manner of illness. I dreamed of opening up a shop or some kind of in-home practice in Ramble. I met a few clients at the health club, but most of the older people around here seem to think . . ."

"That massage is a little steamy?" I offered.

"And that a masseuse is another name for a prostitute," she finished. "I've even had a few offers."

"But she's a good girl," Pastor Seymour said.

"Too good for you," she teased.

Friends and family started to arrive, so I slipped out to the CR-V and changed my shoes. The ground held just enough moisture that the heels sank into the earth unless I forced all my weight to my toes. I can't say the resulting walk was graceful.

Soon mourners filed into every available seat while the musicians played soothing classical pieces and old hymns, while clamping their music to the stands with clothespins against the wind. The overflow crowd, perhaps equal numbers familiar Ramblers and strangers, stood around the circumference of the rippling tent, providing a windbreak, I was sure, for everyone inside. Liv and I were among those stuck standing, having staked out a side position not far from the front, since the Rawlings had asked us to distribute single flowers to the mourners at the close of the service.

Larry mingled among the stragglers in the back. I'd never seen him in a suit before, only in jeans and overalls. His field-worn face and callused hands seemed awkward in a starched white shirt and tie. When he caught my eye, he smiled, then turned back to talk to Worthington, the Rawlings' butler.

Pastor Seymour delivered a wonderful sermon, somehow still managing to project his voice farther than he could walk unassisted. By wonderful, I mean coherent and short, my enthusiasm for his brevity encouraged by the pressure now increasing on my toes from my unnatural stance and the wind gusting at my back and plastering the skirt of my dress to the backs of my legs.

Brief eulogies from friends and family members followed. I listened intently as everyone from relatives to fraternity buddies gave brief statements. But it seemed unlikely that anyone would let a motive for murder slip at the funeral of the victim—and that was how it turned out. From the public comments, one might suspect Derek was up for canonization.

Miranda and Jonathan Rawling perched in the front row. They did not speak, but Jonathan wrapped an arm around his wife's shoulder and Miranda dabbed at her eyes daintily with a genuine lace handkerchief.

At the close of the service the musicians played while attendants lowered Derek's body to its final resting place.

"Friends," Lorne Jans said in his official sober tone, "the family has provided flowers for you to place on the casket as you say your final good-byes."

Liv and I took our positions on either side of the center aisle, where we'd placed large urns of assorted long-stemmed flowers. As mourners approached the coffin row by row, we handed a single flower to each person who came. Not to be irreverent, but with the number of flowers they'd requested, I was going to be surprised if there was any room left over for dirt.

Jonathan and Miranda were the first to approach, and we

halted the line while they stood over the cavern that now held their only child. Miranda, looking more frail than petite in her feminine black suit, swayed for a moment as she stood. Her husband's grip on her arm tightened.

I'd heard all kinds of stories, mainly from other florists, about funeral theatrics: fainting wives and mothers, sudden heart attacks, and even a story or two of grief-stricken wives or lovers—sometimes both—throwing themselves into caskets. Nothing like that happened here, not that I expected it to. Rather, Miranda whispered the beginning of a child's bedside prayer, then melted into her husband's arms.

I blinked back a tear and swallowed hard, forcing down the acid that rose in my throat.

After Jonathan steered Miranda to the side of the casket, where they could greet those who came up, Liv and I resumed the distribution of flowers to the remaining friends and family. The next man through bore a striking resemblance to Jonathan, so I assumed it must be his brother. Which got me thinking, since Derek was the Rawlings' only son, and presumably their heir, could someone have killed him to move up their position in line? It always worked out that way on *Perry Mason*.

As the rest of the mourners followed, Liv and I somehow assumed that cloak of invisibility worn by those carrying out a service. People in line chatted about everything from their grocery lists to their sex lives. Yeah, ick. But the main topic of hushed conversation was the murder. Several talked about Jenny as if she were already tried and convicted and sitting on death row, waiting for her last meal.

Still, I forced myself to eavesdrop, hoping maybe I could glean something that would lead to more suspects. I also wondered if the mystery woman—the woman who'd written the threatening letters—could be in attendance.

Carolyn, the mayor's daughter, had taken time out of her day-before-the-wedding plans to be here and stood in line with her parents. A pout formed on her lips as she pulled blowing hair from her face.

"But the manicurist appointment was for ten minutes ago." She inspected her already perfect nails. "Are you sure she'll wait?"

"She'll wait," Mayor Watkins said. "If she wants to keep the variance for her shop."

"And we still should have time to get our hair done before the rehearsal," his wife, Rita, added.

They seemed less than concerned about the dearly departed. I scanned the remaining group of mourners.

Near the back, his gaze roaming over the crowd, stood Bixby. I suspected he stayed in back to keep as much distance as possible from the allergens. I could tell that strategy wasn't working, especially with the swirling winds. He looked as red eyed as Miranda Rawling.

As I handed the last of my flowers, a daisy, to a young girl (who began plucking off the petals to a cadence of "he loves me, he loves me not"), I glanced at Liv, whose urn still held half its blooms. I drew her attention to my empty urn, then headed to the truck for more.

On the way back, my hands filled with more pollen-laden flowers, I stopped to talk to Bixby. Insensitive and probably a little petty of me, I know, but I guess I still bore a bit of a grudge.

"Chief." I casually shifted the flowers from one hand to the other, sending unseen allergens swirling into the air. At least, that was my willful and malicious attempt. "Anything new on the investigation?"

"Hello, Audrey." He took one step back and pulled a handkerchief from his pocket. "Nothing I'm able to divulge to the general public, I'm afraid."

"I see." I took one step toward him. "I just hoped that you'd found something that could clear Jenny."

"Ah, your friend." He ran his handkerchief under his nose. "I'm afraid not. There's just so much evidence—the knife, for example. The knife you gave her."

That did it. I stepped forward until I cornered him against one of the tent's support poles. I went to stick an accusing finger in his face, then realized that hand still held the flowers. Even better.

I hate to admit I stooped to something so petty, but in my defense, I was sleep deprived and more than a little cranky and a bit unbalanced—with my heels still sinking into the soft dirt. Besides, what could he do? Charge me with assault with a deadly delphinium?

"That's circumstantial," I said, "and you know it."

He recoiled in horror from the advancing flowers, plastering himself against the tent pole. "Who else had access to the knife, then, huh? You yourself said you gave it to her."

Why did I give her that knife? Because I was trying to help a friend in need, to give the kid a break. That was why I put the knife, the shears, and the tape in the bag. The bag?

"Wait," I said. "The *bags*. The bags have holes in them."

He looked at me as if I had broken out in a chorus of "The Wells Fargo Wagon" in Swahili. "What?"

"I put the knife, the shears, and the tape in a bag." I stepped back but waved the flowers to illustrate my point. Unconsciously, at this point. Honest.

"The last shipment of bags had holes in them. Liv's been up in arms about it for days now. Customers have been complaining because they're missing items. Think about it. The shears and the bag were in the apartment. The tape was in the car, on the floor. The knife could have fallen out anywhere. The sidewalk, the car. Suppose the knife *was* on the floor of the car—then anyone could have used it to kill

Derek. We need to take a look at that bag. I only hope Sarah hasn't thrown it out."

Bixby crossed his arms in front of him. "*We* don't have to check on anything. Look, I understand you want to help your friend, so I won't even ask how you know what we found on the floor of the car. I have my suspicions there. But I'll tell you this much: Jenny's were the only fingerprints found on the knife."

"So the killer wore latex gloves. You see it on TV all the time." Even as I said it, it didn't make sense. Picking up a knife from the sidewalk or the floor of the car to kill Derek would suggest the killer hadn't planned it that way. Bringing gloves suggested some premeditation. I couldn't have it both ways. My realization must have shown in my eyes.

"See what I mean?" he said. Although his question was punctuated not with a question mark but with a gigantic sneeze.

"I still think the bag should be evidence. I don't understand why you took half our tools but left behind something so crucial." As I swung the flowers around to illustrate my outrage, I realized I'd gone too far. Bixby closed his eyes. Several short breaths failed to bring under control the sneeze that was coming.

What happened next progressed like one of those slow-motion films they showed us in high school, the ones that demonstrate how far a sneeze can travel. I managed to get a step back, but this was a forceful, full-body sneeze. He tried to direct it safely to the ground—and, thankfully, he did. But as the sneeze erupted, his . . . uh . . . posterior portions connected with the tent post. For a second, it flexed, but then the pole disconnected at a joint, and the flap came down, slapping Bixby in the face.

He instinctively lifted his hands to protect his face, or

maybe he got tangled in the rippling flap and panicked. The only thing I know is that, soon after, the next pole let loose. I stood paralyzed as the whole structure listed, then a domino effect ensued. At first the tent remained airborne, supported by the lift created as the air rushed in underneath it. Then it gave a final shudder and deflated, leaving Liv, the string ensemble, the harpist, and a dozen or so mourners trapped underneath the billowing canvas.

As Liv crawled out, the tent rested like a veil on her hair, making her look much like the Virgin Mary in one of our childhood Christmas pageants. (Liv always landed the part of Mary. I, on the other hand, was always cast as Shepherd #2 or some such. Except for the year I had to play a goat.)

Liv rolled her eyes in a very unbeatific manner. Then she started giggling.

The violinist shimmied out of the tent next, but on his back, trying to catch a glimpse up my swirling skirt. My stare of death was met with a wink, as he rose to his feet and began helping others to theirs—mainly women, I noticed.

The crowd dispersed after that. Liv and I stayed around for another hour packing up our equipment. I tried to avoid the Rawlings and Bixby. And the violinist.

The remaining flower arrangements we'd worked for days to construct would be picked up by the local nursing home. The Rawlings apparently found donation an easier alternative to disposing of all this extreme foliage.

Then, with the family gone and only the rental company there trying to make sense of what had happened to their tent, I approached Derek's grave. I pulled a flower from one of the arrangements at random. I glanced at it. A blue rose. A blue rose can mean many things—*impossible* or *unattainable*, since it doesn't occur in nature and must be dyed.

Maybe finding Derek's killer would prove both impossible and unattainable.

But the blue rose also was the symbol of *mystery*. And mysteries were meant to be solved, weren't they?

"I can only do my best, Derek."

I tossed the blue rose on top of the heap of foliage that rested on Derek's coffin, took a deep breath, and walked away.

•

Chapter 12

❧

Amber Lee's laughter filled the shop.

Liv raised exasperated eyes to the spiderwebs on the ceiling. "It's not funny. This could be very bad for business. The whole funeral was ruined."

"First of all," Amber Lee said, "from what you told me, most of the guests were gone. Second of all, I'd think the tent rental company or the weather would get most of the blame."

"Or Bixby," I added, preparing yet another peach rose for the pew decorations. "He's the one who wrestled the tent down."

Liv gave me the look. "Because someone backed him into a corner. Really, kid, what were you thinking?"

"Backed him into a corner? Me?" I flashed her my most innocent look. "I never raised my voice. We had a civil conversation. At least he agreed to look for that bag."

"Civil conversation? Waving those flowers around. I'm surprised he didn't press charges." After a moment or two of silence, Liv's lips pressed together in an expression designed to stifle a giggle.

Growing up, sitting at the table over milk and cookies, we'd often get the affliction Grandma Mae called the giggles. I don't remember anything funny that started these sessions. But one of us would start laughing, and then the other, and then we couldn't control ourselves. Tears ran down our eyes, milk (and sometimes cookies) spurted from our noses, and we had trouble remaining upright in our chairs. The sessions generally ended in hiccups and deep breaths, with more than an occasional relapse.

So it wasn't unusual, when I saw her try to suppress a giggle, that a similar one rose in my throat. When my laughter bubbled over, Liv's chin quivered a brief moment before she caved, and the back room filled with laughter. It spread to our floral design interns, and even Opie cracked a broad smile.

When the bell over the door rang, tears were still running down my face. "I'll get it." I wiped the streaming tears with the back of my hand as I walked out, only to see Nick staring at the offerings in the self-service cooler.

"Hi." He flashed me a dazzling smile. That man missed his calling. He should be doing toothpaste commercials. I wondered how someone who spent his days working with sugar could keep his teeth so perfect.

He opened the cooler and pulled out a small bouquet of delicate dendrobium orchids. A symbol of *beauty*—letting the recipient know she's considered a belle, someone admired for her beauty and charm. The sight plummeted me back to earth. Nick obviously treasured a beautiful woman, and I, with my windblown hair and tears streaming down what was sure to be a rather red face, would never be more than a friend. I was someone to talk shop with, to share wedding plans with—for other people's weddings—and to help tote home drunken matrons.

I forced a smile as I cashed him out.

"These are pretty," he said. "More than pretty. Exotic. Unusual."

"Interesting." I'd long since noticed that what men see in flowers they often see in the women they're enamored with. So Nick went for the unusual and exotic type. *Unusual* was something I could accomplish pretty well. *Exotic* was another story. I pictured some slim, petite Asian woman with pouty red lips. She'd be wearing a sleek silk suit with impossibly high heels and carrying some purse-bound pooch.

I, on the other hand, was more of a homegrown girl: fresh faced, all denim, cotton, flat shoes, and corn bread and apple pie. Nick's sweetheart was probably somebody new to the community—maybe one of those DC types who'd moved into the area in recent years, looking for more affordable housing despite the two-hour rush-hour (an oxymoron, if I ever heard one) commute. Which could also explain why nobody could claim to have seen him with anybody. People who spend four hours a day in the car can spare little time or energy for socializing, especially if they're tossing doggie treats into their purses all day.

"Will you . . . uh . . . be at the wedding tomorrow?" he asked.

"Yes. I've known Carolyn for years now, and we're doing the flowers, too. It never hurts to invite your florist as a guest." I chuckled. My earlier mirth evaporated, however, melting away at the sight of those blasted orchids. I needed to get over this silly infatuation. "It helps in case of any last-minute wilting issues, too."

He laughed as I handed him his change. "Maybe I'll see you there, then. We're doing their cupcakes. And I'll be there to handle any last-minute frosting debacles. Speaking of which, I'd better get back to work myself and let you get to yours."

I waved lamely at Nick as he left, wondering if he'd bring a plus-one to the wedding and we'd finally get a gander at this exotic mystery woman.

With a small sigh I returned to the back room and the mound of wedding work that yet awaited us. I demonstrated how to compose the pew arrangements to the interns, then turned the task over to them before diverting my attention to an arrangement meant to surround the unity candle.

For some reason, the phrase "Always the bridal florist, but never the bride" popped into my mind, and I couldn't shake it. Maybe it was the long hours and little sleep, my aching feet and back, or just coming to earth over my ill-fated crush on Nick, but I could sense a major pity party coming on.

And a pity party without mentally rehashing that whole fiasco with Brad the Cad would be as complete as a Cinco de Mayo party without salsa.

Brad and I had been dating for about a year. Call it a premonition, but I'd tried to cancel our dinner date that night. It was just before Mother's Day, and long hours had left me dead on my feet. But he begged and pleaded, so I knew something was up.

I was standing right at the same workstation, in fact, when I promised him I'd be there. He sounded excited on the phone as he told me to meet him at seven thirty at the restaurant at the Ashbury Inn. Liv and I spent a giddy afternoon speculating. She decided that his excitement on the phone, his insistence that I be there, and his choice of the romantic, expensive venue could only add up to a proposal. And I spent the rest of the afternoon making flower arrangements for other people while planning my own wedding flowers.

That was when I made plans for that now loathsome bouquet—the one scattered over Derek's dead body. I then went on to plan the church decorations, and before quitting time, I'd put finishing touches on my mental plans for the centerpieces for the reception. I ran home, dressed up, treated my face to the rarity of the full makeup routine the stylist suggested that time Liv and I had closed up shop and headed to a pricey salon for a day of pampering. I even pulled the tags off and ironed my new dress and wrestled my feet into heels.

Brad, on the other hand, wore a sports shirt and khakis and had neglected to remove his five o'clock shadow. But I refused to let that dampen the moment. After all, a twinkle of excitement danced in his eyes as I answered his knock at my door. I guess I was so focused on that, I also took no notice that he didn't comment on my appearance.

We ordered and ate our dinner as usual, except for a bit of silence in our ordinarily easy conversation. But I attributed that to nervousness over the upcoming proposal. His frequent wiping of his palms on his napkin confirmed the diagnosis. And mine were getting a little damp as well. Either it was nerves or we were both coming down with the plague.

I spent the silent moments working out more wedding details. If we held the ceremony in the gardens of the Ashbury, I might even arrive in a horse-drawn carriage festooned with roses and ivy. My brother, Philip, could walk me down the aisle, I supposed, as long as Mother didn't mind if I didn't ask her new husband. I'd only met the man a handful of times. Surely she wouldn't expect—

"Audrey, I suppose you're wondering why I asked you here. I mean, besides dinner."

I shrugged and sent him a shy smile.

"It's just that, I think the time has come in our relationship . . ." He started picking at a dry cuticle, a nasty habit I hoped to break him of one day. "Well, I don't know how to say it except to say it."

Here it comes, I thought. I wondered if he would drop to

one knee in the restaurant. And then I'd say yes, and everybody would clap. Maybe they would bring a complimentary dessert. Yeah, my priorities were probably off for thinking that, but then again, I'd tasted the dessert at the Ashbury before. Their cheesecake is to die for.

"Audrey . . ." He didn't kneel but cleared his throat. "I'm moving."

All the blood rushed to my face and my head started to buzz.

"Did you hear what I said?" he asked.

"Moving?"

"Yes. It's what I've been hoping for. A job with the production crew for a new TV show. A real break into the business." He stared out the window. "No more videotaping weddings and transferring dreadful home movies that no one ever wanted to watch in the first place to DVDs that will just gather dust on a shelf."

It might not be that bad to move, I thought. A local TV show filmed in Richmond or even Virginia Beach wouldn't be too terrible. If we moved to Virginia Beach, I still had friends there. I know I said I never wanted to leave Ramble, but maybe we could find a place on the outskirts of town . . . I stopped myself short. Caught up in what he'd said, I'd missed what he hadn't. He hadn't asked me to marry him.

"Where is the job?" I took a sip of my water with shaky hands, then put my nervous energy to work shredding my napkin in my lap. And no, the Ashbury doesn't use paper napkins.

"Manhattan."

"As in New York City? That Manhattan?"

"None other." He gave me one of those quirky grins of his, his head held high and the pride ringing in his voice. He considered this move making the big time.

"That's crazy," I said, popping his balloon. He seemed to shrink into his chair. "There's all kinds of wackos in New

York. Pedophiles and mass murderers and rapists and riff-raff urinating on subways and mugging joggers in the park."

He rolled the salt shaker between his hands and wagged his head. "I've made up my mind, Audrey. I've given notice and sent in my intention letter. One of the guys in the crew had a room to rent, so that's all settled. I start in two weeks."

So everybody and his brother knew about this before me. Without even telling me he'd applied, his plans were all made. It seemed like he had all the details settled but one.

"What about us?" Yes, I'll admit, it was a direct question.

He reached over and laid his hand on mine. "Audrey, you know how I feel about you."

"Enlighten me."

He let out a lungful of air from pursed lips. "I think this is a new beginning for both of us."

"A beginning of what?"

"Audrey, I can't take you to New York, and it wouldn't be fair to ask you to wait for me. Maybe this is a test. Maybe in a few years I can come back to Ramble and be content. But I think it's time to explore what's out there, expand our horizons."

"You mean date other people."

He leaned back in his chair. "Don't you think that's best?"

I studied his face. His expression was somber, but something around the corners of his eyes gave him away. "You *want* to break up."

He held up a hand. "I didn't say that."

"You don't have to. It's written all over your face."

"Audrey, it's about the job."

I shook my head. "No, it's about all the glamorous women you think you'll find in New York City. A bigger pond and more fish to choose from. Well, let me tell you, it's not all *Sex in the City*. Not everyone is a size-two fashion model and they're not going to line up to date some small-town videographer. A big city can also be a lonely place."

"Audrey, keep it down, will you?"

And then it dawned on me why he was dropping this bit of news on me at the Ashbury. So I wouldn't make a scene. Little did he know.

I stood up and pointed my finger in his face. "Well, you listen, Mr. Big-City Show-Biz Tycoon. Go to New York. Expand those horizons of yours. And when you get your fill of the skyscrapers and subways and hookers on every street corner and all that other Yankee foolishness and come back here with your tail between your legs, do me a favor."

Brad winced. "What's that?"

I leaned over the table, until nose to nose with him.

But I had nothing more to say. I yanked my purse over my shoulder and walked out to the applause of our fellow diners.

Kathleen Randolph left the check-in desk, ran out after me, and drove me home.

"You know what I think?" she'd said as she turned onto Ramble's Main Street. "I swear the reason men stink at relationships is because of battle genes. When men go to war, the ones who survive are either very good at fighting or very good at running."

"Brad's never been in the service."

"No, but I bet his father or grandfather has. Think about it. Johnny comes marching home again, gets married, and has little Johnnies. Sometimes I think the ability to sit down and work things out has been totally bred out of the male sex. Especially in Ramble, Audrey. After all, this town was settled by Josiah Carroll."

"The Revolutionary War hero, I know. He was a spy. Brad's a descendant on his father's side."

"Hero and spy, my foot. The only reason Carroll was able to warn the troops about the British presence was because he was running away from them at the time. Take it from me, Audrey. I've been married three times. And all men seem to want to do is fight or run."

I'd thanked her, and as I leaned against my apartment door, I thought for a moment about her theory. Perhaps Brad was bred to fight or run. Or maybe he was just being a jerk. Like my dad.

Either way, I hadn't talked to Brad since.

How I could have been so foolish as to misinterpret a breakup date for a proposal, I'm not sure. Liv suggested that maybe we believed what we wanted to. But the more I thought about it, the more I wondered if I'd wanted to marry Brad after all. Was he the love of my life? Or were we two people thrown together into a comfortable relationship because we were both single in a small town?

Chapter 13

I woke up Saturday morning, the day of Carolyn's wedding, scrunched down under the covers while Chester lounged on my pillows, licking my hair. It's not that I didn't appreciate his efforts, but I had other plans for grooming that morning.

I opened him a can of something that claimed to be pot roast in gravy. I had to admit, the gravy smelled a little like real pot roast, even if the little square nuggets floating in it resembled . . . I don't know. I tried to remember the last time I had the leisure to put a roast in the Crock-Pot before heading in to work. Maybe with some potatoes and baby carrots . . .

And then I cursed the floral business. Not really cursed. Grandma Mae would have had a fit. But I used more than a few of our approved "green" words as I pulled out the sole pair of clean underwear left in my drawer—complete with the smiling face of one Pippa the Penguin (a gag gift from Jenny a few Christmases ago). Not that anyone would see them.

Grandma Mae's admonition to always wear clean under-wear in case you're ever in an accident rolled through my mind. I'd have to make sure I drove especially carefully today. While these were clean, I'd rather keep Pippa under wraps. Still, I had just enough nursing experience to know that in a serious accident, they'd cut them off without a glance. And even if they did get a chuckle out of them, I'd be too ill to care much anyway.

I woke myself up in the shower, belting out the corny theme song from the cartoon supposedly designed to get kids more interested in physical fitness.

> *Pippa the Penguin*
> *Gliding through the sea,*
> *Cruising on an iceberg,*
> *Learning how to ski*
> *With Whoopie the Walrus,*
> *Having flippertastic fun.*
> *Don't glum there*
> *In your comfy chair—*
> *Come on, kids! Let's run!*

Somewhere along the line, my neighbor Tom added per-cussion to my vocals by pounding on the bathroom wall. As if I complain—or even tell anybody—when he belts out the latest Justin Bieber tune.

But even that gleeful melody couldn't shake off the mel-ancholy. I grumbled more as I yanked on my scrubby work clothes on a day when most of the rest of the world slept in, lolled over their Saturday papers, or consumed humongous bowls of sugar-coated cereal while watching the fitness escapades of Pippa and Whoopie.

One look in the mirror and I knew no amount of con-cealer would cover the dark circles forming under my eyes. Flippertastic. Of course, when you set your alarm clock for two hours after you went to bed, and start doing that on a regular basis, those circles are bound to happen. So I packed my makeup in a bag with my dress shoes, grabbed one of my Liv-approved wedding-attendance dresses out of the closet, and booked it to the shop.

I hoped that the flower fairies—maybe the ones from all those Victorian children's books—had come in during the night and finished our work. But no, they're a fickle bunch, those flower fairies, and just as lazy as the laundry fairies and the housework fairies.

The empty shop was as we left it the night before—cut stems rising to flood level on the floor, our arrangements stacked in the coolers. The completed arrangements looked good, though. Our interns had gotten the hang of it quickly. The unfinished arrangements made me worry.

I microwaved some instant coffee. Someone besides the wedding coordinator would have to put a full pot on. It would be safer for them anyway. Sniffing the instant brought back a modicum of consciousness along with a long-buried memory.

As a child, Liv was a late sleeper, but Grandma Mae and I were early risers. I remembered sitting in her darkened kitchen, waiting for the teakettle to boil.

Grandma Mae never drank hot tea. In accordance with her Southern roots, tea was iced tea. But she would put the old copper teakettle on the electric stove, then rescue it just as it was beginning to whistle. She'd make us both a cup of instant coffee and we'd sit in the dark, half-awake, waiting for the brew to bring on whispered conversation. To accommodate my child's palate, mine was weak, half milk, and with enough sugar to make a dentist go into cardiac shock. I prefer it the same way to this day. I'm still not sure I even like the taste of coffee.

But I found a moment of peace in the recollections of that hushed kitchen, a feeling of being loved and cared for. Of being encouraged. "You can do anything you've a mind to," she told me on more than one occasion. "And don't slouch," on even more. So I forced a smile to my face, threw my shoulders back, and held my head high, just as Amber Lee stumbled in the door.

"My, don't you look chipper," she said. "It's not natural."

I chuckled and took my first trip to the cooler for peach roses.

Liv arrived a half hour later, again uncharacteristically late. Her dark circles drooped lower than mine, if that were possible, and seemed twice as deep. Which was probably why Eric had accompanied her to the shop. If she looked any worse, he'd be pushing her in a wheelchair or rolling her on a gurney. But I knew Liv would be there regardless.

"This is ridiculous, you know that," he said. "Y'all have to sleep at some point, or you're going to collapse."

"Can't collapse." Liv kissed Eric on his scruffy cheek. "It's too much work to get up. Besides, you know what it's like to run your own business, the hours you put in to make it thrive."

Eric couldn't say much to that. While he'd been building his construction business, Liv poured her life into the shop. I wondered how they had found enough time to meet, court, and marry between all the business obligations. I barely had time to get a haircut, which was why my hair spent so much time in a ponytail.

Liv assigned Eric to floor duty, while the rest of us got to work. Dressed in his typical plaid shirt, jeans, and work boots, he looked more ready to toenail in a stud somewhere, whatever that means.

Eric isn't a tall man—only five seven. Five eight if you count the heels on his work boots. But he was the perfect complement to Liv. He sported a perpetual stubble, which he'd shaved off just once since I'd known him, for his wedding day. Unfortunately, he resembled an overgrown ring bearer in his pictures. So the stubble remains, by their mutual consent, to hide his boyish looks. And their wedding pictures are kept under lock and key.

On the job site, I've seen him wearing a constant frown while barking orders. But when Liv appears, that melts away, his green eyes twinkle, and a smile appears under that jungle of stubble. Perfect teddy bear.

At nine o'clock, our team of interns arrived, looking refreshed and rejuvenated in the way only youth can. Melanie and Opie chatted like old friends as Opie showed off a new tattoo. It was nice to see her smile more. I wondered how much of the goth exterior was a lifestyle choice and how much of it was to protect herself against a society that she thought didn't care. A little caring and those walls came tumbling down.

Once we'd finished the large altar arrangement, the boys loaded everything into the van and Eric's truck. Leaving the shop in the capable hands of Amber Lee, the rest of us drove to the church. Liv and Eric helped unload the extensive church flowers—well, Eric unloaded under Liv's supervision. Every time she tried to move a muscle, he jumped in and took over. When he wasn't looking, Liv rearranged everything.

After all the church flowers were packed inside, Liv and I split up the interns in a method similar to choosing dodgeball teams back in elementary school. She and her team scurried off to the Ashbury to decorate for the reception, while my team and I started work on the church.

The First Baptist Church of Ramble was the only church in Ramble proper. Not counting the nondenominational New Hope Zion Prophetic Episcopal Missionary Pentecostal Alliance of Prayer, which met in a storefront next to the dry cleaner's. I suspect the real name was longer, but they ran out of room when they hand-painted the sign on the windows.

But inside the historic First Baptist, a high, arched ceiling was reinforced by long wood beams jutting from side to side, beams that Carolyn wanted strung with swags of ivy and roses. Candle arrangements were to adorn the sills of the stained glass windows. And, of course, there were copious flowers for the altar and pews.

The mayor had blanched as he'd written a substantial check for the flowers. Then the family had learned that our service included only dropping off the flowers. Suddenly the mayor's wife declared there just wouldn't be time to put them into place and asked if we could decorate for them. Which we agreed to do . . . for a price. But that was before we knew the wedding would be the day after a major funeral.

I was grateful to have the football players to climb the ladders and hang the swags. I only hoped Carolyn and her mother had made arrangements with someone else to take them down, since that was not included in our commission. And although the overhead floral swags might survive one Sunday, after that they'd begin to wither and rot. And I doubted Pastor Seymour would appreciate that.

I had just started placing the windowsill arrangements in the stained glass windows when Carolyn's mother, Rita, stormed in.

Rita Watkins has a habit of storming in, whether it be a light drizzle just to dampen everybody else's enthusiasm or a full gale with flashes of anger and rolling rumbles of sarcasm. But the worst storm, the one the social meteorologists feared the most, was the sudden calm of an icy gaze. No one knew for sure what lay behind that front, but all agreed it couldn't be good.

And as she rounded the corner and took in our work, still

in its early stages, it was the icy gaze that fell on her face. I
think the temperature in the old church sank by at least ten
degrees.

She approached me, a pained smile forcing its way to the
corners of her thin lips. "Audrey"—she tilted her head to
look up at the empty beams—"I'd think the church would
be done by now."

So would I. "We're making good progress. We were a bit
delayed with all the funeral arrangements, but we—"

"So I gathered." She swept her finger along the outline
of a perfect peach rose, yet scrunched up her nose. "Audrey,
my dear, part of running a business is keeping those con-
tracts and establishing a realistic schedule for getting things
done."

I forced a similar smile to my face. I suspect with the
lack of sleep it must have been pretty scary, because she
stopped talking.

"Mrs. Watkins," I began, my words coming out flavored
like a nauseating treacle, perhaps an impersonation of hers,
"I assure you that your flowers will be done in plenty of time
before the wedding. Yes, I admit, we're a tad behind schedule." The understatement of the year. I'd planned to finish
the church the day before. "But we've brought on extra help
to compensate, and they're doing a marvelous job. You have
nothing to worry about."

Rita stood frozen to the ground, either trying to evaluate
the sincerity of my assurances or trying to come up with
another complaint. "I suppose you have been busy with the
funeral. I can't fault you that. Just an unfortunate coinci-
dence that the poor boy died so close to the wedding. And
this is a large job."

For a moment I wondered how they would have managed
if Rita had gone ahead with her initial plan to order online
flowers and arrange them herself. I doubted the FedEx man
would have stayed around to help her decorate.

But then my mind went back to Amber Lee's statement about Derek's long string of girlfriends, including the mayor's daughter.

"Did you know Derek well?" I ventured.

"Oh, you know how it is with small towns," she said. "You get to know everybody."

"I'd heard that he and Carolyn were once close."

"Oh, that." She waved the question off as one would wave off a fly at the church supper. "She might have gone out with him a few times, but I told her I didn't see that turning into something."

"Just didn't get along, did they?"

"Well, I hate to speak ill of the dead, but Derek . . ."

I cocked my head and raised an eyebrow.

"I told Carolyn I thought Derek was cheating on her."

"Oh," I said, hoping she'd elaborate. Of course, her allegation that Derek had cheated betrayed the lie that his and Carolyn's relationship consisted of only a few dates. They must have been seeing each other exclusively. At least on Carolyn's part.

Rita leaned in closer and lowered her voice. "Red hair."

"Excuse me?"

"That's how we found out about the other woman. Flaming orange-red hair. He must have seen her the same day he saw my daughter, because I spotted several strands on his suit coat. And Carolyn found more of it in his car."

"Oh, my." I tried to think if I knew any redheads in Ramble.

"Derek denied it, of course. But I think he was seeing her the whole time he pretended to be interested in Carolyn. And . . ." She trailed off and bit her bottom lip.

Come on, Rita, don't shut down on me now. "And?"

"And I'd hate to say more, especially since he just passed on."

She was killing me.

"Rita, I can see something is bothering you, and nobody is going to blame you for saying something now—just one friend to another. This is a special day for you. Don't walk into it burdened with someone else's baggage." It was meaningless psychobabble, gathered from more than one college afternoon watching daytime television between classes—oh, the value of a college education.

I could see her beginning to cave, so I launched another volley. "Nothing you say can hurt Derek now—or his memory in the minds of those who loved him. And you'll feel better when you get it off your shoulders."

Rita's eyes lit up. "Just between you and me, I don't think he stopped seeing the redhead, even after he proposed to Jenny."

"Why do you think that?"

"I have insomnia at times, you see. And last week the weather was so mild at night that I took a walk. It must have been three in the morning when Derek's sports car sped past on Main Street. And in the streetlights I could just make out a woman in the passenger seat."

"Not Jenny?"

"I couldn't see the face well, but whoever it was had flaming red, curly hair."

A longtime clandestine relationship with a mystery woman . . . I wondered if the elusive redhead might be the author of those lurid letters, the ones that turned threatening. I'd keep my eyes open for redheads.

"You're right, Audrey." Rita's smile widened. "I do feel better after unburdening myself." She pulled me into a half-thawed hug.

At that moment cruel fate, combined with the unconquerable force of gravity, deigned that one single peach rose fall from the swags above. And where else would it land? Yes, smack-dab on Rita's shoulder.

In close procession, two more plopped down in other parts of the church, flowers raining from above.

In slow motion, Rita picked up the rose from her shoulder, crushed it in a tight fist, then handed it to me. "Fix it," she said, with a refrozen smile, then turned and walked away.

"Yes, ma'am." There was no other response.

Chapter 14

❧

My promise to complete the church decorations on time was sorely challenged by the falling roses. In the end, the boys took down all the swags so I could check that the roses were secured. But I stood back to survey the completely decorated sanctuary—the veritable garden I'd promised Carolyn—just as the organist and bell ringer arrived.

First Baptist of Ramble, on special occasions, still rang its steeple bell the old-fashioned way, using the same historic cast-iron bell that some said hearkened back to colonial days. Others claimed it was added in the early 1800s. But a few tourists still came through every now and then begging to see the old bell, despite the cobwebs that invariably filled the narrow staircase that led to it.

As the interns carried the empty boxes and supplies out to the truck and put the ladder back in the church's maintenance closet, I darted into the ladies' room to slip into my dress and try to look more like a wedding guest and less like a sweaty contractor.

I dabbed on a little extra antiperspirant, slipped into a soft scoop-necked floral dress, accented it with a sage green chunky necklace, and stepped into heels. I wish I could say the tired face disappeared under the application of makeup. I did my best, anyhow.

When I exited the ladies' room, the sound of feminine voices echoed from a nearby Sunday school classroom. I recognized Carolyn and Rita among them, even if I couldn't make out the words. These were not happy voices. I hoped all the peach roses hadn't fallen from the swags while I changed. I suspected I'd better check in and make sure everything was okay from the floral perspective. Maybe I'd get lucky and find out that an usher had rented the wrong size tux or that no one could find the groom.

One of the bridesmaids, dressed in a polka-dotted tea-length peach dress, opened the top of the Dutch door at my knock.

"There, there, peaches," Mayor Watkins crooned. Looking dapper in a tux and already sporting his peach boutonniere, he placed a comforting hand on his daughter's shoulder. His nickname explained Carolyn's flower choice. While she'd insisted on peach roses, she hadn't given a reason why. Touching, that she would choose a flower based on her father's pet name for her. Then again, he was paying for the wedding.

"It's just a little snag," he said. "Everything is going to work out all right. No one will even notice."

Even as he reassured her, Carolyn's lower lip jutted out and quavered. She looked like a pouting child in her pure white re-creation of a 1950s tea-length dress in satin with a lace overlay. Not that I knew much about wedding fashions, but that was how her mother described it when they placed the orders for her flowers. The fifties theme was a new one for me, but they explained they wanted modern flowers—that the arrangements they'd seen in the old wedding books and magazines they'd picked up from the library used book sale were dreary. I suspected the yellowing pages and the old-style photography made them appear that way, but I gave in to their wishes anyway.

The photographer snapped a picture of her, but Rita waved him off. I recognized him as the photographer for the *On*. I'd encountered him doubling as a wedding photographer on more than one occasion.

"Don't cry." Rita took Carolyn by the shoulders. "You'll ruin your makeup for the pictures. If you do anything, scream. But smile while you're doing it, lamb chop." If that was her mother's nickname for her, I wondered what we'd be eating at the reception.

"Dress, shoes, and gloves," Carolyn almost spat out, her face twisted into a maniacal grin. "Was that too much to ask?"

I let out a sigh of relief. This was not a flower issue. The bridesmaids, however, scurried to the far corners of the room, like cockroaches when you turn the light on in a fleabag motel—not that I'd been in too many fleabag motels.

"Oh, Audrey, there you are." Rita rushed over and took my hands. "I'm so sorry I doubted you. The church looks lovely, and so do the bouquets."

"At least something's gone right," Carolyn muttered. "First we're missing a whole bridesmaid, and now this."

"Don't worry about it." Rita turned back to Carolyn. "There's nothing you can do at this point except have all the bridesmaids take them off. You can't have some with and some without."

I hazarded a quick glance at the cowering bridesmaids. Most of the girls were Carolyn's friends from the health club set, so I imagined the missing bridesmaid was Jenny. I wondered what it was that each would have to "take off" and was relieved to see they were all sporting their dresses and dyed-to-match shoes. So at least the group wouldn't be standing up in their slips or bare feet, a thought which made me smile.

"And there's still no answer at the bridal shop?" Carolyn said. "I'm sure Jenny never got around to picking hers up. They have to be there. The shop should have an emergency number."

Mayor Watkins shook his head. "Even if I did get through to them, there just isn't time to get them here. The girls will just have to go without."

Carolyn rolled her eyes. "They'd look so much better with the gloves. I can still wear mine, though. Right?" It was more of a demand than a question.

"Of course, peaches," her father said. "You're the bride. You can do anything you want."

Step one in the manual entitled *How to Create a Bridezilla*: Make her the center of the universe and demand that everyone succumb to her wishes. At least it looked like she'd managed to get her manicure just in time to stuff her hands into gloves. Thankfully, our part in this affair was completed and deemed acceptable.

"Congratulations again," I said. "And Carolyn, you look gorgeous."

"Thanks." Carolyn picked up her bouquet for a picture.

"Oh, and, Audrey, I hope everything is okay at the reception, too," Rita added as I was almost out the door.

"Yes, just lovely," I said with a wave. Guessing. More of an educated guess since I knew Liv wouldn't leave there until it met with her stamp of approval. Then again, I hadn't seen her yet.

A teenage usher with a face full of acne and the barest hint of fuzzy stubble—which he seemed to wear more proudly than he did his rented tuxedo—escorted me to a seat at the end of a pew. In the front corner of the church, the same chamber group who'd performed at the funeral, including that vile violinist, played similar classical and religious pieces. If he held a grudge, it didn't show. He winked at me as he caught my gaze.

The church was approaching capacity when Liv arrived on Eric's arm. She gave me the thumbs-up sign as an usher directed them to a nearly full row.

"Excuse me, miss?" The teenage usher was back. "Could you please slide over? We're full up, and I think we can fit one more person in this row."

I did the required sliding, squeezing next to a matronly woman I didn't recognize (out of town family maybe?) wearing way too much perfume. The space between me and the end of the pew would be perfect for one person, provided that person was three years old, an elf, or an anorexic supermodel. Preferably a three-year-old anorexic elf.

The usher returned a moment later and directed Nick Maxwell into the space next to me.

"Hi." He eased into the allotted space, clearly not enough. His legs contacted mine, as did his hips and torso. It left no room at all, however, for his arms and shoulders, so he hoisted one arm over the end of the pew, then awkwardly draped the other on the pew back behind me. "Sorry. Tight squeeze."

I nodded, wondering if I should be feeling one of those "electric shocks" the romance novelists are always writing about, or some stirring deep within or whatever the current jargon is. Instead, I felt a little like a sardine traveling in steerage. In the boiler room. This scenario could only have been more awkward had Nick brought a plus-one. She'd be sitting in his lap.

The matronly woman slid over, giving us all another two inches. Now I could sit comfortably without touching—as long as I didn't try any excessive movements, like breathing.

"Funny," Nick said, "we were just talking about you."

"We?" I asked. My ability to hold a coherent conversation evaporated.

"Your cousin, I guess. Liv. I ran into her over at the Ashbury when I dropped off the cupcakes. It's amazing. I would have never picked you two for cousins."

"I'll admit, there's not much of a physical resemblance." I turned to glance at Liv. She mouthed, "Nice," and gave me another thumbs-up.

"What was that?" Nick asked.

"What?"

"What Liv said to you?"

"Oh, that . . ." I felt my face color. "She just . . . said the reception flowers are nice."

"They sure are, and I must say, the church is fantastic." He craned his neck to get a good view of the overhead swags, and his extended arm slid forward to rest along my back.

Do I lean forward to break contact? And spend the entire ceremony in an unnaturally erect posture? Or do I remain in place and pretend that the feeling of his hand on my back isn't having an effect? It didn't measure up to the hype of an electrical shock—and maybe that was a good thing. I'd suffered a bad shock from a frayed toaster cord before and it wasn't a pleasant experience. I decided to go for nonchalance.

He chatted on, asking occasional polite questions about the flowers. He did seem to possess a superior knowledge of wedding planning, perhaps as a result of his research through the bridal magazines. Before long, my brain kicked in again, and our conversation from the time the wedding was supposed to begin until twenty minutes later—when it did begin—flowed cheerfully and naturally.

The procession must have lasted ten minutes. Eight bridesmaids, all dressed in the same polka-dotted peach dresses with matching shoes and fascinators—although sans the gloves—carried their bouquets of peach and white roses, daisies, and ivy. Very 1950s, although I agreed with Carolyn: I was missing the gloves.

A ring bearer, who must have been about two, sprinted down the aisle and tossed his pillow onto the platform before running to his mother. Then a flower girl walked down the aisle with her basket of peach and white rose petals. I knew Carolyn wanted the child to scatter them on the aisle runner, but instead she clung possessively to the basket and gave defiant looks to the audience as she toddled her way to the front— daring them to take her precious petals away from her.

We all rose as Carolyn walked down the aisle, looking radiant on the arm of her father. Her groom stood innocuously at the front of the church, looking pale and wavering from foot to foot. I sure hoped he wouldn't go down. Not only for Carolyn's sake, but it would only mean more time packed into the increasingly warm church as they attempted to revive him.

He seemed to rally as Carolyn approached, and even managed a smile.

"Dearly beloved . . . ," Pastor Seymour began, and thus commenced the traditional vows I'd heard countless times in the little church. If they'd asked for anything different, they didn't get it. But with an octogenarian pastor, it's better not to ask. He could officiate a traditional wedding in his sleep—I think I even saw him do it once. But throw him a curve, as Ellen Whitney had tried to do, and you just never knew what you'd get.

Of course, thinking of Ellen made me think of Jenny. They all traveled in the same group—the "health club set" was what I'd nicknamed them. All that exercise and juicing. The closest I got to juicing was an occasional chocolate-covered strawberry Blizzard at the Dairy Queen.

While the woman next to me started fanning herself, sending more of her cloying perfume in my direction, I found myself staring at the bridesmaids. A quick count showed eight bridesmaids and nine groomsmen, but I doubt anyone would have noticed a missing bridesmaid if they hadn't been looking. Shirley, Pastor Seymour's girl Friday, stood about midway down the row. I hadn't placed her as one of Carolyn's clique, but I did recall her saying something about finding massage clients at the club. She was whispering something to a blonde who looked familiar.

And then I recognized the blonde. Sarah Anderson, of course, Jenny's roommate. With her hair down and her face made up—and her body not covered in spandex and sweat—I hadn't placed her. She cleaned up nicely.

Two bridesmaids had red hair, Shirley and another girl, but she was a pudgy little thing, bless her heart, with eyebrows that almost touched in the middle of her forehead. I couldn't imagine her or Pastor Seymour's assistant as Derek's secret inamorata.

When the new couple kissed and were introduced to us as husband and wife, we all rose and clapped, while the groomsmen erupted into old-fashioned hoots. After they all filed down the aisle, Nick turned to me. "I suppose I should head over to the reception to make sure the cupcake tower is still standing. Need a ride?"

"No, we need to take some of the flowers over in the truck. Some of them do double duty."

"See you over there, then."

I waved impotently as he darted out the back door. Liv squeezed her way through the crowd and made her way over to me.

"I see we've made some progress on the confectionary front." She took my arm as we inched toward the foyer.

"Nonsense, Liv. Don't read anything into it. He didn't choose this seat, after all."

"Maybe not, but you weren't at the reception hall this morning."

I crossed my arms. "Where you steered the conversation in my direction."

"No steering necessary. He coasted right into it. Hard to talk to him about anything *but* you."

"To quote Grandma Mae, 'pshaw.' " I held the door open and we exited to the porch. Even though the temperature soared outside, it felt much more comfortable than the over-packed, stuffy church.

An usher handed each of us a little tulle bag of grass seed encased in peach-tinted fluff.

"I'm telling you," she insisted in a whisper, "he's interested."

"Interested in collaborating. In having a business relationship." I found a spot in the shade of a cherry tree where we could launch our grass seed without getting doused with it ourselves. Eric squeezed through to join us.

"No, he didn't have the business look in his eyes," Liv insisted. "Eric, you were there. You saw it, too. Tell her."

Eric exhaled. "Liv, don't go doing this."

"What?"

"This infernal matchmaking." He eased the tie about his neck. "It never works, and someone is bound to get hurt every time. Why don't you let it go? If it's meant to be, it will take a natural course. Like you and me."

Liv and I burst into hysterics that drew the attention of those around us. And Eric only knew the tip of the iceberg. Liv had been matching up couples, with uncanny success, since her first junior high dance. Of course, I'd since forgiven her for pushing Brad in my direction.

"What?" he said.

"If you only knew." I wagged my head. "Natural course. Sure."

Shouts erupted closer to the church, and Carolyn and her groom darted out. After the new couple traveled about three feet, Carolyn got a faceful of grass seed, grimaced, and then scurried back inside.

"Daddy!" was all that we heard, and then hushed whispers, as the bride and her parents huddled just inside the open doors of the church.

The groom stood red faced, planted momentarily as he looked at the sea of faces, and then he backtracked into the church. He never seemed to manage to gain access to the huddle. Instead, he loped awkwardly to the side.

"Hi, Audrey." Little Joe had sneaked up on me. His polyester black suit, the same that he wore for all his work at the funeral home—or maybe he owned more than one of them—shone in the sunlight.

"Hey, Little Joe. Nice wedding."

"Yes, you did a fantastic job on the flowers. Real pretty."

"Thanks."

"Going to the reception?"

"I'll be there."

"Good." He smiled and pulled out his invitation—printed like an old 45 record with the names of the bride and groom as the song title. "I'll be there, too. Save me a dance, huh? I've been studying up some new moves online."

I'd live to regret what came out of my mouth next, but he was so hopeful and sweet, and I was so sleep deprived. "Sure, Little Joe. I'd be happy to dance with you." What would be a few minutes wandering around the dance floor while he tried to remember something he read on the Internet, compared to breaking the man's heart? I was a little leery of his new moves, but if Little Joe could learn it online, I was certain I could fake it for a few minutes.

Finally the huddle inside the church dispersed, and Mayor Watkins stepped outside.

"Ladies and gentlemen," he said, "we thank you all for coming today. And we appreciate you sticking around to send the couple off. However, the grass seed you've been given is much harder than the samples we were provided, and we'd ask that you not throw it at the bride and groom, to avoid injury. Please feel free to take it with you and fill in any bare patches in your lawn, as I was assured it is very fine grass seed.

"Thank you very much for your cooperation, and we'll see you over at the reception in"—he glanced at his watch—"a little over two hours."

The couple then sprinted to their car, a huge boat of a red convertible with loads of chrome and fins on the back end—a fully restored 1957 Pontiac Star Chief, Eric reported with awe—to a round of weak applause.

Eric shook his head as he stuck his grass seed back into his pocket. "I don't know, Audrey. You got your work cut out for you."

"Most of the work is done. All we have to do is run a few flowers over . . ."

"No, I meant keeping your perfect record. That boy needs to get some gumption, or this marriage might not last much past the reception."

I was holding out for a cupcake.

Otherwise I would have been home in my bed, sound asleep, and would have missed the forty-five minutes of speeches and congratulatory toasts, plus the thirty seconds of the choreographed dance extravaganza that the bridal party had worked on for "simply months"—the mashed potato, the emcee called it—and that might have been better if they'd performed it before all those toasts. Aptly named because the bridal party was, at that stage, toasted.

The venue was spectacular—or a spectacle, depending on personal preference. I saw Kathleen Randolph, the owner and manager, peeking her head in a few times with a strained expression on her face. Whether she was not fond of weddings or if she thought the historic inn should only be decorated in the period-appropriate fashion, I couldn't tell.

But for this reception, the inn looked more like it might be haunted by Arthur Fonzarelli than George Washington. The guests were seated at traditional round banquet tables, each replete with a tall peach arrangement. Diner-style tables were set up for the wedding party. Yes, 1950s chrome and Formica diner tables, and the bride and groom ate at a sweetheart table that looked like a soda counter with high chrome stools.

Instead of a DJ or band, they'd somehow appropriated an old Wurlitzer jukebox, chock-full of fifties favorites. Guests picked the songs, which were then pumped out over the sound system. "Jailhouse Rock" seemed to be a particular favorite among the groom's friends for some reason.

Of course, the fifth time it played, another chorus drowned it out, one that became familiar as the evening wore on. "Daddy, make them stop."

Carolyn whined her line when the waitstaff tried to bring out the food during the dance time (which explained the cold chicken), repeated it when the groom's brother started to tell an old story of his childhood, and perfected it when guests clinked their glasses, requesting the couple to kiss.

Of course, the evening did have its moments. Cocktail hour featured diner food of sliders, fries, and mini chocolate milk shakes. The nonalcoholic drinks were provided for the kids, I was sure, but popular with many adults. I had one. Okay, more than one.

It was the cupcake tower that kept me from sneaking out. About four feet of sugar overload, it sat near the dance floor on a round table draped with peach satin. The table itself was also covered with cupcakes, and Nick stood by it almost the whole evening, chasing away dancers who got too close and those who wanted to partake too early, mainly the pouty flower girl, who still held on to her basket of petals.

I wasn't sure which was more scrumptious looking, Nick in a suit and tie or those cupcakes with mounds of swirly frosting—in white, chocolate, and peach hues. They just sang from the tower, topped by a small sweetheart cake for that ceremonial cut. Liv had also lent a few peach roses to augment the design.

Throughout the evening flashes went off as people took pictures of the cupcakes, the flowers, the jukebox, and, if they dared, the bride and groom.

"Daddy, make them stop," Carolyn demanded as she shielded her eyes from the flash of a cell phone camera.

"How about you go ahead and cut the cake, now, peaches?" the mayor asked.

Yes, why don't you?

"I want more pictures first. By the jukebox."

I turned to Liv. "I wonder if there are any more of those little chocolate milk shakes."

"I'll come with you." She patted a sleepy Eric on the shoulder.

As Liv and I approached the soda bar, I spotted Little Joe, the mad mortician, heading for me, so I pulled Liv into the shrubbery. Well, not really shrubbery, more of a forest of plastic ficuses. These seemed to be disguising an unused closet. A tad too tacky for the Ashbury. Maybe I should talk with Kathleen Randolph about fresh floral alternatives.

"What's going on?" Liv spat a plastic leaf out of her mouth. "What are we doing in the bushes?"

"Little Joe. He's been after me to dance with him."

"Then dance with him."

"My feet are killing me already. I don't need his added weight on top of them."

"He's a bad dancer?"

"I don't know. I've never danced with him before. But how good can he be if he learned to dance from an online course? Is he still out there?"

Liv peeked through the dense leaves. "Yes, he's still there, talking to another man with a handkerchief over his face. I think it's Chief Bixby."

"Oh, great. Little Joe's probably put out an APB on me, and Bixby is going to arrest us for some obscure excess pollen violation."

"There's no such thing."

"Then he'll make up something."

"Audrey, what if they find us here? How are we going to explain hiding in these ficuses?"

"We're not hiding. We're conversing."

"And of course we like to do that in the privacy of silk camouflage. Um . . . Audrey . . . I hate to say it, but these plants are quite dusty. I think I need to sneeze."

"Try to hold it in. Are they still out there?"

Liv braved the jungle once more. "I don't see Little Joe, but Bixby's headed this way."

"Shhh."

And so we stood, stock-still, trying to blend into the plastic jungle.

"There you are." This was a female voice: Mrs. June's. I could just make out the top of her poufy hair through the leaves in front of me. She stopped less than two feet away.

"June," Bixby said. "Nice wedding."

"So what are you doing standing out here like some party pooper?"

"It's those blasted flowers. Must be a ton of them in there. I'd have stayed home if it was anyone else but the mayor's daughter."

"I thought the flowers were splendid. Mae's girls did a nice job on them, didn't they? Considering . . ."

"Considering?"

"Considering some rat absconded with half of their tools."

"That's funny, they didn't report any theft."

Mrs. June's silence drove the point home.

Bixby sighed. "Just part of the investigation. I have to do my job."

"No, I think you took pleasure in it."

Bixby grunted. "Maybe a little. But between all those flowers at the crime scene and our other *growing* problem."

"You still think someone is farming that marijuana around here?"

"Yeah, I do. We've never had such a problem before. And you have to admit, the flower girls are new in town, and they'd know how to grow the stuff."

"Preposterous. They've been here five years—and a lot longer than that if you count summers. You just want it to be them so you can blame it on someone you don't consider local. You've got no evidence. Oh . . . is that why you took a bunch of their plants? Using the murder investigation to get a look around their back room? Don't you know what marijuana looks like by now?"

"I do, but that Lafferty kid doesn't. I told him to bag up anything that looked suspicious. Still, we'll see what the state lab says about the residue on the cutting tools."

Liv reached over and squeezed my hand. I swallowed hard. It stank to be suspected for something like that, not to mention to be called flower girls and worse: nonlocals. But at least Bixby's tests should exonerate us.

"So that's why you took all their tools," Mrs. June went on. "They were pretty worked up over that, you know. Look, if you've got allergies, you'll have to find some way to cope. You can't blame everything that goes wrong in Ramble on Audrey and Liv, like you're on some crusade to rid the world of flowers. There are medications—"

"I'm sensitive to a lot of medications. You know—" His argument was interrupted by several quick inhalations, followed by one humongous sneeze.

A split second later Liv sneezed as well.

Mrs. June turned around and locked eyes with me through the bushes. I shrugged.

"Did you hear that echo?" Bixby said.

"Yes. Yes, I did." Mrs. June took Bixby's arm. "Odd acoustics in here. Say, I want to find that wife of yours and say hello." Mrs. June was a dear and led him away back into the reception room. Now Bixby's actions made a little more sense. If someone was growing and distributing marijuana in Ramble, I supposed we'd have means. It could be a pretty lucrative side "business," too, considering the number of retired hippies who'd bought up the struggling farms outlying the town and now raised organic crops, meat, eggs, and cheese and sold them at the local farmers' market under tie-dyed psychedelic tents.

"Is the coast clear?" I asked.

"Clear enough." Liv grabbed my hand and pulled me out into the open.

"Oh, hello. Audrey, was it?" Sarah Anderson, Jenny's roommate, stood gazing at us, tottering a bit on those high peach heels.

"Hello, Sarah." I wiped a couple of dust bunnies from my shoulder.

"Is there anything good back there?" Sarah, still decked out in her polka-dotted peach bridesmaid dress, leaned into the ficus, losing her balance. "Just a door." She giggled and wagged a finger at me. "Trying to get away? Trust me, it's not going to work. Nobody leaves until little Miss Peaches gets all her stupid pictures. C'mon, I'll buy you a drink."

We followed her to the bar and helped her onto a stool. "Any milk shakes left?" I asked the server.

"Ooh. Good idea," Sarah said. "It's a little warm in here. How about a wee bit of schnapps in mine?"

The server smiled and scooped more ice cream into the blender carafe. "You?"

Liv and I declined the addition.

"I'm going to need an extra hour on the treadmill to work this off," Sarah said as the server sprayed whipped cream on top of her schnapps-laden shake and presented it. Sarah tore one end from her straw and launched the remaining paper across the room. "I think I hate weddings now. Don't you hate weddings?" She twirled around on the stool.

"They're okay." And then a thought hit me. "A good chance to run into old friends. I've been looking for one person in particular, but I can't remember her name. You probably know her. She was a friend of Derek's, too, I think. A redhead?"

"Nope. Never saw Derek with a redhead." She scrunched up her nose. "Not that I didn't see him with horses of every other color."

"So Derek was unfaithful to Jenny?"

"Derek was . . . Derek." Sarah toyed with the straw. "Jenny shouldn't have done that, though."

"Done what? Been in a relationship with him or kill him?"

"Jenny and Derek weren't in the same league. It was doomed from the beginning." She stared into her shake morosely.

I'm not sure why people celebrated a wedding by consuming copious amounts of a depressant. Raised by teetotalers, I'd imbibed only once in college. I spent the majority of the evening weeping on a friend's shoulder over the way my jeans fit and the next morning camped out in the bathroom with my head on the toilet seat.

"I tried to tell her," Sarah muttered. "Tried to tell him.

They liked each other all right, but it wasn't love. Anyone could see that."

Shirley came to fetch her. "We're being summoned for more pictures. This time Carolyn wants us all in the car."

Sarah saluted and then tumbled off the bar seat. "How do I look?" She plastered on a sad smile then followed Shirley to the exit.

"She's going to be hurting tomorrow." Liv pushed Sarah's deserted drink back toward the server.

The milk shakes, or malteds, as the server explained the difference, were luscious and rich, and I relaxed as I drained the dregs from the glass. Unfortunately, that was when my guard fell.

"Audrey!" Little Joe's excited voice cut straight through to my backbone, if I possessed one. "I've been looking all over for you. Where have you been?"

"Hiding."

"Such a kidder." Little Joe grabbed my hand and pulled me from my stool. "Ready to take that spin on the dance floor?"

I should have realized he meant "spin" literally. He stopped at the jukebox long enough to make a selection before leading me to the crowded dance floor. "The next song is a jitterbug," he said, perhaps in way of apology for the awkward waltz. "Well, not really a jitterbug. It's a swing dance. Jitterbug technically refers to the people who dance it and can't stop. Did you know there was supposed to be a song in *The Wizard of Oz* about a jitterbug? I found that online, too."

I tuned him out as we swayed to Elvis's "Are You Lonesome Tonight?" A question I didn't want to ponder, either. So when I heard an older couple mention the name Rawling, I maneuvered in their direction.

"At least we're spared another wedding. It would have been appalling," the woman said in an accent I could only identify as old money. Funny how economics often transcends geography.

"I heard that Whitney woman say they were planning the wedding of the century."

"Not if the Whitneys were paying for it. And from what I hear, the Rawlings weren't going to pitch in much, either."

"I thought they liked that girl."

"At one time they did, but I heard they're a little strapped for cash."

Little Joe tried a move in a direction away from the couple, but I stood my ground and yanked him back toward me. Misinterpreting my move, he drew me into a tighter embrace. "Maybe I like waltzes after all," he said, his breath heavy with the onion rings from the diner bar.

"What do you mean, blackmail?" the man said.

The woman shushed him, and I steered Little Joe a little closer so I could hear. Good thing the dance floor was crowded at the moment.

". . . business dealings . . . implicate the whole family . . ." I caught only a few words. So I pulled Little Joe and edged as close to the couple as I dared. If we were any closer, we'd be dancing a foursome.

". . . million dollars," the woman said.

"No way Jonathan would part with that kind of money."

I wanted to hear more, but at that moment Elvis finished his crooning and the dancers applauded. The older couple headed toward their table.

"Here it comes!" Little Joe said, a maniacal fire in his eyes. I had just enough time to recognize the song as "Shake, Rattle, and Roll" before everything started shaking, rattling, and rolling.

First the shaking. Little Joe's long legs started pounding the dance floor. I tried to keep up with him, mirroring the steps, but they were just too fast for me. I think I caught every other one.

Then came the rattling. That was my teeth coming together as Little Joe grabbed my hand and led a series of wild swings that sent me bumping into more than one person. Soon the dance floor cleared around us, and, between spins, I could just make out an audience forming around the perimeter, gaping at us. Any more spinning, and I'd not be able to walk.

But that didn't prove to be a problem, because then came the rolling. Perhaps cheered on by the spectators now clapping to the music and the occasional flashbulb, Little Joe latched on to my arms and soon I was airborne.

Moving dead bodies around all day must be a great strength-training routine. He swung my legs to each side of him, and I could feel my dress ride up to my hips as he swung me between his legs. One shoe flew off as he picked me up and twirled me around his shoulders, knocking the wind out of me as my diaphragm struck his clavicle and scapula. I struggled for the breath to protest, yet he kept on tossing me around as if I were a Raggedy Ann doll smeared with bacon grease and he were a pit bull terrier.

Finally he let me go. But it was not the relief I was looking for, because, as a finale to his routine, he sent me sliding along the dance floor, feet first. I can describe everything that happened after that, because my brain videotaped it in slow motion, storing it under the title "Most Embarrassing Moment Ever."

As I hurtled along the dance floor to the closing chords of the music, I got my bearings enough to see Nick Maxwell leap out of the way. And then I saw nothing but the billowing peach satin of the cupcake table. My body slid under the table, my ankle wrenching as my one remaining heel snagged in the table cover, slowing my momentum.

The table above me tilted; the crowd gasped. I had visions of the whole thing coming down, but that didn't happen.

Rather the cloth shifted, as if pulled by an amateur magician, and one lone peach cupcake teetered on the edge of the table. Then it fell, somersaulting like an Olympic diver before landing, frosting side down, right in my . . . um . . . décolletage.

Chapter 15

At eleven in the morning, I could delay it no longer. I plucked clean underwear from my dryer—non-Pippa-the-Penguin variety. I'd tossed those as soon as I slunk into my apartment Saturday night.

I paid extra attention to my makeup. If I couldn't summon an air of dignity after my public humiliation, at least I could fake it.

"Well, Chester, it's been fun." I scratched him behind the ears as he lounged on my dresser. "But it's time to face the human race again."

Why would you want to do a thing like that? he said, or maybe I inferred it, because I wanted to dive back into bed, pull the covers over my head, and stay there. But that had been the previous day's agenda. Besides, even though Liv's message had said she had the shop under control and to take as much time as I needed, I'd have to get back to work sometime.

"G'morning," my neighbor Tom said. He headed up the steps as I headed down. "Nice picture in the paper."

"Thanks." It brought a smile to my face. Sure, the article appeared in the *On* over a week ago, but Tom and I had never hit it off, so it was nice of him to mention it. Maybe the human race was worth rejoining after all. "And good morning to you, too," I called out with a pleasant wave.

When I arrived at the shop I discovered that Liv was an incredible liar. The shop was still a disaster.

"I wanted to clean up Saturday," Amber Lee explained, "but customers kept coming in. And then I was dead on my feet."

"Not a problem." Liv patted her on the shoulder. "A dirty shop doesn't matter when we're closed. Thanks for manning the store on Saturday."

"I heard I missed a humdinger of a wedding."

I squinted at her. "What did you hear?"

"Well, let's just say I never picked you as a Pippa the Penguin fan. Meanwhile the town is divided, fifty-fifty. Half of Ramble is laying odds that you and Little Joe are going to settle down in a little house outside town. The other half insists that you're going to strangle him with your bare hands." Her bright smile dimmed as she considered her words. "Not that we need any more of that kind of thing in town."

"If given the opportunity, you could set the record straight that I'm going to do neither. I'd appreciate it."

"Already doing that, sugar. I've got your back. The hoopla will blow over pretty quick. It probably would have already if it weren't for that picture."

Liv cleared her throat.

"What picture?" I asked.

"Good grief." Amber Lee turned on Liv. "You didn't tell her about the picture?"

I backed Liv into a corner. "What picture?"

"Don't get mad. It's not my fault. I didn't take it. It was that photographer from the *On*."

"The photographer . . . the wedding photographer." I could feel all the color seep out of my face, drain out my toes, and hide under the rubber matting. "How bad is it?"

Amber Lee reached under the counter and pulled out a folded copy of the paper. She handed it to Liv.

"It could be worse," Liv said.

I closed my eyes and concentrated on breathing. When I opened my eyes, the picture was in front of me.

There I was, in all my glory, suspended on Little Joe's shoulders, floral dress flapping in the breeze, with just enough of a happy penguin showing to confirm her identity. "How could this be worse, again?"

"At least you shaved your legs," Amber Lee said.

"Or they could have printed a picture of you under the table. Or got your face in the shot."

I plopped down on a stool for support. Yes, I'd asked, but I didn't want to hear that it could have been worse. This was bad enough.

The camera hadn't caught my face in the picture, but the caption below hinted at my identity. "Local mortician tosses bouquet maker." I wondered if anybody would notice if I hid in the back room working on flowers and had everything I needed delivered UPS. Or maybe Juneau, Alaska, needed a florist shop. Or maybe not that far. Somewhere beyond the reach of the *On*, at least.

"I'm going to cancel my subscription," I said.

"I didn't know you had a subscription," Liv said.

"I'll take out one and then cancel it."

"That's showing 'em." Amber Lee punched me playfully in the upper arm.

"Aw, honey." Liv took my shoulders. "It's not as bad as all that. Yeah, people will have a laugh for a little while, then they'll forget." She lifted my chin so she could look into my eyes. "And besides, we have sweets in the back room today. Nick stopped by this morning with a box—"

"If you say cupcakes, I'm going to scream."

"Nope, no cupcakes. He thought you might not be too keen on cupcakes right now. He brought scones. Said he got the idea at the Rawling wake."

And so the power of the scones lifted my depression. Not completely, mind you. That would have taken a lifetime supply of scones. But enough to power me to get working, and as Grandma Mae always said, "A good day of work could cure just about anything."

We cleaned, stocked coolers, looked over future orders, and put the shop back to rights. Meanwhile, Liv pored over the books, pencils behind both ears, to see where this recent upsurge in business left us financially. It must have been good, because the longer she worked, the happier she got. When she ordered in tacos for lunch, I suspected we'd turned a tidy profit. When I saw she'd ordered extra *queso*, I knew we'd hit pay dirt.

So as we cleared off a workstation and doled out extra salsa, Amber Lee asked, "So besides the dancing, how was the wedding?"

"It went fine, as far as the flowers were concerned," Liv said. "More than fine. I heard all kinds of positive feedback. It could be very good for business."

"We already have the wedding business in Ramble sewn up," Amber Lee said.

"Yes," Liv added, "but the mayor is very well connected. It could bring us in more countywide business, now that people know we can pull off big events like that."

"Did we clear enough to give all our interns a bonus?" I asked. "They worked hard and long hours, with such little notice."

Liv grinned. "I was just about to say the same thing. I think there's a bonus in there for all of us."

"Good," Amber Lee said. "In addition to the roof, I need a new water heater."

I'd be spending mine on underwear, just in case.

"Speaking of the wedding," I said, "I learned something from the mayor's wife."

"This ought to be good. What could you have learned from Rita? Wait, let me guess," Amber Lee said. "How to . . . curtsy like a debutante?"

"I'll have you know Audrey can curtsy with the best of them," Liv said. "Maybe Rita gave you lessons in mastering the snail fork? You never know when that can come in handy."

I smiled. Great how my coworkers were able to take a day I dreaded and turn it around. "Actually, she told me a little more about Derek. Carolyn broke up with him because Derek cheated on her."

"Wouldn't surprise me," Amber Lee said. "He was known for that kind of thing."

"With a redhead."

Amber Lee's eyebrows rose. "Not many redheads in Ramble." She raised tented hands to her lips. "A natural redhead?"

"No idea," I said. "Only that Rita saw Derek with a red-head in his car a week or so before he was killed."

Amber Lee rubbed her hands together. "I can't think of anybody offhand."

"What do you think the chances are of finding out?" I asked.

"Well, clandestine relationships are just that. If they were trying to keep it a secret, it might be a bit harder, but . . . there's an old Bible saying, 'Be sure your sin will find you out.' Anything that juicy will come out in the end. Let me put a few feelers out."

I smiled at Amber Lee's new twist on a Bible verse that Grandma Mae had shared with us often—usually whenever something got broken or baked goods went missing. "Thanks. And while you're doing that, have you heard any-thing about old man Rawling being blackmailed?"

"Blackmailed?" Liv shot up out of her seat. "There you go with the blackmail idea again. Look, kid, you're watching too much television. People on soap operas and detective shows get blackmailed, not folks here in Ramble." She put both hands on her cheeks, doing her best impression of that famous painting *The Scream*. "What makes you think someone was blackmailing him?"

"Something I overheard on the dance—at the wedding. An older couple I didn't recognize. They were talking about a million dollars."

Amber Lee whistled. "That's a chunk of change."

"Nonsense," Liv said.

"Well . . . maybe not," Amber Lee said. "The Rawlings and the mayor run in the same circles. They're both members of the same party and go to all the highfalutin fundraisers, hobnobbing with those high-profile DC types. You know, those hundreds-of-dollars-a-plate shindigs."

"Which is why they'd keep their noses clean," Liv said.

"Or why they'd want to *appear* to keep their noses clean," Amber Lee amended. "That would make them prime candidates for blackmail, when you think about it."

Liv was still shaking her head when her cell phone rang. She plucked it from her apron pocket, checked the caller ID, and answered. "Eric?" She listened for a moment, then stepped away for some privacy.

While she was gone I helped myself to her nachos. And maybe another scone.

"You know, I can see someone trying to blackmail old man Rawling." Amber Lee crumpled her taco wrapper into the take-out bag. "What I can't see is him paying it. That man is tight. And a million dollars? He'd kill first."

I recalled Jonathan Rawling's words spoken over the casket of his son. *You really mucked it up this time, son.* What had Derek mucked up? Did it have to do with the Rawling family's business practices? Derek's gambling or his engagement to Jenny? His relationship with the mysterious redhead? Or some other obscure failing we'd no inkling of?

And could old man Rawling have something to do with it? A son with sins as wide and varied as Derek's couldn't remain hidden for long. Could Jonathan Rawling be as ambitious and coldhearted as to consider his son a liability and eliminate him?

Maybe Liv was right. Maybe I watched too much television.

Speaking of Liv, she walked back in with a huge smile on her face.

Amber Lee and I shared glances.

"It looks like someone has good news," Amber Lee said.

"Spill," I added. "We need some good news about now."

"Well, it's mostly good news. Eric got a call from Jonathan Rawling this morning. I guess the bad news is that he needed someone to manage his properties now that . . ."

Liv started to tear and wiped a drop from one cheek. "Sorry," she said. "I feel a little like we're profiting from the dead again. But Mr. Rawling wants Eric to manage his property."

"Just out of the blue?" Amber Lee asked.

"Well, Eric did some work on local properties for Derek. I guess he got points for coming in on time and within budget. And he'll still be able to keep his construction business going. In fact, Rawling wants him to use his own guys whenever possible. He'll just have to keep it at a union scale, so everything is aboveboard, and hire a supervisor when he can't be on-site."

"Wow," Amber Lee said. "Sounds like he's considering it."

"He has to. The offer was just that good." Liv bit her lower lip. "My reservation is what would happen if Rawling sold off his property. Where would that leave Eric? But since he's able to keep his own construction company operating, it shouldn't be a problem.

"Anyway, Eric is meeting with Rawling and his lawyer this afternoon. If everything looks okay, I told him to go for it."

We congratulated her and worked normally for the rest of the afternoon. Well, they worked normally. I darted into the back room whenever the bell over the door sounded. I still wasn't ready to face customers.

Just before closing, the bell sounded again, but Eric's booming voice drew me from my exile.

"Where's that enchanting wife of mine?" he said.

Liv stepped out of the cooler and walked into his embrace. He swirled her around—a bit more gently than Little Joe had me.

"And her lovely cousin." He kissed me on the cheek.

"And what am I?" Amber Lee teased. She and Eric maintained an easy relationship.

Eric put his hand on his hips and eyed Amber Lee up and down. "And hail to the stalwart minion." He removed his ball cap and bowed.

"Stalwart?" Amber Lee said with a pout. She spun around and struck a pose. "Do these pants really make me look stalwart?"

Eric laughed and reached into a shopping bag hung around his arm. He presented Liv with a box of her favorite chocolate truffles. One can hardly give a bouquet to a florist, but chocolate is always fair game. Especially if you leave it out in the open. Or in an unlocked desk.

"I take it the meeting went well," I said.

"Tell me all about it." Liv flipped the sign to "Closed" and turned the lock on the door.

"I met with Rawling and the lawyer, and his main accountant was there, too. His secretary even sat in, taking notes. The job looks just as good on paper as he described it over the phone. It comes with a steady salary and some nice benefits that will come in handy about now. He even offered to put me and my guys on his corporate health insurance."

"Did you ask if he has any plans to sell?" Liv asked.

"He said the properties were doing well and he had no current plans to divest. That's about as secure as you can get these days."

Liv nodded, but her eyes narrowed. Whether she was counting dollar signs or computing the risk involved, I couldn't tell. But I hoped she'd quit before the smoke alarms went off from all that gear-turning in her head.

"So I took it. Signed the papers this afternoon and even jumped into some of the paperwork." Eric thoughtfully rubbed his scruffy chin.

"Uh-oh," Amber Lee said. "That doesn't look like it's all good news."

"You found something," I said.

"It's just . . . I don't want to say too much about Derek. He was always nice to me and my guys. And it was such a shock to find him like that. Only Derek always bragged about going to some Ivy League school for business management, but his books just don't show a whole lot of, well, competence in that area."

"Derek was in over his head?" Liv asked.

Eric thought for a moment and shook his head. "More like he wanted to appear that way. But he neglected a number of the properties. Other times he overcharged renters and local businesses. I found a couple of incidents where he claimed he paid us more than I remember getting."

"That's not going to be a problem for you, is it?" I asked.

"No, not for me. I kept good records, and there's a clear paper trail starting from here on out. I'll leave it to the accountants to reconcile any of Derek's past financial dealings. Since the company spent less than reported and earned more than Mr. Rawling ever saw, they're going to have to fix that with the IRS. But I got a good feeling that they would do that now."

"So Derek stole from his own father."

"That's about right," Eric said.

"Shameful." Amber Lee wagged her head. "I wonder what got into that boy."

"Maybe it was—" I started.

Liv put her hand up. "Don't say blackmail."

"What's this?" Eric asked.

Liv laughed. "Audrey's got this harebrained idea that someone was blackmailing the Rawlings."

But Eric wasn't laughing. He went back to chin rubbing.

"Actually . . ." I gave Liv the stare. "I was going to say gambling. We learned from Mrs. Whitney that Derek had a gambling problem."

"What kind of gambling?" Eric asked.

"What do you mean?" On the old shows on television, people with gambling problems always "played the ponies" and avoided dark alleys and some bookie named Mick. And there was still quite a bit of horse racing in Virginia, just not right in Ramble.

"Well, there's online gaming." Eric began ticking off items on his fingers. "And casinos just over in West Virginia. Then there's the local sports pools, friendly poker games . . . or not so friendly."

"Or maybe he was spending money on the mysterious redhead," Amber Lee said, "and maybe she was obsessed with him or maybe even angry about his upcoming nuptials with Jenny."

"But Jenny had already called off the wedding," Liv said.

"But could she have known that?" I added. "And did the mysterious redhead even write the letters?"

"And since we're playing armchair detective," Eric said, "I suppose any of the business owners that Derek ripped off might have motive to get him out of the way."

I bit my lower lip. "How much money are we talking here?"

Eric shrugged. "Maybe not much individually, but old man Rawling owns half the town of Ramble, and Derek managed it."

Amber Lee snorted.

Liv shot her a sideways look.

"Sorry." Amber Lee wiped her eye. "I just think it odd that the suspect list now includes the Ramble Chamber of Commerce."

I couldn't help but smile. "You know," I said, with a sobering thought, "even if Derek didn't misappropriate much, what he took could be a huge burden for a struggling business." I turned to Liv. "How would you feel if Derek had been our landlord in those early months, when we were first starting to get off the ground?"

Liv sighed. "A few hundred dollars in Derek's pocket could mean the end of someone's life's ambition and labor." Liv turned to Eric. "Any way you could find out who was hurt most by Derek's financial finagling?"

A dark shadow fell over Eric's face. "I can. But I'm a little concerned that this is turning into more than idle conversation." He placed his hand atop Liv's. "Promise me you're not getting involved in this. It could be dangerous."

"She's not," I said. "I am. Someone needs to help Jenny."

"Is that supposed to make me feel better?" Eric said. "I'd hate anything to happen to my favorite cousin."

I shrugged. "Not likely. For one, I'm no threat to the killer since I seem to be getting nowhere. The suspect list just keeps growing. The more I learn about Derek, it seems half of Ramble had a motive to kill him, including his own family."

"His family?" Eric asked.

"Here it comes." Liv thrust her hands over her ears. "I'm sick of this whole stupid blackmail idea."

I explained to Eric what I'd overheard at the wedding.

"Business dealings that implicate the whole family," Eric repeated.

"Could be nothing more than idle rumor," Liv said.

"But Derek is dead," Amber Lee said. "Liv, I know you don't like the gossip, but it's true that someone out there is a killer. Assuming it's not Jenny."

"It's not." The more I repeated it, however, the less conviction it contained.

"So why not look at the gossip—not as gospel, but as a direction of inquiry?" Amber Lee countered. "Okay, for instance blackmail. That could mean a lot of things, especially if it implicated the whole family."

"Derek's gambling," I said. "Someone could have threatened to reveal that to his father."

"Or threatened his father with making it public," Eric said. "Or Derek's mismanagement, for that matter. It would have hurt Rawling's business."

"And his high-profile contacts," I said. "But what if it wasn't Derek's indiscretions that were about to be exposed? What if something implicated another family member? His father. His mother."

"Audrey," Liv chided, "the Rawlings have reigned as king and queen of Ramble society for decades."

"But the bigger they are, the harder they fall," Amber Lee added. "And neither old man Rawling nor the duchess would have appreciated being knocked off their thrones."

"Could they have . . . no," I said.

"Finish the sentence," Amber Lee coaxed. "I left my secret mind-reading glasses at home."

"I was about to ask whether Jonathan or Miranda could have killed their own son to avoid a public scandal."

Liv turned away again in a huff and Amber Lee let out a slow breath.

"You asked," I said. "I was more than willing to let that thought pass."

"No," Amber Lee said. "It's coldhearted, yes, but when's the last time you associated warm and fuzzy with the Rawling family? I say, leave it on the table."

Liv banged her coffee mug on the counter. "Maybe Derek blackmailed his parents, and they killed him so they wouldn't have to pay." The look on her face betrayed the intended sarcasm, but the idea took root.

The rest of us shared glances.

Liv thrust a hand on her hip and shook her head. "You're considering it."

"If Derek knew of some kind of business impropriety of old man Rawling's *and* needed money to pay a gambling debt . . . ," I said softly.

Liv thrust her arms into her sweater and stormed out the door.

"She'll calm down," Eric said. "It's just that . . . I suppose I should go."

I waved him off, and he followed after her.

I poured myself a cup of coffee. I guessed finding out who killed Derek wouldn't be quite as easy as finding the nearest dark alley and looking for shady figures named Mick.

Chapter 16

It was Liv's day to start late, so I arrived at the shop bright and early at seven. Okay, maybe it was seven twenty. It would have been seven thirty, but I saved a few minutes by scarfing down my partially thawed frozen bagel on the way. I'd finished my long-neglected laundry, but grocery shopping was next on my list.

Larry stood by the back door, cradling a cup of coffee in his hands.

"What are you doing out in the cold?" I turned the key in the lock.

"Bixby took my key," he said. "That whole business with the knife, I guess."

I rolled my eyes. "Then sorry I'm late. We'll get you another."

He smiled his Kewpie doll smile, set down his coffee on the back of his truck, and opened the hatch. I helped him unload the flowers, including some delectable snapdragons.

"Those are from the new greenhouse," he said with an air of pride.

"The one you're renting from Rawling?" I asked. "You know, it's funny, but I don't recall anyone else growing flowers around here."

"They didn't use it for flowers," Larry said. "It was used for tobacco transplants." He smiled. "Flowers is better, though."

"I've heard people say they had problems doing business with Derek."

Larry shrugged and pulled down the hatch of his truck.

"You didn't have any problems with him?"

"None worth speaking of now," he said. "That's for sure."

So much for the direct approach. Larry's reluctance meshed with what I knew about him. I'd never heard him say an ill word about anybody. "It's just that . . ." At that moment a dry bagel crumb seemed to catch in my throat. I swallowed to dislodge it and, when that didn't work, cleared my throat while tears started running down my cheeks.

"Oh, Audrey." Larry came up behind me and laid a hand on my shoulder. "How stupid of me. Of course you want to know more about Derek, and it's not out of meanness. Your friend . . ."

While his words trailed off, I struggled with the idea of telling him the truth about why tears were still streaming down my face. But at the moment, with that crumb catching in the back of my throat, I couldn't say much of anything.

"Here, let me buy you a cup of coffee and I'll tell you about the whole business."

I nodded, then fished a crumpled fast-food napkin from my purse to wipe my streaming face. After locking the shop doors, we walked back to Brew-Ha-Ha at the end of the alley. I cleared my throat the whole way.

The outside air was still just a little too cool and the tables were laden with dew, so we went inside. The aromas of fresh coffee and yeasty breads and cinnamon . . . if I could find a candle with that scent, I'd buy a case of them. No, ten cases. While he went to the counter to place our order, I plucked more napkins from the holder on the table and blew my nose. Then I shoved another wad of napkins into my purse to replace my depleted supply.

Larry handed me my cup, just the way I liked it. Larry had been a frequent guest around the table when Grandma Mae instilled me with a tolerance for coffee. Touching that he remembered.

I took several sips of the hot brew. It did the trick. Bagel dislodged. So great was my relief, I started ogling the fresh bagels in the showcase. Maybe on the way out.

"You okay?" Larry asked.

"Yeah, fine." I lifted my coffee cup. "Thanks."

"About Derek. At first I thought he was an okay guy. Kept telling myself that there was no way he could have known."

"Known what?"

"When I rented the greenhouse from Derek, I made a point of asking if it had heat. He said it did. And I guess there was no lie in that. The heater was a big old propane bugger—and it worked fine when I tested it. So I signed the contract and shelled out first and last months' rent plus a hefty security deposit. My guys cleaned out a crop of dead tobacco seedlings someone had left behind and refitted it for flowers."

"He didn't even clean it out for you?" I asked.

"Said something about how he would do it if I waited a week or two, but I wanted to get started. Fools rush in, you see."

I patted his hand. "You're not a fool."

He stared into his coffee cup for a moment, then took a sip. "I should've started small, put in a few dozen plants. But I figured with that big propane heater, it didn't make sense to heat that whole building if I didn't fill it up. Wouldn't pay. So I seeded up and packed the place. For three weeks everything was great. Then I got my first heating bill and nearly went into shock. Propane's a lot more expensive than the natural gas heaters at the other place. So I started thinking that maybe this was a three-season place. It wouldn't be too bad if I didn't run it in the dead of winter. But that was kind of my fault, too, you see. Should've asked Derek if I could see the old heating bills."

"I'm not sure I would have thought of it, either."

"Then came that cold spell. Remember that?"

"In January." The month had brought unusually frigid temperatures.

"Some wiring on the heater overloaded, and the whole thing shut down overnight. When we got there, the inside temperature had bottomed out. By the time we rigged up some temporary propane burners, we'd lost half the seedlings. So I called Derek. Took him a couple days to call back, and a couple more to bring in some guy I'd never laid eyes on. They got the heater running again. Derek apologized, and that was the end of it."

"But you lost half your plants," I said.

"And spent more money buying those temporary heaters—and all that propane. Not to mention man-hours, since someone needed to stay and adjust them to maintain a proper temperature around the clock for four days."

"Did Derek offer to replace any—"

Larry wagged his head.

I let out a breath. Just the seedlings alone could have cost him thousands.

Larry shrugged. "The cost of doing business. There's always a risk. But I thought we were good at that point. I figured Derek couldn't have known the heater was about to go." He bit his lip and looked up to the ceiling.

"Uh-oh," I said.

"Yeah. Two weeks later came that second cold snap. I woke up in the middle of the night with this feeling, you know? Couldn't shake it. So I drove over to the greenhouse and, sure enough, the dang heater cut out again. Only this time I got the burners going before the temperature dropped too much. Didn't lose but one or two plants."

"That's good, then, right?"

"Well . . ." Larry exhaled through clenched teeth. "Here's the thing. I knew it would take a while to get Derek to call back, and I kinda wanted another opinion on that heater, so I called in Jimmy Gorden and asked him to take a peek for me. No offense against outsiders, but everybody knows and trusts Jimmy. I was surprised that Derek didn't use him for his heating repairs."

"What did Jimmy say when he'd seen it?"

"He didn't have to see it. He already had. And he'd told Derek months earlier that it needed to be replaced. Every time it runs on full, it melts half the wires. Not only couldn't it be fixed but, in his opinion, it was a serious fire hazard."

"And Derek knew this when he rented it to you."

Larry studied his empty cup while his jaw twitched, ever so slightly.

"That's fraudulent. You could have sued him."

"I should've walked away. Sometimes you need to cut your losses. Instead, I got the estimate for the new heater—a natural gas variety that was supposed to be a model of fuel efficiency. I told Derek I would pay the initial cost if he would take some off my rent each month until it was paid off."

"Reasonable."

"Derek agreed, and again I thought we were golden." He rose and went to the counter for a refill on his coffee.

Once he'd settled back in his seat, I said, "But that wasn't the end of the story, was it?"

"Hardly. Everything was fine for a couple months there.

New heater worked great and cost me a lot less money to run. Thought I might be able to turn a profit after all. Then a few weeks ago, Derek ups and raises my rent. At first I thought it was a mistake, that he forgot to take the heater payment out. Then he shoved our lease agreement in my face and showed where he could charge an increase in rent based on user-requested capital improvements." Larry shook his head. "He was charging me more rent for the new heater. Even though I still owned most of it."

"Oh, my."

"Audrey, I pride myself on keeping my calm." And he proved it. His exterior showed nothing but a serious visage. Only his white-knuckled grip on the coffee cup exposed the anger he still felt.

"Oh, my."

"Larry?" Liv said. "Audrey, that's a new low." Liv tried to force a gerbera daisy into an already full vase and ended up bending the stem.

"I didn't say I suspected Larry of killing Derek," I said. "Just that he had motive."

Amber Lee paused and rested her hands on the top of the broom she had been pushing. "Only . . ."

"Only what?" I asked.

But Amber Lee remained quiet for a while, as if trying to sort out and catalog all the gossip from the past millennia.

"See what you did?" Liv quipped. "You broke her."

"No," she said, "I just remembered. Years ago . . . long before your time. Larry was sweet on a girl. It got real serious, too. At least in his mind. Buying-a-ring serious."

"But he never married," Liv said.

"He used to hang around Grandma Mae's a lot," I said. "When we were kids, we used to think they were going to get married. I guess we didn't consider that Grandma was a good twenty years older than Larry, and they were just friends."

Amber Lee smiled. "No, not your grandmother. Before they were friends." Her smile fell. "For once I almost gave up gossiping. Gossip in Ramble's not usually that cruel. From what I remember of the story, Larry got dressed in his best suit—well, he only owned one suit—and he dropped on one knee in the town square after the Sunday afternoon band concert. He pulled out a ring and professed his undying love. It was one of those public proposals, like you see at ball parks and such, and you wonder what will happen if the girl doesn't say yes."

"And she didn't say yes," Liv said.

Amber Lee shook her head. "She didn't say no at first, either. Just a prim and proper 'I'll let you know, Lawrence.'"

"How long did she leave him hanging?" I asked, already feeling sorry for the sweet man who supplied so many of our flowers.

"Not long," she said. "Her folks announced her engagement less than a week later. Put a full-page spread in the *On* and announcements in the regional papers. Larry found out like everybody else did. It made him a laughingstock for weeks. I remember them saying, 'Hey, Larry, I see your girlfriend made the paper.' And 'Hey, Larry, what are you going to do with that rock?' Mean-spirited, if you ask me. But if they were mean to him, they were brutal to her. Said the only way Larry didn't measure up was in the wallet area. Most folk thought he was better off without her. A few told him that, but that didn't go over so well, either."

I took a deep breath. I had to ask, but I had a feeling I already knew the answer. "Who was the girl?"

"Miranda . . . now Miranda Rawling."

As we continued to work, I struggled to get my head around the idea of sweet, quiet, man-of-the-soil Larry with the queen-of-ice social matron Miranda Rawling. Kind of like *Green Acres* in real life. Except that on television the couple managed to make it work.

Instead, Amber Lee explained, Miranda quickly married Jonathan Rawling, and the two of them left for several years while he gained experience in business in DC. When Jonathan's father passed away, they moved back to Ramble to manage the family's holdings, bringing little Derek with them.

"I never would have got that connection," I said.

"Honey, this is Ramble." Amber Lee sent her knife through a foam block. "We don't have six degrees of separation here. There's always a connection."

I stared at the knife. I hated to think it, but Larry had more motive than I'd even imagined. Not only his recent run-in with Derek, but Miranda had jilted him. But no way could I put Larry's cherubic face on top of the body of a cold-blooded killer. Then again, I couldn't place him side by side with Miranda Rawling, either.

"I'm going to pay Larry a call," I said.

"What on earth for?" Liv asked.

"I told him I'd give him a new key to the shop since Bixby took his." I placed the master key in my purse. "I can make a copy at the hardware store before heading over."

"Why not give it to him the next time he comes to deliver flowers?" Liv asked.

I shrugged.

"Wait until we close up, and I'll go with you," Liv said. "It's been a while since I've been out to the greenhouses."

"You just want to go to make sure I don't do anything that would embarrass you."

Liv smiled. "And there's that."

Amber Lee laughed. "I don't know what you guys have up your sleeves, but why don't you head on out? Shelby and Darnell are due in any minute, and I can close up."

"You sure?" I said. "I mean, I know you *can*. You've been doing a marvelous job. I just don't want to impose."

But she shooed us on, and soon Liv and I were cruising across Ramble in the CR-V—if you can call the five-minute trip a cruise. We checked at Larry's main greenhouses.

"He's at the new site," one of Larry's employees said.

Even better. We could get a look at the lemon Derek had stuck him with.

"Want me to call him?" he asked.

"No, that's okay. We'll find it."

He gave us directions, then added, "I hope I got that right. I haven't been up there since we cleaned it out."

"He has different guys working there?" Liv asked.

"No," he said. "He put us all here and he does all the work up there himself. He keeps telling us to wait, that it'll all make sense. Said he found a way to make that place pay for itself after all."

Liv remained silent as we headed out to the rented greenhouse. I surmised she was dying to tell me "I told you so," but this new added bit of secrecy in the otherwise transparent gentleman seemed to throw her a curve. It was throwing me a curve, and I was the one who'd wanted to go see him.

But what could he be hiding in that greenhouse?

We bumped along the old road that led to the place: deep country, potholed, and narrow, with the shoulders overgrown with weeds. A single-lane gravel driveway led up a steep incline, where we could make out Larry's truck. I gunned the Honda up the drive, parked behind him, and pulled the parking brake. Even then, the CR-V jerked back a few inches when I lifted my foot off the brake pedal.

The massive greenhouse was the sole asset on this property, and the weeds grew high right to the structure. A small field nearby might be suited for seasonal cut flowers but would need a good clearing, and it didn't look like any work had been put into the endeavor.

"Do you see him?" Liv asked.

I shook my head. I walked to the greenhouse and tented my eyes to peer inside. I could see row after row of seedlings and plants in various stages—roses in the back. Midway through stood a worktable, and I could just spy the shape of a knife resting on its surface and wondered if it could be one of the twelve. Of course, if the Rose in Bloom knife were present, that would clear Larry, right?

"I'm going in there," I said.

"I'd rather you didn't," Larry's voice rumbled, humorless and firm.

I turned around. "Oh, hi. We were just looking for you." I smiled. "I . . . uh . . ." I dug into my purse, fingered a bottle of mace that Brad once gave me for my protection, then left it to fish out the key we had made on the way over. "We brought you a new door key for the shop."

He stared at the key in my open palm for a few moments, then stepped forward to accept it. "Thanks, but you didn't need to bring it out here."

"It was no problem," Liv said with a nervous giggle.

"No problem at all," I added.

Larry pulled out a ring of keys and added the new one to the mix.

"You know"—I forced a lighthearted tone—"I've never seen these greenhouses. Care to give us the grand tour?" I took two steps toward the door.

Larry shuffled to bar my way. Grim faced, he looked at me, then at Liv, then back to me. "Sorry," he said. "I'd rather not. Not today, anyway. The . . . temperature. Opening the doors too much causes temperature fluctuation, and these plants have been stressed enough as it is. Maybe some other time, eh?"

"Sure." Liv inched backward. "We'll just . . . be heading back to town. Right, Audrey?"

"Sure," I said.

"Audrey?" He looked pained. "Is that why you drove out here? To bring me the key?"

I managed a nod.

He ran a hand through his shock of hair. "All right, then. Take care going down that drive. It's pretty steep. And I'll let you know when I'm ready to show you around. It's only . . ."

I shrugged. "No problem. Some other time, then. See you later, Larry."

Larry smiled and waved as I took care backing the CR-V down the long gravel drive. We were halfway to town before either of us spoke.

Liv broke the ice first. "I don't know what to think. Grandma Mae was always such a good judge of character. But that . . . that was creepy weird."

A chill ran up my spine. "Yeah."

Chapter 17

I dropped Liv back at the shop to pick up her car, but I couldn't prevent her from going in to do more work. And since I couldn't let her work alone, I followed her. I figured I might as well look over my appointment book and put together some ideas for the bridal appointments scheduled for later in the week. Time to start shifting my focus back to that aspect of my work.

Amber Lee rolled her eyes when we trudged back in through the door. "Can't live without the place, or don't you love that husband of yours anymore?"

Liv shuffled through the mail on the counter. "He's working late tonight, so I might as well get a jump on things as well."

I hung up my purse and glanced at the takeout menus on the bulletin board. "Barbecue?" I said hopefully.

"Sounds good," Liv said. "With extra honey corn bread. I'm famished."

"Well, all right," I said. "Amber Lee, you staying?"

"As much as I'd like to . . . I have a date."

"Ooh, a date, is it?" Liv asked, always the matchmaker.

Amber Lee shook her head. "None of your business." She teased us with a smile as she closed the door behind her.

Liv and I stared at each other with raised eyebrows. But then hunger won over, so I called in our order. Liv kept adding things to the menu before I could hang up. Baked beans, corn on the cob, slaw, and their red-skinned potato salad. Good thing, too, because Eric arrived just as the food came.

We set up a buffet on the checkout counter and took our plates into the gazebo to eat. Quite the trendy picnic spot of late.

"I thought you were working tonight." Liv poured lemonade into foam cups.

"I am." Eric pointed to the file of paperwork he'd set on the table next to him. "I just realized I could spare time to eat. And I wanted to discuss something with you."

"Maybe I should let you two have some time alone." I picked up my plate. I was willing to leave, but not without my pulled pork.

"No, Audrey. This concerns you, too." He stopped to spoon a huge heap of slaw onto his pork. "Mainly you, I think."

"Me?" His serious visage made me feel like I'd been called down to the principal's office. If he started lecturing me on making Liv work too hard, he'd get an earful on the real identity of the taskmaster in our organizational chart.

"I took a good look at some of Derek's paperwork," he said. "Trying to get an idea of the job ahead of me."

"How does it look?" I opened a pat of butter and slathered it on my corn, then licked a couple drops that escaped onto my fingers.

"Odd," Eric said. "He was skimming, all right, taking just enough from each business to not get noticed. Other properties he just left to fall apart, like he didn't care."

"He probably didn't." Liv snagged another slice of corn bread. "If he didn't think they were going to make him money."

"Or if he had to invest ready cash into them to make a go of them," I added.

"Right," Eric said. "It seemed to be a matter of spending as little as possible, even if a small investment would have turned a big profit later on. For example . . ." He wiped his hands on one of the moistened towelettes the restaurant had provided, then dried them on a clean napkin before pulling a page from his folder and holding it up for me to see.

I leaned in for a better view. It seemed to be a rental listing for an old restaurant. Only the condition of the building, with the weeds grown up and the cracked parking lot, would have made renting almost impossible. "I don't recognize that place," I said.

"No," Eric said. "It's closer to DC. But it's a good property remaining vacant, when a little elbow grease could make it hugely profitable."

"Real estate out that way is through the roof," Liv said. "Are you going to fix it up and try to rent it?"

"I'd like to," Eric said. "Except Mr. Rawling told me not to worry about it, to focus my concentration on buildings closer to Ramble. I don't know, maybe he'll get someone else to manage his more distant holdings. But I'll ask him about it again, maybe after I have a few weeks or months to gain his confidence. The building's got good bones, even if it needs some work. It shouldn't go empty like that."

A knock at the door interrupted our conversation. Liv started to rise, but I told her that I'd get it. As I rounded the corner, I couldn't make out the face in the gathering twilight, but I knew of only one regular customer who wore white.

"I saw the light on," Nick said. "And wondered if you wouldn't mind an off-hours sale to a tired businessman."

Oh, yes, his regular bouquet for whomever.

He stopped to sniff. "What is that?"

"Barbecue," I said. "Would you like some? Liv ordered enough for a small army."

"My mother would be appalled at my manners, but yes, I'd love some. Anything not made of flour and sugar would be great right about now." He followed me up to the gazebo.

Eric shifted his file over to make room for Nick, and Liv poured him a lemonade.

"I'm afraid the corn bread is gone," she said.

"No matter." Nick squinted at the rental listing Eric had set down. "What's this?"

"Oh, just a property that Derek managed," Eric said.

"Eric is going to be the new property manager for Rawling Properties." Liv's voice held more than a hint of pride.

"Well, that's good news for me, too, then." Nick reached across the table to shake hands with Eric.

Eric wiped his hands well with a napkin before accepting the handshake.

"That's right," I said. "You'd mentioned that you rented from Rawling."

"Most business owners here do," Nick said. "I was a bit surprised to find out he didn't own this place. Frankly, I wouldn't mind buying my building, if Rawling would ever think about parting with it. I mentioned it to Derek a few times, but . . ."

"Give me a chance to get my feet wet in this job," Eric said, "and maybe we could run some numbers."

"Fair enough." Nick tapped the rental listing. "You know, I think I recognize that place. That used to be *the* place for a romantic dinner." Nick glanced at me, and his face colored a little bit. "But it's been closed down for years now. Even in its sad state, I'm surprised no one rented it." Then he took a closer look at the listing and whistled. "This is way overpriced for the condition it's in."

Eric snatched the paper back. "I hadn't noticed that. Maybe that's why it's still vacant. But it's not my problem, I guess."

I had difficulty swallowing my pulled pork, and it had nothing to do with the meat, tender and tasty as always. "Did Rawling have many properties he didn't want you to 'worry about'?"

"No, as a matter of fact, just this one."

I bit my lip. "Isn't that odd? A building that close to DC could be taking in a heap of revenue. I can see why Derek didn't bother with it, if it needed work, but I can't see Rawling passing up a buck like that."

"What are you thinking?" Liv asked.

"I'm thinking something's fishy about it, like he's trying to hide the place."

"Hide?" Nick said. "A whole restaurant?"

"Well, not hide it," I said. "But keep people from becoming too interested in it."

"Deliberately keep it vacant?" Eric said, studying the listing. "Why?"

"I don't know, but I wouldn't mind taking a peek around." I shoved my greasy plate and utensils into the empty takeout bag.

"Rawling didn't give me a key, I'm afraid," Eric said.

"See, that's even fishier. What if this is tied into the Rawling secrets? I would kind of like to see what the place looks like."

"It's just an old abandoned restaurant," Eric said.

"And in not the best neighborhood," Nick said. "I mean, it's not a ghetto. More industrial, but . . ."

"But it's a nice night for a drive," I said. "Clear skies and supposed to be a full moon. I'll be fine."

"You're going now?" Liv said. "Hold up. I'll ride along with you."

"Not a good idea." Eric turned to his wife. "I don't want you running around all hours. You've been working hard. Look"—his voice softened as he took her by her shoulders—"I need to get back to the office for a couple hours, but I want to know you're safe at home, catching up on your sleep, not running half across Virginia on a goose chase."

Liv's lip jutted out, just for a split second, but then she nodded.

I headed to the back room for my purse. I was precisely in the mood for chasing geese. When I came out, Nick was tossing his keys in the air.

"Ready?" he said.

"For what?" I asked.

"Nick agreed to go with you." The corners of Liv's mouth betrayed the smile I knew she tried to hide. "Isn't that nice?"

"I think it's a good idea," Eric said. "Besides, he knows the neighborhood." And yes, Eric had become well familiar with my uncanny ability to get lost, even with a GPS.

"I don't want to trouble you," I said. "It could be just a silly hunch."

"No trouble," he said. "Like you said, it's a nice night for a drive, and it would be kind of interesting to see the old place again."

And then I wondered. Nick said it was once the romantic place to go. Had he taken her there? The recipient of the flowers?

Chapter 18

❧

"You got cake back there or something?" I asked. I can't say we went for a romantic drive in the country. No romantic drive I'd ever been on—not that I counted myself an expert in these things—ever involved sitting in the passenger seat of a bakery truck inhaling the intoxicating scents of sugar, vanilla, and . . . was that almond extract? Then again, maybe they should.

"Yes," he said. "Last-minute cancellation. I was supposed to deliver two sheet cakes over to the assisted-living complex just outside of town. Fiftieth anniversary party." He shook his head and sighed. "Sad thing."

"Don't tell me one of them died on their anniversary."

"Nope. He caught her cheating on him with her canasta partner. Canceled the whole party."

"You know, that's almost worse."

He chuckled. "Still, they made it forty-nine years, three hundred and sixty-four days. They might figure it out yet."

"I suppose."

"Some humdinger of a wedding the mayor threw for his daughter."

I bristled in my seat. Better to face it head-on. "Not my most stellar moment."

"Yeah," he said. "I'm afraid the photographer didn't get your good side this time."

What did that mean? Did Pippa make my butt look big?

"I mean," he said, "not that you have a bad side. I didn't mean to say the picture was unflattering . . . I . . ."

"Nice try. I'm just glad I didn't take down the whole cupcake tower. I'd have to change my name and move."

"It wasn't that bad. Although Carolyn seemed a little upset that you were stealing her spotlight. I heard her talking to her father midway through that little dance-a-thon—"

"Let me guess." I attempted my best Carolyn impression. " 'Daddy, make them stop.' " Then I tried her laugh, that nasal titter her poor groom would endure the rest of his life, unless Carolyn took up canasta.

Nick's genuine laughter filled the truck, and it made me laugh, too, the tension-relieving laughter that doctors say is good for you. I hadn't wiped away the tears of laughter when his next words came.

"So," he said, "are you and that mortician guy serious?"

"Serious about what?"

"I mean, are you an item?"

"Little Joe and me?" I let out a sigh. "I suppose he's interested, and there's more than a few people in Ramble who'd like to see us together. He's tall, you see, and somehow they think that makes us an ideal couple. But he's not my type, so I try not to encourage him. Besides, the first time he asked me out, it was still too soon after . . ."

"After?"

I scrambled for an answer. I felt so relaxed in the truck, joking and laughing and inhaling almond fumes, that I'd let my guard down. And I didn't want to talk about Brad. I waved it off. "Just an old relationship turned south. Say, what about you? You sure have been buying up the bouquets lately. Who's the lucky girl?"

Grandma Mae would have had a fit to see me asking such a direct question. "Ladies don't pry," she'd told us. "At least not obviously. Prying just shuts people down."

And maybe Grandma was right, because instead of answering, he just said, "Oh, there's our turnoff."

I didn't need to press for an answer. In a small town like Ramble, I was sure to run into her. But as Nick deftly maneuvered the truck through the maze of industrial streets, I decided he could still be a friend. I was at ease with him, as he seemed to be with me. We shared work interests in common, a similar sense of humor. All in addition to being tall. Hey, height wasn't the most important thing, but it meant I could hang out with him, wearing actual shoes, without looking like an Amazon princess or the Jolly Green-Thumbed Giant. As long as the girlfriend didn't prove to be the jealous type.

"Here it is," he said as we drove past the old building. It looked just like the picture, only creepier—like a trendy catering hall for the Addams family. The windows were dark and filled with birds' nests and spiderwebs that glistened in the streetlights. The picture was broken by a pale shaft of light and the silhouette of a man as he squeezed in the front door.

"Someone just went inside," I said. "A squatter, do you think?"

"I don't know. Let me circle the block and see if I can find a place to park."

"Where did all these cars come from?" I asked. Cars lined the street and filled the weed-pocked parking lot.

"Maybe one of the businesses nearby?" he suggested. "They probably figured since the lot was vacant . . ."

"But the factory building looks dark." I scanned the area

for other signs of life. "And these cars don't look like they belong to any factory workers I know." We'd passed BMWs, a Bentley, and two cars with diplomatic plates. Nick stopped to let a stretch limo pull out of a long parking spot before easing the bakery truck into it. From this vantage point on the side of the restaurant, we could see both the front and back doors.

"Someone else is coming," he said. "Get down."

I scrunched down in the upholstered seat and peeked out the bottom of the window. A couple, arm in arm, climbed the steps of the supposedly deserted restaurant. The pale shaft of light returned, setting the young blond woman's jewelry and short sequined dress glittering. They entered the building and all was dark again.

"They've got blackout or something on the windows and doors," Nick said. "It looks dark and empty, but I bet the whole place is filled with people." He turned to me. "Some hunch you had. Something is going on in that building."

"But what?"

He grabbed the door handle. "You want me to go find out?"

"What?"

"Let me just go to the door. Maybe I can get a peek inside."

"Are you crazy?"

"What?" He pointed to all the cars. "People means safety. The worst thing that could happen is that they don't let me in. But maybe I can get a good enough look to find out why all these people are coming to a deserted restaurant in the middle of the night."

"You think something illegal can be going on in there?" I asked.

"Audrey, it's a deserted building. I doubt they have a valid business license. *Of course* there's something illegal going on in there."

"Then don't go. You could get hurt. Let's just call the police."

"And tell them there are cars parked outside a deserted building? Even if they took me seriously, by the time they got a warrant, anything going on in there would be swept under the carpet. No, let me just check it out. If I can get a gander inside, then we might have something to tell them. If I can get a cell phone picture, better yet."

"But if this building has anything to do with why Derek died . . ." I grabbed on to his wrist. "I'm going with you."

"Then if you're right, and it's dangerous, we'll both be put in harm's way."

"Wait, you can't argue both sides."

He chuckled. "Sorry, captain of my high school debating team. An old habit to break. Tell you what . . . we both want to know what's going on in there, right?"

"Right."

"Then you wait here. I'll call you on my cell phone and put it in my pocket. You'll be able to hear me talk and hear anything I hear. We'll pick an emergency word. If I use that word, you call 911 right away." He tossed me the keys. "And hightail it out of here while you're doing that."

I didn't like it, but I agreed.

"Wait," I said.

"Are we going to argue this again?" His voice carried a note of exasperation.

"No," I said. "Except it looks like a classy party. And you look . . ." I reached over to straighten his collar. Although he'd changed out of his baker's whites, he couldn't be mistaken for couture, just dreamy, and as my hand accidentally brushed up against his stubbly cheek I doubted this friend thing was going to work.

"Do you have a suit coat?" I asked.

"Just a leather jacket." He reached behind my seat to pick it up. "What do you think?"

"That'll have to work," I said.

He dialed my number. We tested the connection, then he climbed out of the truck.

"Nick, wait," I said.

He looked back. "Audrey, it's the best way."

"No, I . . . We need the emergency word."

"Oh, right." He ran a hand through his hair. "How about 'pfeffernüsse'?"

"Pfeffernüsse?"

"It's a cookie. And I won't be saying that by accident." He smiled one of those paralyzing smiles of his, then headed to the restaurant while the *Mission: Impossible* theme played in my head.

I scrunched down in the seat with my cell phone pasted to my ear and watched as he tried the front door. Locked. But moments later, just a slit of light became visible.

"Yes?" A gruff male voice echoed through the cell phone, sending a wave of adrenaline through me. Just what in the world did we think we were doing? A baker and a florist trying to gain access to a possible criminal hot spot? We must have been out of our minds.

"I heard there's some action here tonight," Nick said.

"Sorry. Private party." And then the slit of light disappeared.

I waited until Nick pulled open the door of the truck. "Did you see anything?"

"One eyeball." Nick tossed the leather jacket into the space behind the driver's seat.

A wave of relief flooded me. Something about that not-so-deserted building gave me the willies. We watched as the back door opened and a man stepped outside. His white apron glowed in the moonlight and a small flare, then a smaller glow near his face, showed that he'd stepped out for a smoke.

Minutes later, the glow was extinguished and the man

passed back into the building, leaving a narrow band of light around the outside of the door betraying the fact that it was ajar.

"Bingo." Nick opened the truck door again.

"Where are you going?"

"They said they're having a party. Let's make it a party."

"What are you talking about?" I climbed out of my seat and followed him to the back of the truck, where he raised the hatch.

"Get in here, out of sight." He pulled me up into the mini kitchen that was the back of his truck and closed the hatch before flipping on a light. He wrapped himself in an apron, shoved a couple of food service gloves into a pocket, then put on a cheesy baker's hat, one of those paper ones that look like the hats Liv and I once folded using pages of the *Ramble On.*

"What are you doing?"

"What's a party without cake?"

He pulled a sheet cake out of the stainless steel racks in the back of the truck and hoisted it onto the counter.

"You're taking them a cake? Like that's going to get you in there."

"Ah, my dear." He pulled out a pastry bag and wafted it under my nose. "Never doubt the power of cake. I just need to change it up a bit."

I watched as he artfully pulled icing from the top of the cake. "Happy 50th Anniversary!" became "Happy Birthday!"

"What if it's not anybody's birthday?" I asked.

"In a group of any size, it's always somebody's birthday. Or near a birthday, anyways. If I'm not out in fifteen minutes, dial 911." He turned off the lights, tugged open the hatch, and headed toward the back door of the old restaurant.

As my eyes readjusted to the darkness, I slipped out of

the back of the truck and felt my way to the cab. As I checked my phone for the time, I realized that he hadn't called me like he had earlier. I wouldn't be able to hear what was happening.

I hazarded a glance around the back of the truck, but he was gone.

Chapter 19

✧

Time refused to budge. Seconds became minutes, and minutes seemed like hours, sitting in the darkened truck, 911 already keyed into my phone, thumb hovering over the send button. After ten minutes, I dialed. Liv, that is.

I explained what Nick had done and that I was supposed to call emergency if he wasn't out in the next . . . four minutes and thirty-nine seconds. How could it have taken only twenty-one seconds to tell the whole story?

"Calm down," Liv said. "You're talking a mile a minute. Nick's a big boy, and I'm sure he'll be fine."

"How can you be so sure? Something's going on in there, and he's right in the middle of it, and it's all my fault." My brain painted images of illegal activity ranging from political conspiracy to cockfighting to unlicensed puppy mills. At that point, two couples exited the front door, talking and laughing. I scrunched down again, wishing I had binoculars. Maybe I could spot one of those designer pooches stashed in the designer bag of one of those ladies leaving. Or a stray chicken feather on a lapel.

"You didn't make him go in there," Liv said.

"No, but I dragged him all the way out here in the first place for no good reason."

"Because you were curious. And you're trying to help Jenny and figure out what happened to Derek. Those are good things. And it sounds like Nick just wants to help you do that. And how could you say it was for no good reason if you discovered something going on in a deserted building? I'd just go with it."

I stared down at the phone. This from the woman who has a conniption every time we spot a mouse in the back of the shop?

I checked the time again. Four minutes and ten seconds.

"Besides," Liv said as I put the phone back up to my ear, "would you hurt anyone who brought you cake?"

"Probably not, I—"

A knock on the truck door caused me to juggle the phone. Through the window I could only see the torso of a large man dressed in black. He stood just outside the door. I crammed the phone, call still active, into my pocket and rolled down the window, just a crack. "Yes?" I said, my voice trembling.

"You need to grab the other cake and come with me."

"The other . . . ?"

"Cake," he said. "They ran short. The boss sent me to get you. Said something about there being an extra one out here."

I glanced at the keys dangling in the ignition and considered booking it out of there. But I couldn't leave Nick alone to face any danger I'd put him in.

"All right." I pulled the keys from the ignition and walked around to the back, trying to look out of the corner of my eyes to see if he held a blunt weapon—or a not-so-blunt weapon—not that he'd need it. This guy was built like Lurch. I tugged open the hatch, flipped on the lights, and found the remaining cake. I couldn't take the writing off like I'd seen Nick do. "It says Happy Anniversary, I'm afraid."

He shrugged. "They already saw the other one. Real pretty. The boss just wanted more to cut so everybody gets some. Good thing you had extra, huh?" He smiled at me, showing a mouthful of crooked, yellowed teeth, and I could see him eye me up and down. Was he trying to figure out if I looked like a baker? Or did he have something else on his mind? The thought made me shudder.

I found another paper hat, flicked it open on two tries, and shoved it on my head, then wrapped a spare apron around me. Might as well look the part.

The hulk held the cake while I jumped down from the truck. I wished he'd done the genteel thing and carried it to the building. That sheet cake was heavy. Kind of like a large urn full of water, except flat and more awkward to carry, especially if I didn't want to end up wearing it. No wonder Nick preferred cupcakes.

Liv had grown quiet. I hoped that she'd stay that way and that the call hadn't disconnected when I shoved the phone into my pocket. There would be a witness, at least, if anything happened to me.

Lurch held open the back door. After a blind hallway, we passed through a small room. Diners sat at elaborately set, candlelit tables. A secret five-star restaurant? What in the world? I couldn't think of any reason why someone would run a clandestine restaurant, unless they were serving food the health inspectors wouldn't approve of—like puffer fish. I tried to focus on a nearby plate, but it held only a familiar-looking piece of cake.

Unless illegal spirits was their game. A bartender poured drinks behind a gleaming wood counter set up in the corner. Operating without a liquor license? Avoiding the taxes involved? Music played, and couples on a small dance floor swayed to Rat Pack music.

Lurch sped ahead to a door and opened it, ushering me into a more well-lit area filled with stainless steel. Welcome to the kitchen. Plates of food sat under warmers. White-clad kitchen staff hustled over grills, pans, and pots, cooking and plating food. Scrumptious odors wafted around—garlic, steak, the yeasty smell of warm bread—making me hungry, despite the fear and the recent barbecue meal. What can I say? I'm a stress eater.

Lurch stopped at a blind corner and ushered me on. "The boss is around here."

I prayed every prayer I knew, then headed around the corner, wondering whether "the boss" would resemble Al Capone. Only to see the back of Nick Maxwell. "You?" I managed.

He was the boss? I was in deep trouble.

He turned around, seemingly in slow motion, a knife in his hand gleaming against the harsh fluorescent lights.

The room started to spin. Nick and Lurch came at me at once. I tried to jump back but found myself up against a cold, bare, and unfortunately solid wall.

"What is wrong with you?" Lurch said. "You almost dropped the cake."

It took a moment to realize that no knife pressed up against my flesh; rather, both men had an arm on me, an arm on the cake, and concerned expressions on their faces.

"Are you okay?" Nick said. "You're awfully pale."

I caught my balance. "I'm fine." The wall helped hold me up. Maybe solid was not such a bad characteristic after all.

Nick took the cake in both hands. "I got it," he said. He slid it onto the stainless steel counter behind him, next to the ravaged remains of the other cake and a stack of empty plates.

Lurch grabbed a tray of cut cake and rounded the corner.

"What in the world?" I watched as Nick plunged the knife into the new cake.

"Just trying to buy more time," he said. "This is why I like cupcakes. So much easier to serve. But I wanted to stop you before you called 911. I still haven't figured out all that's going on here."

"It looks like a restaurant. A nice one, at that."

"It looks the same as it did when it was open years ago. Except for the blacked-over windows and the guard at the front door." He slid a piece of cake onto a plate. "And the early bird special was to die for."

"Not a good choice of words," I said.

"Sorry," he whispered, then he paused as a server came and whisked away another tray of cake. "Once the cake is cut, we might be able to get a better look around the place."

"I hope you saw more than I did," I said.

"After they let me in, I was escorted to a couple of dining areas until they found someone with a birthday." He smirked. "Some woman threw her arms around her husband, and I knew I was golden. Everyone likes to think someone is sending them a cake. After that fuss, the guy didn't even try to deny he'd sent it. I should get his name and bill him."

He fell silent when Lurch returned with an empty tray and grabbed a full one.

I started setting clean plates on the new tray.

"Thanks." Nick shoveled cake onto the first plate. Then he lowered his voice again. "All I saw on this floor was people eating and drinking. Illegal to do without the proper licenses, and not lucrative unless you're advertising. This place looks deserted, yet it's filled with customers, so something is drawing them here. There's another floor they used for wedding receptions and such. I saw people on the stairs, but I haven't been able to get up there." He paused while the other server dropped off a tray and whisked away a full one.

"So whatever they're trying to hide is going on up there," I said. "What's the plan?"

"Can't say I've had time to come up with one," he said. "Maybe you could finish up cutting while I try to sneak up there. There's another staircase at the back of the kitchen. If they come back you can cover for me. Tell them I went looking for the men's room or something."

I grabbed his wrist. "I don't like it. For one thing, I don't like the way Lurch has been eyeing me. And what if they catch you sneaking around?"

"You have another plan?"

"How about we finish cutting this cake and sneak up together? Maybe they'll assume we just left."

"And if we get caught?"

"Then we think of something."

Lurch came back for another tray. He eyed the remaining cake. "I think we're going to come out about even, maybe a little left over."

"Make sure the staff all get a piece," Nick said.

Lurch gave him a yellow-toothed smile. "Sure will. Thanks!" I'd have sworn he skipped off. But the floor didn't shake, so it must have been my imagination.

"See, what did I tell you?" He slid the last piece onto a plate. "Here's our chance. Ready?"

He pulled off his gloves and led me around the blind corner. Two members of the kitchen staff looked up. "There's extra cake here. I *hope* there's enough to go around. Help yourself," he said.

The two cooks scurried to claim their cake. Nick grabbed my hand and led me to a staircase, probably the way they'd once carried food up to the wedding receptions upstairs. Now the staircase didn't seem like it got much use, as I surmised based upon the dust and spiderwebs. Shoddy way to do business. Then again, this place didn't get regular health inspections, either.

The staircase opened up to a dim area with stainless steel shelves lining the wall. I imagined waiters once used them to queue the plates to carry them to reception guests.

Doors were closed to the room beyond, but the windows leading into it weren't blacked out like those leading to the outside. Nick and I crept to the doors, each of us claiming a window to peek into, when a loud alarm sounded and the lights began to flash.

Chapter 20

I jumped back *almost* just in time. The doors swung open and mine smacked me in the shoulder. Better than the nose, I guess, which was where the door would have hit had I not seen the mass exodus headed toward us.

But I grabbed hold of the door to give me a little cover as people streamed out of the room and down the dusty staircase. No one seemed to look beyond the glass to notice me, but in the short gaps between the well-dressed people filing out of the building, I could see Nick's face pressed against the tiny glass window of the opposite door, like looking out of a porthole of a cruise ship and seeing someone stare at you from the porthole of an adjacent ship. Except there was no water, no sun, and no buffet. I didn't even get cake.

When the stream of people dried up and the landing was empty, Nick let his door swing shut. I followed suit but remained pressed up against the wall, afraid to move. Nick returned to the window and peered into the room. He waved me back to the door.

A few people remained in the banquet room. Or I should say "casino." And the casino parts were disappearing fast, as black-clad workers flipped tabletops and rolled large items through a door. Only it wasn't a door, because when they swung it shut, it disappeared completely into the moldings of the wall.

I looked up at Nick and could see the tightness of his jaw. Then I remembered the story about his uncle's gambling. He pointed to the stairs and mouthed, "Let's get out of here."

I followed Nick. As we crept down the steps, I turned every few seconds to glance behind me.

He paused on a bend in the staircase and put a finger to his lips. Voices ascended the stairs. I strained to hear what they were saying, and I hoped it wasn't "Find that baker and his assistant in the doofy paper hats and kill them."

". . . police won't be searching the place tonight," an authoritative voice said. "Getting a warrant takes time. The party line is that you're doing some work for the owners, checking if the property is still viable as a restaurant. Depending on who answers the call, that may not be an issue anyway."

A muffled question was followed by the first speaker. "No, the key thing is not to panic. The minimum of people should be visible at the door, which is where I hope to hold them. Should that not work, just go about your business as if you have a right to be here. You want everything you do to show that you belong here, not that you're afraid or hiding. Be polite, but not overly friendly. If questioned, you know what the answers are supposed to be. Stick to them. Don't volunteer anything. Got it?"

The voices grew quiet and more distant, replaced instead by the clinking of dishware.

Nick craned his neck around the corner, then leaned back to report. "It looks like they're doing dishes now," he whispered. "I don't think we're going to be able to get out through the kitchen."

"The other stairs?" I asked.

He considered this for a moment, then led the way as we crept back up the stairs. We surveyed the area through the porthole windows again. The upper banquet room now looked like nothing but an empty reception space. He pushed open one of the doors and stuck his head in. I followed him inside. I could make out the staircase at the other end of the large room. We were halfway across, standing under the large chandelier, when the lights went out.

"Lovely," he said.

Then his hand—warm and admittedly a little sweaty—closed on mine. We inched our way through the rest of the banquet room toward the little bit of light that showed from the staircase. His foot creaked on the first step of what turned out to be an elegant curved staircase with an oak banister. We paused and waited in the dim light. I think I'd already stopped breathing five minutes earlier, so I concentrated on that, breathing in and out as rhythmically and quietly as possible.

"You okay?" he asked in a whisper, his grip on my hand tightening.

I sent him an artificial smile, and we took the next few steps without incident. The front door came into view. We froze for a moment when an apron-clad server ran past with more dishes, but she never looked in our direction. As soon as she exited the room, Nick said, "Go!" and we ran the rest of the way down the stairs. He pulled open the door and I ran out—right into the chest of a uniformed police officer.

"So, is there a problem here or not?" The officer looked back and forth from me to the "authoritative voice" we'd overheard prepping his crew for the police. The voice was now connected to a body and answered to the name of Cecil.

"I don't understand why you're here," Cecil said smoothly. "I can't imagine what would have alarmed anyone to call the police."

"I got a call that a woman named Audrey was in trouble here." He turned to me. "And you're Audrey. Are you in trouble?"

I certainly hoped not. "I didn't call the police."

"I know," the officer said. "The call came from someone named Olivia Rose. Do you know an Olivia?"

"She's my . . ." My voice cracked. "She's my cousin."

The cop rolled his eyes. "Yeah, now everything makes sense." He turned back to Cecil. "So what are you and your people doing here?"

"Well, Officer, the owners asked me to check out the property, to make sure all the kitchen equipment was in working order. And what better way to do that than cook a meal?"

"That makes sense," the cop said.

Although now Nick rolled his eyes. I jabbed him with my elbow as a warning. I wasn't sure if he understood the significance of what Cecil said earlier, about their claim not mattering *depending on who answered the call*. To me it suggested that certain cops, maybe this one, might be connected to the gambling operation somehow.

And here Liv thought I was being overly dramatic to suggest blackmail as a motive. Instead we'd stumbled into a gambling den, if they still called them that. Not that this elegant environment suggested anything dennish. But this qualified as organized crime, at least.

"And what are you doing here?" the cop asked me. I considered telling him we had checked into the property for Eric, Rawling's new property manager, but then thought better of it. I didn't want to jeopardize Eric's new job—which was probably why Liv used her maiden name when she called the police. "We . . . uh . . ." I looked at Nick.

"I used to come here, years ago." Fortunately he seemed to read minds and didn't mention Eric, either. "And I wanted to see what had become of the place."

"I thought you were delivering a cake," Cecil said.

"That, too," Nick said. "But it's why I stayed to take a look around."

"Taking your assistant with you?" the cop asked.

Nick put his arm around my shoulder. "Not my assistant." The words were true, but the gestures and the tone of voice suggested something different. I blushed at the implication.

"I'd always thought," he went on, "that the upstairs reception area would be the perfect spot for a wedding reception. Isn't that right, dear?"

I nodded numbly.

Nick turned to Cecil. "It's good news for us, then, if they're thinking of reopening the place."

Cecil cleared his throat. "That hasn't been decided yet."

"So we're good here?" the officer asked.

Cecil sent him an ingratiating smile. "Of course, Officer."

The cop turned to me with raised eyebrows.

"Fine," I managed. "My cousin just gets a little overdramatic at times, I guess." And as soon as the words were out of my mouth, I wondered if my phone was still connected and Liv had heard that. I winced.

"Then I'll be off," the officer said. "Make sure you lock up tight. We don't want vagrants making homes in these empty buildings."

Cecil agreed as he held open the door, then closed it after the officer strode out.

I took a step for the exit.

"Just a minute," Cecil stood, arms crossed, in front of the door, blocking it. "Thanks for playing it cool, but I want to know what you're after. If you came to see the reception area, I know you got an eyeful."

"We know about the gambling, if that's what you mean," I said.

"Don't think you're going to profit on that knowledge."

Nick took a step forward, so much tension in his jaw he was in danger of snapping a tooth or two. "Is that right?"

Cecil raised a hand. Lurch stepped closer, a splotch of frosting still decorating his lapel.

"We wouldn't . . ." I cleared my throat and started over. "We wouldn't dream of it."

"No," Nick said. "But it's getting late, and the lady and I should be going."

Cecil looked him up and down, then gave me a passing glance, before a half smile crept up his oily face. "But of course." He stepped out of the way.

Nick grabbed the handle. We were almost free. But was there more to learn here? Something to help Jenny? I suspected the opportunity wouldn't arise again, since I'd have wagered that every bit of gambling equipment in that building would be gone before the sun rose. And maybe Cecil would trust us, since we hadn't spilled everything we'd seen to the cops. At least, hopefully, he wouldn't hurt us.

"Oh," I said to Cecil, "my condolences on your boss's son." It was a hunch, but I wanted to see how it played out.

The corner of his mouth twitched. "Thank you," he said. "You knew Derek, then?"

Bingo. "Did he come here often?" Yes, I'd connected the dots. Derek's gambling. An illegal club belonging to his father.

"More than the old man wanted," Cecil said.

"Any idea who might have wanted him dead?"

Cecil shrugged. "He was no more than a nuisance to me. Now I don't need to chase him out anymore. His father didn't like him hanging around the place."

"Or having to pay his debts," I added.

Cecil smiled, "That, too. I can't imagine Rawling is all that choked up about it, but you didn't hear that from me. He used to get in Derek's face all the time. 'Gambling,'" he said, imitating Jonathan Rawling's aristocratic accent, "'is for suckers. You only win if you're the house. Be the house, boy.'" Cecil shook his head. "Good advice, but the kid wouldn't heed it. Everything was about the game to Derek. He knew all about the odds, but for some reason he didn't think they applied to him. That redhead must be devastated, though."

"Redhead?" I asked.

"Yeah, slinky dresser, always hanging all over him. What was her name?" Cecil asked.

"Lucy," Lurch suggested.

"Yeah, that's it. She called herself Lucy, and then laughed like her name was funny," Cecil said.

"She been here since Derek's death?" I asked.

Cecil shook his head. "Strictly with Derek."

And now that Derek was dead, where did that leave Lucy?

Nick was silent on the way home. Whenever I got a glimpse of him in the headlights of oncoming traffic, he had that same tight-jawed look about him. Stewing in his own juices, Grandma Mae would have called it. The thought of stew just made my stomach rumble.

"Is there any cake left?" I asked.

"Nope." Then he grew quiet again.

We drove past a cluster of fast-food restaurants just off the highway. I thought of asking him to stop but decided that wasn't a good idea given his current mood.

So, we'd found the place where Derek gambled and lost all that money that he'd skimmed from the properties he'd managed. And since his father owned the place, all the money went back into the family coffers anyway. So old man Rawling wouldn't have had a motive to kill his son, except to spare himself the embarrassment of having a son who gambled and lost.

The idea that Derek could have blackmailed his father sprang to mind. Could he have threatened to expose his father's whole illegal operation if, say, he wasn't allowed credit or access to the games?

Or maybe Cecil had just tired of having the boss's kid around, having to kowtow to him and cover up for him. Didn't professional hit men go for the carotid? I remembered something like that from an episode of *NCIS*. Either Rawling or Cecil could have hired someone to do the deed.

And then there was the mysterious Lucy. Could Lucy be the same woman who'd written the letters found in Derek's closet? The ones signed "Bunny"? And if not, where did she fit into all of this?

And then add half the town of Ramble who were being swindled by Derek. Even Nick, sitting silently next to me, had motive. Could he be pretending to be helpful, leading me out of town to divert suspicion from someone closer to home?

And I had a sinking pit in my stomach over Larry's sudden secrecy. What was he hiding in that greenhouse?

Pastor Seymour's words rang in my ears. *She could have been stuck with that man for life.* Did someone kill Derek to protect Jenny? Maybe Mrs. Whitney saw through him and decided to put an end to Derek before he ruined Jenny's life. And since Ellen didn't know the wedding had been canceled . . .

As we pulled into Ramble, the town took on a sinister appearance. Rather than the friendly hamlet I saw every day, I now saw a town with a secret. Shadows loomed in every corner, and Derek's blood still cried from the deserted streets.

Nick pulled into the alley behind the florist shop.

"Do you still want those flowers?" I hopped out and stretched my back.

"Flowers?"

I forced a smile. "You came to buy flowers earlier."

Nick shook his head. "No, it's okay. It's late. I'll . . . Good night." And he drove off.

My gaze followed the vapor trail the truck left behind, then a chill ran up my spine as a mouse scurried across the alley in front of me.

As the noise of the diesel engine faded away, I started walking toward the apartment. I should have asked Nick to drop me at home, but he seemed too distracted. Now I was paying for it. Every noise, every gust of breeze that stirred the surroundings had me doing a double take. I had made this two-block walk before, in all kinds of weather, at all hours of the day and night, and it had never been so terrifying. I didn't think I had any adrenaline left after our encounter in the gambling den, but my body proved me wrong as my heart and head pounded out of control.

I rounded the corner, glad to see the light streaming from the porch—of my neighbor's apartment at least. I half ran the remaining distance to my door, keys in hand. Movement at my living room window drew my attention as my curtains flicked ever so slightly. A gray paw seemed to be the source of the momentum. I let out the breath I'd been holding.

I turned my key in the lock and swung open the door of my darkened apartment. Flipping on the overhead light, I surveyed . . . pure devastation. Magazines had been splayed over the floor and a lamp dangled from the end table, supported by only its cord.

I rounded the corner into the kitchen. Two chairs lay on their sides, as did the kitchen garbage can. Plastic storage bowls were strewn across the floor, and a shredded streamer of paper towels weaved around everything.

Either someone was trying to send me a message or I owned a cat.

"Chester!" He trotted from the bedroom, sweet as can be, and circled my legs. I hoisted him up and stroked his gray furry head. He began to purr and dug his claws into my shoulder.

"What am I going to do with you?"

Feed me, he seemed to say as he jumped out of my arms and trotted over to his food dish.

"All right, buddy." I opened a can of cat food and slid it across the floor with little ceremony. Tonight he'd have to eat out of the can and like it. And judging from the way he buried his head in the can, I think he liked it.

While he chowed down, I poured cereal and milk into a bowl and wandered back into the living room. I picked up a small stack of bridal magazines and righted the lamp before plopping down on the sofa.

Normally while I thumbed through a bridal magazine my eyes were drawn to the flowers. But tonight, not so much. I saw a picture of a bridal couple dancing at their wedding and thought back to the reception-area-turned-casino. I spied a cupcake tower and thought of a certain baker, holding a knife . . . then minutes later grasping my hand as we tried to find a way out of the old restaurant. I saw a picture of a jukebox for rent, similar to the one Carolyn had rented, and thought back to the unfortunate jitterbug almost forgotten in the excitement of the evening.

There were just too many loose pieces to this puzzle. It wasn't like a bouquet with a missing flower. It was more like a vase with too many mismatched blooms just shoved together. Maybe the key wasn't looking for more clues but trying to pull out the ones that didn't fit.

I slammed the magazine shut, pulled my knees to my chest, and moped for a good thirty seconds before Chester hopped up on the couch and climbed my knees, trying to force a lap for sitting. Instead, I lay back on the couch and he sprawled on my belly. I drifted into an exhausted but troubled sleep amid thoughts of marriage and murder, flowers and felonies, and cake and catastrophe.

Chapter 21

"No, I think poinsettia bracts are fine for a Christmas bridal bouquet," I said to a clearly relieved bride. "Most people say the meaning has to do with *celebration* or *Christmas cheer*. What would you think of pairing that with a white rose? Or a white poinsettia with a red rose?"

"Ooh," she said, as I flipped to a page in my holiday bridal book. I explained the differences in meanings between pine (*hope* or *pity*) and ivy (*friendship* or *fidelity*) as possible greenery. And I told her no, I didn't think pine-cones had a negative meaning, and yes, we could wire a few into the bouquet.

I tucked her deposit check into my order book and walked her to the door. I barely had a chance to wave good-bye when I heard my name.

"Audrey." Liv pressed her hand over the mouthpiece of the phone. "It's Mrs. June for you. News about Jenny, I think."

"I'll, uh . . ." I looked around the shop. "I'll take it in the back room."

I picked up the receiver. "Hello?"

"Audrey, when can you get free?"

"Why? What's up?"

"Jenny's up, at least for a little while. You can get in for a visit if you go before two."

"Why, what happens at two?"

"Bixby will want to drive over and question her again when he finds out she's speaking in coherent sentences. Can you make it?"

"I'm on my way."

I left by the front door, hopped in the CR-V, sent Nick a wave as I drove past the bakery, then used the GPS to find the county regional jail. I remembered the lively public debate on whether to allocate funds to build the place, but I can't say I ever had reason to visit before. I guessed now I'd see my tax dollars at work.

The facilities looked a lot newer and more secure than the Ramble Police Department. I was buzzed in twice, carded, signed in—and prayed when I saw the sign that elaborated about how visitors could be subjected to various searches.

"You don't have any weapons on you, do you?" a guard asked before I stepped into the scanner.

"Of course not," I said. "I . . ." Yeah, I did have one of the new floral knives in my purse, so I handed her my whole purse. She shoved it into an empty locker in the hallway.

I expected to see a long, dingy white room with a glass divider separating orange-clad prisoners and weeping visitors, chairs set on either side, and phones to speak into. Except for the fact that the walls were painted a vibrant blue, I was not disappointed.

I sat on a fixed round stool opposite Jenny, sent her a shaky smile, and picked up the telephone. It felt sticky and I tried not to cringe. Although I'm not normally a germaphobe, I longed for one of those little moistened towelettes from the barbecue place, but my purse was hanging in a locker.

I looked at Jenny. Dark circles, reddened eyes, pale skin, matted hair, and a hunted look. She could be an extra for *The Hunger Games.*

"Audrey, thanks for coming. And thanks for the underwear and stuff."

I wished I could have leaned in and given her a hug. "You're welcome." Even under the orange jumpsuit, I could see she wasn't the plump healthy thing I remembered, but skeletal. And no, I wasn't envious of her new shape, any more than you could be envious of the emaciated kids shown on those world aid commercials. I tried to recall if she'd lost much weight from the time—was it about a week ago when she arrived at the shop to order wedding flowers?

"How are you holding up?" I asked.

She nodded and pushed a strand of dirty brown hair behind her ear.

"I don't know that I can stay long." I felt guilty that I couldn't just spend the afternoon sitting with her, like you do when you go to a wake and words just don't come, and wouldn't make any difference if they could. "About Derek . . ."

My words opened the fountain, and tears started streaming. "I didn't kill him."

"Shh . . ." I leaned toward the glass. "I didn't say you did. I *know* you. I know you wouldn't kill Derek."

"I still can't believe he's dead." She rocked forward and raked her hair with her hand. "It's like this terrible nightmare, and if I could only wake up, everything would be okay. Why can't I wake up, Audrey? Help me wake up."

I let her cry into the phone for a few moments. I leaned my head back and stared at the dirty fluorescent panels in the cold white ceiling. I felt so powerless.

"Jenny, listen to me. I know it's bad. I wish I could make it all go away for you, but I can't. I do want to help, though.

Can you tell me what happened that night? Everything, from when I saw you pulling away with Derek."

She took a deep, shuddering breath. "I . . . When I got into the car, Derek asked me where I wanted to go eat. I told him I was a little tired and asked him if he wouldn't mind eating in. See, I wanted to break up, but I didn't want to just blurt it out in the car or in a restaurant. I figured I owed him a little more than that.

"I cooked him dinner—just pasta and a salad, but the good stuff, you know what I mean."

I did. Jenny had inherited her mother's Italian cooking skills.

"Then we went into the living room and sat on the couch. I almost chickened out. He has such lovely pale blue eyes, like some kind of gemstone." She frowned and shook her head. "Had."

I hoped the compassion I felt was evident in my eyes. I wanted that fixed glass wall to melt away, so I could hug her and rock her and tell her everything would be okay.

She stared at her hands. "Everything came out sounding a little stiff and formal, but I said, 'Derek, I like you very much, and I hoped, in time, my feelings would develop into love. But I'm afraid they haven't, and I don't think I can marry you.'"

"And what did he say?" I remembered Bixby's theory that the breakup triggered a fight and that she killed him in self-defense.

"He didn't say anything. This odd look crossed his face. At the time I couldn't identify it, but that look keeps coming back to me—it's probably how I'll always remember Derek." She lifted her gaze to meet mine. "It was relief, I'm sure of it. I don't think he wanted to marry me any more than I wanted to marry him.

"He just squeezed my hand, then he gave me a hug."

"Then what?" I asked.

She shrugged. "Nothing. Sarah came home." Jenny laughed hollowly. "I felt almost embarrassed to be hugging him on the couch. While she took a shower, Derek and I talked. I gave him back his ring. He hugged me again at the door. We parted as friends."

She bit her lip. "Nobody seems to believe that, though."

"I believe you," I said. "And I'll do my best to try to get you out of here."

"To what, Audrey? My roommate won't talk to me. My own mother is too busy to come see me."

"Not too busy," I said. "I know she's taking it hard."

"Then why won't she . . . ?"

I must be easy to read, because one look into my eyes and Jenny knew. Or maybe she just knew her mother.

"Audrey, you have to help her. If she's drinking again . . . You've no idea how much it took to get her off that stuff in the first place." She leaned back and pleaded to the god in the ceiling. "What have I done to her?"

"You didn't do anything. But I want you to help me. Focus. What happened to the bag of tools I gave you? And the bouquet. Can you tell me?"

But Jenny's expression clouded over with grief. No wonder Bixby was so convinced she'd killed Derek. She was a poster child for guilt. "Tell me."

"We stopped for groceries," she said. "The pasta and tomatoes and a bunch of other things I needed. I thought I grabbed everything out of the car. I put the bouquet in a bag, too," she confessed. "I know it probably wasn't the best way to keep it looking nice, but we both had our hands full. I don't *think* I left it in the car, but I don't remember seeing it the next morning. I can't see why it's so important."

I met her eyes. "Trust me."

She quirked her head, as if trying to see through the haze. "I half remember Derek running a glass of tap water and saying something about flowers, only I was so busy cooking.

And so tired. And so worried about how he'd react. And it's all one jumbled mess now. Maybe we did leave some of the bags in the car."

She furrowed her brows. "I half remember Bixby asking me about the flowers and tools, too. Audrey, why are they important?"

"You don't know?"

She squinted at me, a pained look that suggested she needed to know but didn't want to. I'm sure it was the same look I had on my face whenever I stepped on the scale. Why didn't she have a lawyer here going over the case with her, telling her what to say and what not to say?

I swallowed. "Derek was stabbed with a knife—a florist knife, possibly the one I sent home with you. The blade severed his carotid artery."

Jenny's hand flew to her heart.

Not her neck, her *heart*.

"Jenny, do you know where the carotid artery is?"

"The heart, right?"

I couldn't help a small smile. That one action confirmed my faith in Jenny's innocence. Someone had sliced into Derek's carotid artery with surgical precision. And while, yes, all arteries originate at the heart, Jenny's reaction proved she had no idea where Derek had been struck.

But how could I help get her out of prison—both the prison of her guilt and the literal bars? And why had she been so unresponsive when first arrested?

"Jenny, something else. I want you to know I trust you and I care, but I must ask this. Have you been taking drugs?"

Jenny's jaw dropped, but it took several moments for any speech to follow. "Of course not! Audrey, you know what I think about that stuff."

"I know, but I'm not talking about just illegal drugs. Anything prescribed or even over-the-counter?"

"No, I . . ."

When she trailed off, I knew there was something.

"With all the stress of the wedding, I'd been having trouble sleeping. I took a sleeping pill that night, after the breakup, and almost every night for a few weeks before that. I remember thinking that when the wedding plans were over, maybe I'd be able to get back to sleeping without it."

"What kind of sleeping pill?" My stomach did acrobatics. When I was still in nursing school, we'd read case studies of certain prescription sleep meds that had gained notoriety by causing a small number of patients to sleepwalk, strolling around, eating, sometimes even driving while asleep. The class had laughed uproariously over the account of one man who disrobed and went to work—as a roofer.

Could Jenny have murdered Derek while asleep? I shuddered. People have been absolved of crimes committed when it could be proven they were asleep, but proving it would be difficult.

"What pills, Jenny?"

Jenny shrugged. "I don't remember the name. I have more of them, though. In my room." Her countenance brightened. "I was out like a light. Do you think that could clear me?"

I didn't answer her question. No need to give her more to worry about or make her wonder if she could have killed Derek in her sleep. Bixby had searched the room, though, and no medications were found, at least according to the inventory that Mrs. June had shared. But in the event he'd missed it . . . "Where in your room?"

She blushed. "You know that stuffed Pippa the Penguin you bought me?"

"You kept it?" I had bought it for her one Christmas after I learned of her passion for penguins. I swear that bird haunted me.

"Of course," she said. "It had a little pouch for the official Pippa the Penguin pedometer. I put the pills inside so they'd be handy if I woke up in the middle of the night."

Yeah, the perfect place to keep your meds. In a stuffed animal. It made Jenny-sense.

"You can go get them. Just tell Sarah I gave you permission."

I spent the next few minutes trying to encourage her to eat, sleep, and not to worry.

I only wished I could do the same.

"That report of the apartment search is here somewhere," Mrs. June said, as I leaned on the corner of her desk keeping a lookout while she paged through files she had been recruited to make copies of.

I had driven back to the Ramble Police Station right after my visit with Jenny.

She licked her fingers and thumbed through a few more pages. "Here it is. No, there's no record of a diamond engagement ring."

"You said there's no record of any pills, either. Was there a stuffed penguin? Did Bixby place it in evidence?"

"What is it with you and that penguin?" Mrs. June said.

"You saw that photo, didn't you?"

"In all its flippertastic glory," she said. "You're not involved with that mortician fellow, are you?"

"Little Joe? No, he's just a friend."

"Good. I'd hate to see one of you girls taking up with such a morbid fellow. Your grandmother would have had a fit. Although he always seemed to have a soft spot for Jenny."

"Little Joe and Jenny? I never saw any interest there." And I might have appreciated it at the time, when Little Joe was following me around like a puppy dog.

"For a while, but not until after she lost the weight."

Right about the time she bade me farewell.

"Not that she gave him the time of day," Mrs. June added, "after Derek started coming to call."

Which gave my former dance partner a hint of a motive, if he'd been spurned by Jenny and supplanted by Derek. He had the strength. And as a mortician, he'd be well acquainted with the carotid artery. When we talked at Derek's viewing, he was rather enthused by spatter patterns.

But I couldn't see Derek allowing Little Joe into that expensive car of his and risking getting formaldehyde stink in his leather seat cushions.

Mrs. June had been scanning the report as she talked. She shook her head. "No record of any penguin in the report." She flipped through a series of photographs. "But"—she slapped one photograph down on the desk and pointed to a spot on the bed—"I think that might be your little feathered friend right there."

I leaned over to take a closer look. There was Pippa, lounging on Jenny's unmade bed.

Our conversation broke up as Bixby walked in. He gave the flower arrangement I'd set on Mrs. June's desk a wide berth, almost hugging the walls as he made his way to his office, then shut the door.

Mrs. June winked at me. "Thanks for the flowers, Audrey."

"I might just stop by and bring you some more often. They brighten this place up."

Mrs. June's words echoed in my head as I drove over to Jenny's apartment. If Grandma Mae would have had a fit if one of her granddaughters took up with a mortician, I wondered what she would think of me walking around Ramble pretending to be some kind of detective. I hoped she'd understand I was trying to help a friend. Grandma Mae was all about helping people.

I eyed the flowerpot critters on Jenny's front porch and wondered if Sarah had replaced the key. But I was not to find out, because she yanked open the door at my first knock.

"Oh, Audrey."

"Hey, Sarah. I just visited Jenny."

Sarah stared at me from the crack in the door and shrugged.

"And she wanted me to pick up something from her room."

Sarah just shook her head. "Even if I wanted to let you into my apartment, which I don't, Jenny's mom came and picked up all her stuff today."

"Today? That's quick." I was surprised Ellen had been sober enough. "I wonder why the hurry."

"I asked her to. If you must know, I'm looking for a new roommate. Jenny sure isn't going to pay her share of the rent in jail with no job—not that I feel comfortable with her anymore. And her mother had no interest in paying, either. I mean, I'm not sure I could quite afford the rent for this place by myself, even with what I make at the health club and from my private clients." She eyed me up and down. "You wouldn't be interested in a personal trainer, would you? Or an apartment?"

I let the offer of a private trainer pass without a thought. If I wanted someone to torture me, I'm sure I could find a wacko to do it without expecting to be paid. But I considered the apartment for a moment. A roommate would help me save money faster, and maybe some of Sarah's healthier habits would rub off on me.

But I couldn't imagine taking Jenny's apartment or living with someone so cold as to move her roommate out just because she'd spent a few days in jail.

Then I caught myself. Lots of people wouldn't be comfortable sharing an apartment with someone accused of such a violent crime.

"I'm afraid not," I said.

"If you know of anybody, let me know." The door shut in my face.

I checked the time on my cell phone. Ellen wouldn't be

home yet, so I went back to the shop and filled in Liv and Amber Lee on my visit with Jenny and my shorter visit with Sarah.

"That poor girl," Amber Lee said.

"Which one?" I asked. "Jenny or Sarah?"

"Both, really," Amber Lee said. "It would be terrible for Jenny if she found out she did kill Derek, even if she did it in her sleep. Can you imagine the guilt?"

The thought caught in my throat. Hypothetically, I didn't think people should be held responsible if they weren't conscious. Although, if something similar happened to me, I'd hold myself responsible. A double standard, I'm sure.

"I don't know Sarah well," Liv said.

"I don't think anybody does," Amber Lee said. "She moved here when they opened the health club. I mean, she has friends, but no close ones. No boyfriend."

"But she's a very pretty girl," I said.

"Pretty is as pretty does," Liv reminded me, repeating one of Grandma Mae's old axioms.

"What does that even mean?" I asked.

"It means personality does count," Amber Lee said.

"Fat lot of good it did Jenny," I said.

"Hey." Liv came up behind me and put an arm around my shoulder. "That didn't sound like it was about Jenny or Sarah. The pretty girls get picked for the cheerleading squad and get the hunkiest dates to the prom. That's high school. But we're adults now. Being in a relationship isn't an achievement earned by being pretty—and if guys choose their mate that way, they get what they deserve. A miracle happens when two people suited to each other—maybe even made for each other—meet, let down their guards, and then commit to a relationship. And that can happen to the homeliest person alive and can elude even the most beautiful of women. It's a mystery."

I did mention Liv was an idealist.

Amber Lee seemed to take her side. "And Sarah is a pretty girl, but she'll always be the bridesmaid and never the bride until she learns to be kind. Shoving Jenny out of the apartment isn't kind. And good guys will see through that."

"Just as the right man will appreciate you for who you are," Liv said.

"I thought that was where I was getting with Brad," I said.

Liv stroked her chin thoughtfully. "Brad appreciated you, and I think you were well suited. But he obviously just wanted something different."

"Who?"

She shook her head. "Who says it's a who? I think he just wanted out of Ramble. Small-town life isn't for everybody. I mean, lots of people grow up in small towns and just want to shake the dust off their feet and move to the big cities."

"And folk in the big cities," Amber Lee added, "want to leave the rat race and become farmers and vintners. Mark my words. Brad will get his fill of the big city and be back."

"I won't be waiting for him," I added, wondering how we'd gotten so far afield of Jenny and Sarah. I glanced at the clock and put the finishing touches on a small vase arrangement before hanging up my apron and gathering my purse.

"Mind if I head out a little early?" I asked. "Ellen should be home by now, and I want to see her before she . . ."

"Starts drinking?" Liv suggested. "Good idea. Is that for her?"

I looked at the small arrangement of purple anemones. "I knew she liked the flower from the bridal appointment, but I wanted the color to be different enough not to remind her of the bridal flowers."

"It's perfect," Liv said. "Want some company?"

"I can close up," Amber Lee said, obviously enjoying her new status in the shop.

"Sure." I smiled.

I can't say I was still smiling when Ellen opened her door. She'd managed to start her drinking early. She swayed as she took in our appearance, gaze flitting from the flowers to my face to Liv's without ever focusing on anything. But she pushed open the door and let us in without a word.

"Hi, Ellen. How are you feeling today?" Liv said. "We brought you some flowers."

Ellen plopped down on the couch. Good thing. At least we wouldn't have to catch her today. She wore lime green capris with a brown blouse and no shoes. Her nails were pink and her toes natural. In some way, her normal monochromatic look worked for her, at least better than her "untidy drunk" ensemble.

She scowled at the flowers.

I set them on a table near the sofa, and Liv and I slid onto a matching floral love seat without waiting for an invitation.

"I went to see Jenny this morning," I said.

She stared into space for a few moments. "How is she? How's my baby?"

"Doing a little better. But she's confused."

Ellen nodded. She whisked a tissue from a box on the end table, near a pile of used tissues.

"She might appreciate a visit from her mother," I added. "She's worried about you."

"About me?" She searched my eyes. "Why would she be? Oh. You tell her?"

"That you were drinking again? I didn't have to. She figured that out on her own."

"Don't give me that," she said, the belligerent drunk oozing out in her voice. "Always sticking your nose in. How does knowing that help Jenny or me, huh, smarty-pants?"

"It doesn't," Liv started.

"Which is why I didn't tell her," I finished. "But would you rather she believed you're just too busy to go see her?"

She screwed up her face. "Always sticking your nose in."

"Which is why I'm here. She asked me to get something from her room. I went by her apartment, and Sarah said you'd been by to collect her things."

"I thought Princess Sarah had more class than that. Jenny sure can pick friends, can't she?" Ellen rolled her eyes. "Not gone but a few days and she calls me up demanding that I get Jenny's stuff out of there. As if I don't have enough to do. Maybe if I hadn't been doing that all morning, I could've visited Jenny myself."

"That's right," Liv said. "But you can always go tomorrow. Would you like me to go with you?"

Ellen pushed herself up in her seat. "That's right. I couldn't go today because I was moving her junk and cramming it all in her old bedroom. I'll set her straight on all this drinking stuff. Tell her it isn't true. Maybe I had a little—a moment of weakness. But who doesn't?"

"I'm sure she would find it comforting to know that what happened hadn't set you back," Liv said. I'd give her an A in diplomacy.

"She's a good girl, Jenny is," Ellen said with a hiccup. "Isn't she?"

"Of course." I forced a cheerful smile. "She didn't do this thing. I'd like to help her by finding out who did."

"She's a good girl. Wouldn't hurt a fly." And she burst into tears again, bypassing the tissues by throwing herself down and crying directly into a satin throw pillow.

Liv rushed over and rubbed her back. I watched as

wracking sobs became slow, rhythmic breathing. Ellen cried herself to sleep, probably not for the first time in the last few days.

I rose. "Ellen?"

Liv hushed me. "Poor dear," she whispered.

"I'm going to check Jenny's room. Want to join me?"

"Is it all right to do that?" Liv asked, then lowered her voice. "What if Ellen wakes up and catches us?"

"Jenny said I could look through her stuff. Her stuff is here."

"How about if I just tidy up for Ellen a little?"

"Chicken."

Liv then made a squawking noise like no chicken I'd ever heard.

Ellen stirred, rolled over, and began snoring lightly.

"Okay, then just consider me your backup on this mission."

I tiptoed to Jenny's room. Cardboard boxes rose to chest level, leaving only a narrow walkway. Sarah must have laid claim to the furniture. I pulled one of the new shop knives from my purse, glad that Liv was in the other room so she wouldn't see that I'd absconded with it, and slit open the first box.

Clothes. I shuffled through it, making sure there was nothing else packed inside, and found a scarf I'd lent her, years ago. I wrapped it around my neck, then thought better of it. Although it belonged to me, I didn't want to appear like the vultures descending on an estate sale. I hoped Jenny would be out of jail soon, running around town, even if she was wearing my scarf.

I shoved it aside and opened the next box. More of the same. It wasn't until the fourth box that I found some of Jenny's more personal things, mainly knickknacks and photos. I leafed through a small photo album she must have started back when we used to pal around, because my own face graced some of the opening pictures. Then I suddenly disappeared, as did Jenny's waistline. Carolyn and Jenny and Sarah at the health club, Jenny in a funny strongman pose. Then a photo of Jenny and Little Joe dancing. She might have warned me. Although, it looked like their dance was a little more controlled and refined than the jitterbug he treated me to.

A bunch of pictures of Jenny and Sarah followed: paddling in a canoe, bundled in heavy ski suits, dressed as Lucy Ricardo and Ethel Mertz for a Halloween party. I swallowed hard. Jenny's smiling face made it obvious she counted Sarah as a friend. For a split second I thought of it as cosmic payback. Sarah had dumped Jenny just as Jenny had dumped me. But I stifled that thought. I had missed her, but at least I hadn't lost my fiancé, been accused of murder, and gotten thrown into jail.

I continued thumbing through the album. The next pictures focused on a budding relationship: a snapshot of Jenny and Derek double-dating with Carolyn and her fiancé (now new husband)—a dinner at the Ashbury. Jenny's engagement picture. And another shot of Jenny and Derek smiling between Jonathan and Miranda Rawling. It was funny; though they were all smiling, none of them looked exceedingly happy. Or maybe recent events were making me see something not there. I closed the book and kept digging.

At the bottom of the next box I found Pippa the Penguin, splashed with Jenny's strawberry-scented conditioner, the open bottle haphazardly tossed into the box. I found the compartment hidden underneath and pulled out a small plastic bag of pills.

The plastic bag gave me pause. It didn't suggest prescription to me, unless something had happened to the original container. And I didn't recognize the pills. Then again, it had been a long time since I'd taken pharmacology, and new drugs and generic versions of old ones came out all the time. I could look it up online at the shop to double-check.

"Um, Audrey?" Liv's voice startled me. "Someone just pulled in. I think it's Pastor Seymour."

I shoved the plastic bag in my pocket. "Is Ellen awake?"

"Stirring a little."

Right then the doorbell rang.

"Why don't you see about making coffee," I said, "and I'll answer the door."

By the time I returned to the living room, Ellen was trying to fight her way off of the sofa cushions, the imprint of an upholstery button engraved on her cheek.

"Stay where you are. I'll get it," I chimed.

"What are you doing here?" she muttered.

I swung open the door and greeted Pastor Seymour and Shirley, his assistant, with a smile. Out of the corner of my eye, I saw Ellen jerk to attention and shove her liquor bottle under the couch cushion.

"Audrey, my dear." He grasped my hand with his cold, arthritic fingers. "An unexpected pleasure."

I pulled him into a hug, then shook Shirley's hand. Amber Lee had explained that she'd become an invisible fixture with him whenever he made calls, ever since the previous year, when he drove through the local fast-food chicken restaurant—which unfortunately didn't have a drive-through at the time.

"Hey, Pastor," Ellen said, sitting primly on the couch.

"Don't get up, my dear," Pastor Seymour said as Shirley led him to the love seat and settled him with a pillow behind his back. Not that Ellen tried to stand, a wise decision on her part.

"I came to express my condolences at the loss of your daughter's fiancé," he started, "and to see if I could do anything to help. Of course you all are in my prayers."

"Thank you, Pastor," Ellen said. "Thanks for coming."

As I sank into a rocking chair in front of an electric fireplace, I let my hand slide across the lumps that the pills in the plastic bag caused in my pocket. A similar lump formed in my chest, and I wondered if Pastor Seymour's presence might help soften the blow of the theory I was forming, that Jenny might have attacked Derek while asleep. At least if Ellen tried to kill me, I'd have witnesses.

"I'm glad you're here, too," I found myself saying. "I discovered something, and I want to talk with both of you before I go to the chief about it."

"Something to help Jenny?" Ellen said.

I cocked my head and bit my lip before continuing. "It's something I learned from Jenny today, and it has to do with what I found in Jenny's stuffed penguin."

"You were messing with Jenny's stuff?" Ellen said.

I swallowed hard. "Jenny asked me to retrieve something for her, and you were . . . asleep."

Before Ellen could process that, Liv walked in with a tray of coffee. I used the time she spent doling out cream and sugar to collect my thoughts. Best not to sugarcoat things.

Ellen cast me a frightened look, taking her coffee from Liv with trembling hands. Porcelain clinked on porcelain and liquid jostled out of the cup and landed in the saucer. What was the old proverb about words being like water—once you pour them out, you can't take them back?

I wished I didn't have to say them. I declined coffee. It would roil in my stomach. I cleared my throat instead. "I don't know of any other way of saying this, but did Jenny mention to either of you that she'd been taking sleeping pills?"

The pastor shook his head.

As did Ellen, but then she paused. "She did say something a few weeks back about not being able to sleep. I figured it was just prewedding jitters."

"She seemed stressed during the prewedding counseling," Pastor Seymour said. "More than most of my young ladies.

Derek was . . ." He stopped and considered a cobweb in the corner. "A bit . . . dismissive of her concerns."

You'd have to know Pastor Seymour to know those were fighting words.

"So Derek didn't seem to care," I translated.

Pastor Seymour nodded.

"That's crazy," Ellen said. "Of course he cared. Why else would he have proposed?"

"I suspect Derek was under a lot of pressure from his parents to reform, and I'm sure they felt Jenny was a step in that direction." I looked Ellen squarely in the eyes. "Jenny is a wonderful girl, and I'm sure she would never do anything to consciously hurt anyone."

Liv sank onto the couch next to Ellen Whitney. The movement was accompanied by a crunch of broken glass and the smell of alcohol wafting from the cushions. It must have been obvious to everyone, but we did what anybody in polite society would do—we ignored the pink elephant in the room.

Liv took Ellen's hand.

I cleared my throat. Here goes, I thought. "Ellen, has Jenny ever sleepwalked?"

I already knew the answer to this question. Once, she fell asleep on my couch after a late-night movie and gab session. In the middle of the night, I found her up, opening and closing my dresser drawers. I asked her why, and she said she couldn't find her tights for school. But if I had to go to the bathroom, it was okay, she assured me, since she could use the cat's litter box in a pinch.

I'd herded her back to the couch, wondering if I should hide the litter box. In the morning, she had no recollection of the conversation.

"Mostly when she was a girl." A grimace of apprehension darkened Ellen's face.

I exhaled. "Certain sleep medications have been known to aggravate that."

"Are you saying . . . ?" Ellen started.

"Yes, it's possible that Jenny could have been sleepwalking and killed Derek—without even knowing it—and without being criminally responsible. It's rare, but it happens."

"No . . ." Ellen's face went ashen and she raked two clawed hands through her hair. "Take that back."

"I'm not saying I want to believe it. But it would explain everything—the knife with only Jenny's prints on it, the flowers."

Ellen stood up. "My Jenny is not a killer. Not even in her sleep. Get out of my house."

"But I . . ."

"I said leave," Ellen insisted.

"Maybe you'd better, Audrey," Pastor Seymour said, a grim look on his elfish face. "I'll stay with Ellen for a while."

"Ellen, I'm truly . . ."

But Ellen whipped her head around to face the other direction.

Liv grabbed my elbow. "He's right," she whispered. "Let's go."

Chapter 22

"**What were you thinking?**" Liv jerked her car to a stop in front of my apartment building. "Telling Ellen that Jenny might have killed Derek after all!"

"I said in her sleep. Unconsciously."

"And you don't see how that could upset the woman? What's gotten into you, anyway? Audrey, ever since they arrested Jenny, you've been defending her. And then you flip-flop, spouting some insane theory about Jenny killing Derek while sleepwalking."

I pulled out the bag of pills and dangled it in front of Liv's face. "Not so insane. Look, I hate the idea, too. It would be a hard thing to live with—for both Jenny and Ellen. But it makes a lot of sense—just a tragic accident. Or would you rather believe some deranged killer is lurking in Ramble, stalking his next victim?"

Liv rolled her eyes. "Still, you didn't need to break it to her that way."

"Like Bixby would be any gentler."

Liv sighed. "Okay, fine. What are you going to do now?"

"Get some sleep," I said. "Then, with a clear head, I'll look up the pills online before I take them to Bixby in the morning. I want to make sure they're what I think they are."

"You really should get Internet here. I know you're trying to save money, but—wait, do you mean you're not even *sure* they're sleeping pills?" Liv said.

My turn to roll my eyes. "Of course they're sleeping pills. Jenny told me she took a sleeping pill and said she kept them in the stuffed penguin."

Liv lifted an eyebrow.

"You'd have to know Jenny. It made sense to her. But I want to identify the specific brand before I hand them over. Jenny's defense lawyer will need to be aware, and it might help if she hears about it sooner rather than through proper channels."

Liv sat in the driver's seat, biting her lip while staring at my front stoop.

"I'm still trying to help her," I said. "Can't you see that?"

She grabbed my hand. "Of course you are. You're a good friend. But this will be a hard thing for everyone to come to terms with. Ellen . . . and especially Jenny. Did you discuss your sleepwalking theory with her?"

I shook my head. And then inhaled. Liv was right. Someone needed to. Someone who cared about her. And it looked like that person would have to be me. "I'll see if I can visit with her tomorrow, tell her what I found. If you thought I was too direct with Ellen, can you perhaps recommend a better tactic?"

"I . . . I was wrong," Liv said. "You're right. There's no other way than to come out and say it." She squeezed my hand. "Want me to come with you?"

"I doubt the jail would allow it." I sent her an encouraging smile. "But thanks for offering."

"You'd better get some sleep, then," she said. "Tomorrow is going to be a humdinger of a day."

"Yeah, and Liv?" I opened the car door and swung weary legs to the pavement.

"Yes?"

"Thanks for being my cousin . . . and my friend."

She leaned over and hugged me before I hoisted myself out of the seat. Once I'd unlocked my apartment door, Liv backed out and headed down the road.

I bent down and prevented Chester from making a break for it.

"No, you don't, buster," I said. "I'm not chasing you all over town tonight. I need to get some sleep."

But sleep proved elusive.

Chester took turns between playing Tarzan with the cords from my already askew blinds and trying to snuggle under my covers and attack my toes. Sleep was not on his agenda.

Not that my mind was all that conducive to the idea, either.

I kept imagining Jenny popping a sleeping pill after breaking up with Derek, looking for relief from the stress and thinking that maybe things would be rosier in the morning. But instead, her sleeping body slipped out of bed, grabbed the florist's knife—and maybe the flowers—in the apartment, descended the porch stairs, and hopped into Derek's car.

She would have still been in her pajamas, but I wondered if Derek even knew she'd been asleep.

But why had Derek remained parked in front of her apartment? I couldn't figure that out. Maybe he needed a few minutes to collect himself after the breakup. Or maybe he had to take or make a cell phone call. I doubted we'd ever know, but I wondered if Bixby had Derek's cell phone records.

I must have fallen asleep at one point, because I had a
dream. I was working on Jenny's wedding flowers. Except
instead of the anemones, she had wanted red roses. Tons of
red roses in the bouquets, corsages, centerpieces, altar flowers. Bridesmaids in red dresses and with red hair. Red rose
petals dropped by a cute red-clad flower girl as she skipped
down a white runner. Only they weren't rose petals, they
were drops of blood.

Derek's blood.

I awoke with a start. What had Little Joe said about a
spatter pattern? If Jenny had killed Derek in that awful way,
even while asleep, she would have been covered with his
blood. Could Jenny have showered and changed and cleaned
up and destroyed evidence—all while asleep?

Or could she have awakened covered in blood, panicked,
and cleaned herself off—and been too shocked and afraid
to admit what had happened? Jenny was the type to close
herself off from a stressful situation, huddle under the covers, and wait for everything to pass. Perhaps the shock of
the whole experience had left her in the stupor Mrs. June
interpreted as drug withdrawal.

I glanced at the alarm. Five a.m. Sleep wouldn't come
until this whole mess was sorted out. So I took a quick
scalding shower, dressed, fed Chester, and walked in the
dusky almost-sunrise to the shop.

Ramble was still asleep, and a hazy mist floated near
the ground. It would burn off when the sun rose fully, but the
ghostly ebbs and rises sent a shiver down my spine, and
every sound gave me the heebie-jeebies. A foraging cat
sounded like a footfall. A bird pecking at an open garbage
bag, like someone lurking in the shadows of the alley.

I shook off the feeling. Soon everything would be sorted
out and Ramble could go on its normal sleepy way.

I microwaved a cup of instant coffee while the computer
in the front of the shop booted. My eyes half-focused, I logged

onto the pharmacological website and searched for the names of some of the leading sleep aids. I scrolled through dozens, but nothing looked like the pills in the plastic bag.

Then I used the site's pill identifier tab—handy tool—to enter the shape, color, and markings. And sure enough, found a match.

Only someone must have made a terrible mistake. This wasn't a sleep aid at all. It was an antipsychotic, and a powerful one.

"Jenny," I said to the empty shop walls, "what were you doing with that?" The idea that Jenny had been hiding a mental illness formed, then evaporated pretty quickly. Sure, Jenny and I hadn't kept in touch as we once had, but a psychotic break would be hard to miss. Small towns pick up on that pretty quickly, and I hadn't heard anyone say, "Did you hear about Jenny's breakdown, bless her heart." And if these pills were prescribed for her, why were they in a plastic bag? And why would she refer to them as sleeping pills?

Then the back door shut with a soft thud.

"Larry?" I remained perched on the stool, straining to hear any further sounds. "Is that you?" I swallowed hard. "Liv?" I really should have locked the door behind me.

I walked to the back room. It was empty, and the door was shut, just as I left it. The sound of the back door must have been the product of a sleep-deprived, stressed-out imagination. I walked to the door and locked it behind me, also pulling shut the sticky, seldom-used dead bolt.

I slammed an angry fist against the cold steel.

One act had made the town so jumpy we were all hiding behind locked doors. I resented the loss, the intrusion of violence and the destruction of our security, as much as if a thief had broken in and stolen one of my prized possessions. I guess a sense of safety is right up there on the list of cherished valuables. Too bad nobody offered an insurance policy on that.

I sighed and headed back toward the front of the shop. Might as well read up a little more on that pill. Even though it wasn't a sleeping pill—which negated my whole brilliant theory—I wondered how Jenny had obtained them and what possible effects and side effects they might produce.

Could it be the result of some catastrophic pharmacy mistake? Or might someone have slipped them to her, claiming they were sleep aids? And could they alter Jenny's personality so much that she could become a coldhearted killer—with no one in town noticing? I rubbed my forehead. I couldn't even put my mind around that idea.

As I passed the walk-in, I noticed movement out of the corner of my eye. Those mice again? I pulled open the door. Sarah Anderson stood in the middle of the cooler.

"What are you doing in here?"

She pulled a florist knife from behind her back, the blade dully reflecting the fluorescent light.

We stood still, frozen, probably both stunned for a moment. Then I ran out and slammed the cooler door behind me. I raced to the back door and tugged. Then tried to manage the stubborn dead bolt with trembling fingers. Why had I locked myself in? I tugged harder, as if by sheer force I could breach the heavy steel door. The dead bolt finally gave way.

"Stop it," Sarah said.

I whirled around. She stood three feet away, brandishing the knife.

"I don't understand," I said. "What are you doing?"

"I think you know." She shook her head. "Get back from the door." She grabbed my wrist and pulled me away from the door.

I had to remind myself to breathe. "The pills . . . But how did you know I—?"

"Shirley. She came into the health club last night. Moonlight aerobics." Sarah shifted to stand between me and the door, between me and safety. "During cooldown, the topic of conversation switched to Jenny and the murder. Shirley told everyone that you found sleeping pills among Jenny's things and that you were planning to take them to the police."

"But they're not . . ."

A corner of Sarah's mouth quirked up into what might roughly be described as a smile. She took a step toward me, and I shuffled backward, toward the open cooler door.

"I figured they'd trace the pills to me," she said. "I didn't know what to do next. I waited outside my apartment, expecting the police to show up looking for me. I decided that if they arrived knocking on my doorstep, I could sneak away and start over somewhere else."

She advanced closer. I took another step back.

"When nobody came, I figured you hadn't gone to the police yet. I still had a chance. See, I had to get those pills back, Audrey. They'd discover what they were, who they belonged to, and then it would all come out. I drove over to your place. Saw you leave and walk here. I decided to follow you."

So that wasn't a cat. Maybe someone had been lurking in the alley.

"But those aren't sleeping pills," I said.

"Of course they are," she said. "That's all they're good for. I should know. I've been taking them long enough. Until I got sick of being asleep."

"Listen, if you're sick, we can get help—"

"I am not sick!" She took one menacing step forward. "I'm not sick, so I don't need pills. Why do people keep saying there's something wrong with me? Something is wrong with them."

I stepped back and raised my hands. I was back in the cooler, with no escape, unless I could talk my way out. "Who says something is wrong with you?"

"My parents, the so-called doctors, everybody. I thought I'd left them all behind when I moved here. I didn't need the medicine anymore. I was fine. Derek thought I was fine. More than fine. At first."

Derek. But Sarah couldn't be the elusive redhead. She had blond hair. Unless . . . and then I recalled Jenny's Halloween photographs of Sarah dressed as Lucy Ricardo.

"You . . . you're Lucy. Lucy has red hair." Maybe that was what my subconscious brain tried to tell me with the red roses dream.

"Derek thought it was cute, the red wig. He called me Lucy when I wore it. We'd take long drives in that cute car of his, and he took me to this little club out of town. He'd buy me dinner—steak and lobster with butter sauce and all that fancy stuff. No one at the health club could see me eat all that cholesterol." She chuckled. "And then we'd dance and gamble a little. He let me peek at his cards and blow on the dice, just like in some glamorous movie. He called me his good luck charm. Me. He didn't love Jenny, you know."

I shook my head. "No, he didn't love Jenny."

"Then why was he going to marry her? I'll tell you why. His father put him up to it. Said what a good and wholesome influence Jenny would be. Marriage would settle Derek right down, he said. But why not marry me? Derek loved *me*. I'll bet I'm every bit as wholesome as Jenny is." She pointed the knife to her own chest for emphasis. "I was furious when Jenny showed me that rock of hers. Over two carats, she said. And Ellen smiling and pushing her all the way."

"Hardly seems fair." I scanned the shop walls for something I could use to defend myself if talking it out with Sarah didn't work.

"Look, I know Derek may have seen a lot of girls, played the field, but he always came back to me. Always."

"You were seeing Derek even when he was dating Carolyn, weren't you?"

She straightened her shoulders. "I have been Derek's lover since three days after I moved to this stinking town," she said with unmistakable pride. "He was the first person who was nice to me at the health club. He bought me a smoothie and we talked. Then he parked his car behind the club and we made out. Most of those other girls were his parents' idea. I was just never good enough for them, but Derek didn't think so. I knew him, you see. I was the one he trusted with his secrets."

"You wrote him letters."

"Of course." She gave a vacant nod. "He didn't appreciate the effort."

"He kept them."

She scowled. "To hurt me. You know, I only pretended to take a shower when I got home that night. I listened to Jenny and Derek talking. I always listened to them. I heard them break up. They didn't belong together. And then when Derek left . . ."

"You gave her those pills. Told her they were sleeping pills."

"They *are* sleeping pills! Like I said, that's all they're good for. They make you groggy . . . knock you out for hours. Jenny had been taking them for weeks. Said they calmed her nerves." Sarah laughed. "And they knocked her out completely. She had no idea that whenever Derek dropped her off I'd wait until she took a pill and fell asleep, then Derek and I went out. What a sap."

"Is that what you did the night they broke up? Went out with Derek?"

"Jenny went to sleep. Now that they weren't engaged anymore, I figured it was my chance to be with Derek. He could take *me* to dinner with his parents, put *my* picture in the paper. He could marry me, and then we'd be together forever. I didn't even care if that ring was used. I knew it fit me. I tried it on lots of times when Jenny left it lying around.

"So I put on my white dress, my white shoes, and those white gloves Carolyn made us buy. I saw the bouquet sitting in a glass of water on the table. It was beautiful, Audrey. Really pretty. All purply. I always wanted a bouquet like that when I got married, so I took it. Why should Jenny have that, too? So I was all ready."

"But Derek wasn't."

She winced and sniffled. "He took one look at me, and instead of telling me how pretty I looked in my dress, he said I was demented. 'A real psycho.' He called me a psycho."

"I'm sorry." She did have my sympathy.

"He said he never wanted to see me again. Now that he was free of Jenny, he could move to Las Vegas and gamble full-time. And if I tried to contact him there, he'd take my letters to the police. Said they'd prove I was nuts."

And they would have.

"I couldn't face that again. Couldn't go back there."

"Back there?"

"All that poking and prodding and answering questions and taking pills I didn't need and feeling foggy all the time. I would never go back there."

A mental hospital.

"So I had to stop him," she said. "I didn't want to, you understand. I loved him. But he hated me for it, and I wasn't going back there." Her hands started to tremble.

"Did you take a knife with you?" I asked, almost in a whisper. I hoped she'd find my tone calming. "With the white dress and gloves and bouquet?"

"Of course not," she said. "Who takes a knife with them when they're getting married? That would be crazy.

"I wasn't sure what to do, you know, how I would go on without Derek. I sat in his car and cried for a good long time, not that he cared. Not that he took me in his arms and patted me on the back and told me everything was going to be all right. He just sat there, still as a rock. But then I looked down and saw the knife on the floor of the car. Don't you see, Audrey? It was meant to be."

I swallowed hard. My voice came out husky. "How did you know where to . . . ? I mean, the carotid artery . . ."

"Artery? Is that why it bled like that? Remember, I'm an exercise instructor. I just aimed for the place where you take the pulse. I felt bad right away. I tried to stop the blood. But there was so much. And then he died and left me—he left me alone—sitting in the car in a white dress covered with blood. Gloves covered with blood. Shoes covered with blood. Pretty purple flowers all covered in blood. Everything ruined."

"How did you clean up without anyone seeing you— without leaving any blood in the apartment?"

"Ramble goes to sleep at nine thirty. I just waited until two a.m."

"In the car with Derek's body?"

"Nobody could see me in the dark in that car with the tinted windows. Then I took off my shoes and ran to the health club. I had my own set of keys and know the alarm codes, so I showered and changed there. I wrapped up the dress and gloves and tossed them into the Dumpster." She laughed and shook her head. "I was in plain sight of the club's security cameras almost the whole time. But unless there's a break-in, they record over themselves in twenty-four hours, and garbage collection was due the next morning. I was home and in my own bed before anyone found Derek."

"But when the police arrested Jenny, you didn't feel guilty at all? That she might be sent to prison for a long time, for something she didn't—"

"If it weren't for Jenny, I might be Mrs. Derek Rawling right now, living in a beautiful house, with servants to bring me breakfast. Money makes a difference, you see. If you're poor, they say you're sick and a hazard to society. They lock you up in a hospital, pump you up with pills, and then put you back on the street. When you have money, you have power. Everyone would look up to me, and nobody would dare call me psycho ever again."

A happily-ever-after. "But what does that have to do with me? Why are you here now?"

"You knew about the pills. Shirley told me. Shirley tells everybody everything. I had to get them back."

I had a thing or two to tell Shirley myself, if I ever got out of here.

"I peeked in the front window and saw you with the bag, staring at the pills and staring at the computer. You have no idea how long I searched her room for them. Finally, I figured she'd just used them all."

"Let me get you help." I forced my voice to be braver than I felt. "Because now I know about it, and you can't blame Jenny if something happens to me. Sarah?"

"No, that's just code for going back there. I won't go back there." She took another step forward, pinning me against the wall in the cooler.

Chapter 23

❧

I figured I was going to die right there, just like Derek, my blood spattered in our walk-in cooler like so many red rose petals. I prayed that Larry or Amber Lee would find me, and that Liv would be spared.

Sarah Anderson might be petite, but I'd seen those muscles of hers, from all that working out in the gym. But I didn't plan to go down without a fight. I looked around, grabbed a white rose from a pail nearby, and held it out like a weapon. Pretty pitiful, but at least the thorns might do some damage, maybe help Bixby identify my killer.

Sarah halted, looking confused at the long-stemmed rose.

A flash of movement came from the cooler door. Liv charged into the walk-in. Without stopping, she knocked Sarah to the ground.

Sarah squirmed and turned. She raised her hand, still clutching the knife, poised now to strike Liv in the back.

If my next actions were instinctive, I'll admit to having

strange instincts. I wrapped the rose stem around Sarah's arm and tugged, trying to pull her arm and the knife away from Liv.

The thorns caught hold in her milky skin, sending long catlike scratches up her arm.

Sarah shrieked and dropped the knife before shriveling up into a ball.

I picked up the knife and looked around the back room before grabbing a full spool of two-and-three-quarter-inch poly satin ribbon with a taffeta embossed texture—in daffodil yellow.

When I got back to the cooler, Sarah struggled a little, but the fight was gone out of her and she mostly pouted and whimpered and nursed her scratches. I managed to hold her down while Liv used the ribbon to tie Sarah's arms behind her and then secure her legs. Finishing up, I noticed, with a perfect bow.

I raised my eyebrows.

"Force of habit." She stood and brushed off her hands.

Bixby looked ready to pounce but kept to his chair like someone had chained him down. He settled for drumming the table with his fingertips.

I answered his questions sweetly, with the demure smile Grandma Mae had taught us that every Southern lady should master.

Bixby slapped his hand on the table after I finished my statement. "Just promise me, Audrey, that you'll never do anything like this again."

"Do what? I was only trying to help a fr—"

"Do things like withholding evidence, confronting a suspect. Putting yourself and your cousin in such a dangerous situation."

"Believe me, Chief, it will never happen again." I might have punctuated that with an innocent flutter of my eyelashes. It was an easy promise to make. What were the odds that I would get tangled up in another murder investigation in Ramble? About the same as having a freak snowstorm on the Fourth of July.

Then again, with global warming . . .

Not that I regretted "sticking my nose in," as Bixby put it. Jenny would soon be released, and a dangerous murderer now sat behind bars. Hopefully she'd get the psychological help she needed.

As I exited the interrogation room, I spotted the enclave huddled around Mrs. June's desk. Liv gathered me in a hug and held on. "Are you okay?" I asked. The idea that she could have been hurt brought tears to my eyes.

She pulled back and met my gaze. "Yes, are you?"

Before I could answer, Amber Lee pulled me into a rocking bear hug. "Don't scare me like that," she said. "I can't lose my friends and my job on the same day."

Eric was next to hug me. "I'm glad you're both all right. When Liv called, I nearly went out of my mind." He put his arm around his wife and kissed the top of her head. "I don't know what possessed you to tackle the woman instead of calling the police."

"There wasn't time."

"She's right." I smiled at her. "Liv saved my life."

She hugged me again. "And you saved mine."

"Still," Eric said, "you are going to the doctor's."

"Yes, sir." Liv saluted. "I will, but I'm fine. You see, I led with the shoulder."

"I just want to make sure it didn't hurt the—"

Liv interrupted him with a hand on his arm and looked to me. "Audrey, there's something we've been meaning to tell you, but I didn't expect this would be the place."

"You're expecting a baby!"

"Congratulations!" Mrs. June shouted, and then she and Amber Lee rushed Liv for a group hug.

As soon as Liv extricated herself, she raised her eyebrows in surprise. "How did you know?"

"Decaf, nausea, and you've been a tad . . . emotional."

She cast me a warning glance.

"Just a smidge."

Liv shook her head. "Well, Sherlock, maybe you do have the makings of a detective."

"Oh, no," I said. "Being a wedding florist is more than enough danger and excitement for me."

"I still don't understand what happened," Amber Lee said. "I get that Sarah killed Derek. But why did she come after you?"

"She was after the pills I found. When Jenny took what she thought were sleeping pills, she was actually taking Sarah's antipsychotic meds. Once I found them, Sarah decided the trail would lead to her. And also, I'd figured out that she was the mysterious woman with the red hair."

"But she's a blonde," Eric said.

"But we found the red wig in her locker at the health club," Mrs. June said. "Incidentally, that's also where they found Jenny's missing engagement ring. Apparently Sarah was too sentimental to dispose of them with the rest of the bloody clothing. There are traces of blood on both, so they've been sent to the state labs for DNA testing."

"I guess hell has no fury, and all that," Eric said.

"But it was more than that," Mrs. June said. "Add in a deep-seated psychological problem and a love for money and all she thought it could buy for her."

"Money?" Amber Lee asked.

"Another reason Sarah was so desperate to marry Derek,"

I said. "She figured no one could send her away if she was Mrs. Derek Rawling. No one would dare."

Mrs. June nodded. "And, according to her confession, she was also the one blackmailing Derek's father. She figured if she couldn't have Derek, she could at least have some of his money."

"Blackmailing him for . . . ?" Amber Lee asked.

"For his son's activities, as well as the old man's gambling operation," Mrs. June said.

"Which he's now shut down," Eric said. "Mr. Rawling plopped the file on my desk this morning. Said he wanted me to try to renovate and lease the place as a proper restaurant. I suspect any evidence of gambling has been removed."

"Will the Rawlings be implicated in all this, do you think?" Liv asked.

Eric shrugged. "Money still does talk."

"But I'm sure a lot of people won't," Mrs. June said. "I doubt there'll be enough evidence to tie old man Rawling to the illegal gambling club. Only I suspect a lot of his high-profile political friends won't stick around to find out."

I nodded. "The party's over."

The outside door swung open. Ellen Whitney entered, dressed in teal from her head to the tips of her teal toenails jutting from her teal sandals. To see her looking more like herself made me smile.

I was shocked, however, to see her return my smile.

"It's true, then?" she said. "My baby can come home?"

"Pretty soon," Mrs. June said. "Bixby's waiting on the papers authorizing her release."

"Oh." Ellen's face fell.

"But she should be arriving any moment," Mrs. June said.

Ellen glanced to the door, which opened on cue.

Jenny, looking a little gaunt, but minus the handcuffs and prison garb, walked in escorted by Ken Lafferty.

Ellen swallowed hard as she straightened her silver and teal necklace, then she ran to her daughter and embraced her, rocking her as they clung to each other.

Liv wiped away a tear.

And, despite my promise to Bixby, I knew I'd do it all over again.

Chapter 24

A while would pass before I'd be able to shake the adrenaline rush that occurred whenever anyone opened the alley door. Especially early in the morning when alone in the back room. I froze and watched until I saw Larry's shock of hair and his plaid shirt.

"Hey, Audrey."

"Larry, I didn't know we were expecting a shipment today." Except for people coming into the shop to hear more about the murder, business had returned to normal, and we had plenty of stock to keep our customers in flowers.

"That's not why I'm here." He placed a long box on my workstation. "These are for you . . . and your cousin." His fair complexion burst into a fierce blush.

"Don't say you brought us flowers."

"Open it."

When I did, I beheld the most perfect pale blue roses I'd ever seen. "You did a wonderful job tinting these. You can barely tell—"

"They're not tinted."

I leaned closer and took a better look. Only the palest pink shone through the blue. "What hybrid is this? I don't know if I've ever seen any so blue." The blue rose has been the holy grail of rose developers for years. No one had mastered one.

A broad smile transformed him again into a Kewpie doll. "I just got the registry papers on it."

"Yours? Oh, Larry! That is wonderful! What did you name it?"

"I call it the Mae rose, after the woman who convinced me to never give up. She had confidence in me long before I had any in myself."

I'm afraid I might have gotten his shoulder a little damp with my tears as I gave him a hug. "After our Grandma Mae. That is so sweet."

"That's why I didn't want anyone else in the greenhouses. I needed to keep it a secret until it was safely registered. Not that I don't trust you. But this is a small town, and things get out. But could you do me a favor, Audrey? Could you choose a meaning for it?"

I carefully lifted one of the blooms from the box and examined its delicate texture. "According to florigraphy, blue roses can mean anything from *royalty* to *impossibility* to *mystery*." I smiled. "But not impossible, is it? Maybe something mysterious, but in a positive sense."

"It's a beauty."

"What about *mysterious beauty*, then?"

"Mysterious beauty." He scratched his chin. "I think I like it."

"You're going to sell all of these that you can grow," I said.

"Audrey, I'd like the Rose in Bloom to market the cut roses for me."

"Of course we'd be delighted to carry them."

"I mean, exclusive, like."

"But people from all over the country are going to want these."

"Which is why I need to concentrate on cultivating more. I'm not equipped for retail."

It meant more shipping, but this would be a big boon to our business. Maybe we could keep our new interns. "Liv is going to be ecstatic."

I arranged the blue roses simply, in a clear glass vase with accents of baby's breath. I set them on the counter in the shop, where they were the center of attention all day— well, they shared attention with talk of the murder.

Jenny had moved back home with her mother, and Sarah had been transported to a psychiatric facility for further examination.

Amber Lee busied herself repeating the story of the "knife fight in the walk-in cooler," and how I'd stopped a deranged killer with only the thorns from a rose. It all sounded so much more exciting when she told it. Her former students must have enjoyed story time. I think she would have taken people on paid tours if Liv hadn't nixed the idea.

"Weren't you going to leave early for some hot date?" I asked her.

"Oh, please," she said. "Don't remind me. I could blame you for that disaster."

"What did I do?"

"Remember when you told me to learn more about Worthington?"

"Is that who you've been seeing? You and the Rawlings' butler?"

"Yeah, until Bixby threw him in the clink. Good riddance."

"Why?"

"That cottage and garden plot of his on the Rawling estate? It seems he was growing a healthy crop of marijuana. That's the only reason he joined the garden club. He used all our soil information to increase his crop yield. Even got Larry to come to one of our meetings to show us how to set up an indoor hydroponics system."

"I thought I saw them chatting at the funeral."

"I bet Larry didn't know what he was up to, either. I hate being used like that." She shook her head. "And you know what? He's not even British."

Another customer entered, and Amber Lee plastered on a smile and went to greet her.

In an afternoon lull, as Liv chugged her decaf and I leaned against the counter in a carbohydrate slump, the bell over the door startled me awake.

Nick Maxwell walked in, dressed in those sparkling baker's whites.

"Come to get a bouquet?" It had been several days since his girlfriend had received fresh flowers.

"Yes." He smiled that dazzling smile of his, and I let another refrain of the only-friends mantra cycle through my head.

"Actually, no. I brought you something." He whipped out a cupcake from behind his back and set it on the counter. "I wanted to congratulate you on catching the real killer. I knew you could figure it out, and I'm glad you're safe."

"Thanks, I . . ." I looked at the cupcake with a perfectly formed red sugar tulip on the top. Did he know that the red tulip was a confession of love? Probably not.

Pull yourself together, Audrey. Just a friend, just a friend.

"I have a confession to make," he said.

"A confession?"

"I haven't been buying flowers for a girlfriend."

"You've been using them as models for sugar flowers, haven't you?"

"No . . . well, that's what I ended up doing with them. But

that's not why . . . I mean, I already had all my molds set. I . . . well . . . I wanted to get to know you a little better."

"Me?"

He smiled again, and everything but his face blended into some kaleidoscopic periphery. "Yes, and I wondered if maybe, sometime this weekend when we're both not working, if maybe we could, I don't know, have dinner?"

"I'd like that."

"How about the Ashbury?"

"I . . ." I let out an unconscious breath. How could I tell him that place to me was cursed? The scene of my breakup—and everybody else's wedding.

"Or I could cook." His eyes twinkled. "I've been known to make things other than cake, you know."

"That sounds lovely. I . . ." I went to the self-service cooler and pulled out a perfect garden daisy and handed it to him. *I share your sentiments.*

"Thanks."

The bell rang as another customer entered, but my eyes followed Nick as he saluted me with the daisy and backed out of the store.

I took a sniff of the cupcake. Instead of smelling like flowers, it smelled of vanilla and almond and sugar.

I guess love doesn't always smell like roses.

Turn the page for a preview of Beverly Allen's
next Bridal Bouquet Shop Mystery . . .

For Whom the Bluebell Tolls

Coming soon from Berkley Prime Crime!

"Audrey, I . . ."

I stood on my front stoop, hand-in-hand with Nick Maxwell after one of our sporadic dinner dates. The moon cooperated, already aglow in the dusky sky, and a gentle breeze stirred the leaves in the trees—very welcome after the heat of the day. I closed my eyes, waiting for our good-night kiss.

Chester interrupted our romantic moment, scratching on the glass window and yowling for me to get inside and serve his every whim. (Did I mention Chester is my cat?) My neighbor Tom added percussion to the feline chorus, using the last remaining moments of daylight to tack up a Fourth of July banner a few feet away. Ah, the joys of apartment living. Then my phone started ringing in my living room.

"I should let you get that. Good night, Audrey." Nick planted a chaste kiss on my forehead and gave my hand a squeeze before sending Tom a wave and walking back to his truck.

I leaned against the doorframe for a moment and watched him go. I knew Nick was encouraged by the growth of the bakery, which now supplied fresh baked goods and breads to local restaurants. But his early hours had really taken a toll on our date time.

Meanwhile my phone had stopped ringing. I opened my door as the answering machine picked up. A click proved that the caller declined to leave a message.

I bumped my behemoth of a window air conditioner up to the max, then made my way to the kitchen with Chester nipping at my ankles and weaving around my legs. I spooned out half of a can of something labeled "Fresh Seafood," but which smelled more like the Dumpster behind a sushi restaurant. He didn't seem to mind. I managed to refill his water dish before the phone rang again.

I carried the receiver so I could stand in front of the roaring air conditioner, then lifted my ponytail so the chilled air could hit the back of my neck. "Hello?"

"Audrey, where have you been? I've been calling all night."

Letting my hair fall, I jerked into my full and upright position. "Hey, Brad." Where I'd been was none of his business. Not anymore. Brad the Cad had blown his chance with me. I really needed to get caller ID.

"Listen, Audrey, I'm coming back to Ramble."

Well, let's call the town band and organize a parade, why don't we? But instead of saying that, I sank onto the sofa. "Coming back?"

"Just for a visit. Well, work, really."

"How nice for you."

"Aw, come on, Audrey. I know you're upset with me, but I hoped we could talk. Clear the air. There might be a job in it for you. A huge wedding."

"Are you getting married?" A logical conclusion considering I made my living as a florist and the wedding coordinator at the Rose in Bloom, the shop that my cousin Liv and I owned.

A long pause was followed by a slow inhalation and exhalation. "No, Audrey. I'm not getting married. You were right. New York isn't exactly what I thought it would be. I really messed up when I left you behind."

I swallowed hard. For a long time I'd dreamed of hearing those words. And I'd rehearsed all kinds of reactions ranging from running into his arms—hard to do over the phone— and stomping on his foot with my highest and spikiest pair of heels.

"Yeah?" Okay, so that wasn't one of the reactions I'd practiced.

"Look, I'm coming back with the whole film crew."

"I thought the show you were working on was canceled."

"It was. Who knew *The Lumberjack Logs* would turn out to be such a yawn? But a friend hooked me up with *Fix My Wedding.* I'm the production assistant."

"And they're coming to Ramble?" My ears perked up. *Fix My Wedding* had become one of my favorite guilty pleasures. Gigi Welch's snarky treatment of brides brought them to tears as she mocked their original—and usually tacky— plans. Then her cohort, Gary Davoll, would sweep in like a fairy godfather and whisk the bride away, spoiling her like a princess. I won't say the elaborate weddings they staged were much less tacky than the bride's original plans, but the show had chemistry. And I could justify the hours I spent watching it by labeling the time as work, research for anyone in the bridal industry.

"Yep. And I might have had something to do with that." Pride rang in his voice. "The original venue fell through. The bride in question is nuts—"

"Aren't they usually?"

"Same old Audrey. Quick-witted and never letting me finish a sentence." The tone in his voice was teasing and cheerful. It belonged to the old charming Brad I dated, not the monster I'd recast him as since the break-up. I shifted my emotions to defensive mode. I would not fall for him again. I would not . . .

"Anyway," he continued, "the bride is nutty about bells, and I told her about the hand-rung bell in the old First Baptist. I showed Gary and Gigi pictures of some of the other local assets, so they're going to hold the wedding at the church and the reception at the Ashbury."

Oh, lovely. The Ashbury. The restaurant where Brad dumped me. This was getting better by the minute. "And you said there might be a job for me?"

"Yes, I showed Gigi and Gary the article about you in the paper, and they thought the whole language of flowers thing was cute. Said a local florist with that kind of reputation might make the episode more interesting. Well, *quaint*, they said, but you know Gigi."

"And the bride's crazy about bells?" My brain started turning. I'd seen bell-shaped vases that might work. Maybe campanula, also known as bellflowers, or any of the other flower varieties that resembled bells. Or was that too literal?

The meanings were suitable. Bellflowers signified *constancy*, a great meaning for a marriage, and the small white ones meant *gratitude*. Of course, the bluebell also could signify *sorrowful regret*, but maybe I could steer her away from that color. Not all of the bellflowers are commonly used by many florists, but I was sure I could get my hands on them if needed. And if I couldn't, Liv was a whiz at acquisition.

"Yes, some fetish with bells," he continued. "We're busing in a bell choir to perform at the ceremony. Guests are ringing little silver bells instead of throwing rice. I think Gary is even arranging to have bells woven into her dress.

Crazy, huh? But that's why people watch the show. I hope you're not overbooked and can squeeze in the wedding. Mom said the shop has been real busy."

"When is the wedding?"

"Um, we're coming next week. Like I said, the other venue canceled at the last minute. Can you do it? I know it's the middle of summer. It has to be a busy time for weddings."

Proving once again that Brad never paid attention. July might be a prime time for a wedding in many parts of the country. But in Ramble, Virginia, where most weddings were held at the old First Baptist, which lacked air condition-ing, or outside in the gardens of the Ashbury, local brides tended to opt for late spring or early fall when the tempera-tures were more manageable.

"I should be free. I'll have to see if Liv can source the flowers for a quick delivery. It will cost a bit more."

"No problem," he said. "The show has deep pockets. We'll make sure the cost of anything you need is written into the contract. Should be some nice publicity for your shop, too."

"Of course, I'll have to talk it over with Liv."

"Last time I called Mom, she said that Liv and Eric are going to have a baby. They must be tickled pink."

"Or blue," I said. "They want to be surprised."

"That's great. Give them my best. Or I can do it when I get into town. Oh, Audrey, I've missed you. I'm looking forward to seeing you."

My stomach twisted. He sounded like the same old Brad that I had dated for a year. But did I really want to see him again? And where would that leave my budding relationship (pardon the floral pun) with Nick Maxwell?

"Yes, Brad, I'm looking forward to seeing you again, too."

*With missing money, secret codes,
and the very strange behavior of one resident,
Darling, Alabama, on the eve of Confederate Day,
is anything but a sleepy little town . . .*

FROM NATIONAL BESTSELLING AUTHOR
SUSAN WITTIG ALBERT

THE DARLING DAHLIAS
AND THE CONFEDERATE ROSE

In this small Southern town, Earle Scroggins, the county probate clerk, has got the sheriff thinking that Scroggins' employee Verna Tidwell (also the Darling Dahlias' trusted treasurer) is behind a missing $15,000. But Darling Dahlias president, Liz Lacy, is determined to prove Verna is not a thief.

Meanwhile, Miss Dorothy Rogers has discovered her own mystery—what appears to be a secret code embroidered under the cover of a pillow, the only possession she has from her grandmother. She enlists the help of a local newspaperman, who begins to suspect the family heirloom may have larger significance.

facebook.com/susan.w.albert
facebook.com/TheCrimeSceneBooks
penguin.com

SUSAN WITTIG ALBERT

THE DARLING DAHLIAS AND THE NAKED LADIES

As Darling's town librarian is fond of saying: "Naked ladies is not a respectable name for a plant." A lily by any other name would certainly smell as sweet—and look just as beautiful as the naked ladies decorating Miss Hamer's lawn . . .

It seems Miss Hamer's house may also be home to naked ladies of a different sort. Her niece, Nona Jean Jamison, and Nona's friend, Miss Lake, have come to Darling to stay with the elderly recluse. But rumors sprout that these visitors are actually the Naughty and Nice Sisters from the Ziegfield Frolic, specializing in dancing barely clothed.

When Nona denies her vaudeville past, the Dahlias begin to suspect that it may be more than modesty that's causing both women to lie low. Why has Nona gone to the beauty parlor to change her hair color? Why has Miss Lake not been seen without a veil? And who is the well-dressed man from Chicago who's just arrived, asking about Nona? The Dahlias are convinced that someone is covering up something sinister . . .

INCLUDES RECIPES!

penguin.com